Bib and Tucker

It's 1947, and Ruth Maclean has returned to nursing school at Kingston General Hospital, only to find she is on her own for yet another placement, this time in the former Rockwood Insane Asylum, now the Ontario Hospital. Ruth must confront the moral dilemmas of early mental health treatments, from electroshock to lobotomies. Can she trust herself, her colleagues, and the men who surround her, or will this be a repeat of her troubles of the year before in the TB Sanatorium? As she struggles to understand mental illness in a challenging medical and personal landscape, Ruth finds growth, connection, and hope.

BIB & TUCKER

White Stockings

Book 2

DA BROWN

Copyright © 2025 by Dorothyanne Brown.

"A Visit to the Asylum" was published in *The Harp-Weaver and Other Poems* (Harper Brothers, 1923). This poem is believed to be in the public domain.

Excerpts from medical texts and other health materials are credited where used.

Cover photograph supplied by the Museum of Health Care at Kingston, Ontario, Canada. Used with permission.

All rights reserved. No part of this publication may be reproduced, stored, or transmitted in any form or by any means, electronic, mechanical, photocopying, recording, scanning, or otherwise, without written permission from the author, except in the case of brief quotations embodied in critical articles and reviews. It is illegal to copy this book or, post it to a website, or distribute it by any other means without permission.

No AI training: Without in any way limiting the author's exclusive rights under copyright, any use of this publication to "train" generative artificial intelligence (AI) technologies to generate text is expressly prohibited. The author reserves all rights to license uses of this work for generative AI training and development of similar machine learning language models.

Though based on historical events and institutions, this novel is a work of fiction. The names, characters, locations, and events portrayed in it are either the work of the author's imagination or used in a fictitious manner. Any resemblance to actual persons, living or dead, organizations, localities, or events is entirely coincidental. Any public figures, books, institutions, trade names, or organizations that may be mentioned in the book have not endorsed this book, have not made any payment for mention, and are not otherwise associated with the book, author, or publisher. No generative AI was used in preparing this work.

Published by arrangement with Somewhat Grumpy Press Inc., Halifax, Nova Scotia, Canada. www.SomewhatGrumpyPress.com The Somewhat Grumpy Press name and Pallas' cat logo are registered trademarks.

ISBN 978-1-998555-09-3 (paperback)

ISBN 978-1-998555-10-9 (eBook)

May 2025 v4

Links to resources may become outdated. Author and publisher are not responsible for content at third-party links.

Contents

Author's notes

Language: This is a work of fiction, taking place in 1947-48. As such, some historically accurate terms used are no longer acceptable language. I have attempted to minimize chance of offence, but please read the dialogue as reflecting the attitudes of that time.

Content warning: This is a story of treatment for severe mental illness in 1947-48. Treatments were few and sometimes brutal. Discussions and character behaviours include attacks, abuse, and incidents of self-harm including suicide. Please read with caution, and if anything upsets you or triggers something in you, seek help immediately.

In Ontario, you can contact: https://connexontario.ca or https://www.dcontario.org.

Anywhere in Canada, The Canadian Mental Health Association offers support. If you require assistance, call or text 988, toll-free.

Elsewhere, contact your local emergency services.

You, like the patients in this book, deserve good mental health. Thank heavens we have better approaches to it now.

A Visit to the Asylum

EDNA ST. VINCENT MILLAY

Once from a big, big building,
When I was small, small,
The queer folk in the windows
Would smile at me and call.

And in the hard wee gardens
Such pleasant men would hoe:
"Sir, may we touch the little girl's hair!"—
It was so red, you know.

They cut me coloured asters
With shears so sharp and neat,
They brought me grapes and plums and pears
And pretty cakes to eat.

And out of all the windows,
No matter where we went,
The merriest eyes would follow me
And make me compliment.

There were a thousand windows,
All latticed up and down.
And up to all the windows,
When we went back to town,

The queer folk put their faces,
As gentle as could be;
"Come again, little girl!" they called, and I
Called back, "You come see me!"

Back to school

"Class," said Mrs. Balch, Kingston General Hospital's School of Nursing's first year nursing supervisor, "we have a bit of a problem. One of the second-year students has had to go home because of an illness in her family. That leaves a placement open that we really hate to go to waste. It's tough to get spaces now, don't you know, with all the nursing schools competing for them. I'm asking for a volunteer from this class to take this placement."

The class murmured. "Where is the placement?" one girl asked.

"I'll let you know once we have a volunteer," Mrs. Balch said. "Now, come, come, girls. Surely one of you would be willing to give up your placement at the Sanatorium?"

Ruth Maclean could feel the heads of her classmates turn towards her. They all knew Mrs. Balch meant her. Drat, she thought. She'd been looking forward to an easy placement where she could catch up with her studies, show off her strengths. After being placed at the San last year, she felt reasonably confident she knew what to do. And the head supervisor there, Mrs. Graham, liked her. She'd been looking forward to reconnecting with any of her old patients that were there, too. She shrugged. Apparently, it was not to be. She could only hope for a decent alternative. Maybe maternity? She knew a bit about that, too, given her mother's many deliveries.

She raised her hand.

"Thank you, Miss Maclean. It does seem appropriate, given your prior experience, though I'm sure we will all miss your expert guidance when we are on the wards, don't you know."

Ruth ran her fingers along the side of her anatomy text, ruffling up the papers. Where was she going to be sent?

"We'll talk after class about your placement, Miss Maclean. Now, let's focus on our anatomy. Where can we find the aorta? Anyone?"

It was a long class, and Ruth grew more and more agitated as the time went on. Why couldn't she have told her right away? She couldn't focus with wondering. Why had she volunteered? She'd just spent a year away from classmates and now she was going to be away from them again.

"Don't worry," whispered Betty. "You'll be ahead of all of us. And we can catch up off shift and in class."

Placements started in two weeks, and there were no classes while everyone was on placement. Because of the shortage of senior nurses after the men came back from the war and so many nurses married them, the placements were heavy work, more like an apprenticeship than a student experience. At least for the Kingston General Hospital and Hotel Dieu students. The Queen's students could still work half days.

"No class, remember? And you'll be way over there at the San."

"Yes, but we're living here, most of us. We'll catch up over tiffin."

"Maybe …"

Finally, the class ended, with reminders about the exam the following week and the need to review the circulatory system. So complicated, thought Ruth. But fascinating.

"Miss Maclean, could you come to my office, please?"

Ruth followed the portly Mrs. Balch up the stairs, listening to her wheeze that matched perfectly the sound from Ruth's cheap nursing shoes. They squeezed into Mrs. Balch's tiny office, a cramped place almost under the stairs, filled with books and stethoscopes and all sorts of clutter. Sighing, Mrs. Balch threw herself into her chair, which whined in response.

"Now, Miss Maclean, I know about your history from last year. You had more than a little trouble."

Ruth started to protest, thought better of it, remained standing at attention.

"I know, some of it wasn't your fault, but some of it … well, let's just say we are hoping there will be no repeat of any of it this year."

Ruth waited. She'd learned not to say anything, anyway, but she was simmering.

"I'm grateful you volunteered to switch placements. It seemed redundant to return you to the San and there was always the risk of the men there getting too friendly again, don't you know." Mrs. Balch glowered at Ruth over her glasses. "So, I thank you for being big enough to realize that."

Ruth waited some more.

Mrs. Balch pushed some papers around on her desk, pulled one out from the untidy pile. "Here it is — your placement. You'll be going to Rockwell, don't you know, the asylum. Though they call it the Ontario Hospital now."

Ruth felt a moan creeping up from her toes to her throat, chilling her through. She clamped it down.

"It's a bit unfortunate not going with your class, but there are good senior nurses there and they have their own school, don't you know, so lots of students to share learning with. Your supervisor will be Nurse Thomas. She's a good sort. I used to work with her myself. It's a twelve-week placement. They've just changed that, told us we need more emphasis on mental illness as if that wasn't part of all of nursing …"

"Twelve weeks?" Ruth couldn't help that coming out a bit moany, though she tried to mute it.

Mrs. Balch looked at her sharply. "We're not going to have any complaints this year, are we? Because your file is quite thick enough, don't you know."

"No, Mrs. Balch."

"Good. Now, they like their students to live on campus, so we've arranged a room for you in Leahurst. It's quite pleasant, near the lake, don't you know."

Ruth sagged. Away from everyone else? She'd be so lonely! And if she heard one more "don't you know" she might actually answer it with a loud "Yes, I KNOW," so she knew she had to get out of there. Fast.

"They'll set you up for after your exams here. Just take what you need when you go, the rooms are quite tight. We can store whatever doesn't fit here. After all, you'll be coming back to us in no time at all." Mrs. Balch looked as if she wanted to add a 'don't you know' but reconsidered it.

"Here's all the information," she said, waving the paper at Ruth. "Better let your family in Cloyne know where you are. We don't want another scene like last year."

Ruth took the form and would have stomped out of the room but there really wasn't any space to move quickly unless she knocked over a pile of books. She backed out carefully and speed-walked up the stairs.

"No running," someone shouted.

Ruth carefully swallowed what she'd wanted to say in response. At this rate, she'd be too full for dinner, she thought. She walked carefully over to Betty's door and knocked, then burst in.

"Betty, you'll never guess! I'm going to —"

"Rockwood?" Betty laughed. "I thought that must've been it when she was being all secretive before you spoke up. She knows none of us wanted to go there. And I already have been last year, remember? I'm hoping I'll get a pass for that placement entirely, even though they are making me repeat the rest of the course."

"But it's for twelve whole weeks!"

"Really? When I was there last year, it was only for six. Flew by. Barely even had to talk to anyone."

"The school has lengthened it. And I have to move over there!!"

Betty laughed again. "Oh, my golly, they are punishing you but good. Leahurst is quite nice except for the drafts. And you can sleep in until the very last minute because you are right across the road. Mind you, sometimes the inmates get out and sneak into your room."

"Stop it, Betty. I'm already scared enough."

Betty shrugged, wrapped her afghan around her, tucking her legs underneath. "You probably had worse to deal with at the San, Ruth. They're just sick, but in a different way. The key thing is to avoid doing your placement on one of the locked wards. Those patients are the dangerous ones. Former prisoners, really sick dementia praecox patients, you have to watch them. I only did two days on a locked ward. Didn't like it. But they'll probably put you with the almost-wells, anyway." She patted Ruth on the arm. "Don't you worry."

She pulled out her anatomy text, flipped it open. "Now, are you going to help me study anatomy? I have chocolate." She peered up at Ruth, making such a silly face that Ruth had to burst out laughing.

"Ok, ok. Let's get to work." Ruth sat down on Betty's bed and pulled out her anatomy book. In no time they were puzzling over the circulation in the ankle and foot, and Ruth could almost forget what was coming around the corner.

TWO

Entry

___

R uth wrapped her cloak around herself and shivered. The mid-October wind off Lake Ontario was whipping around the building as she stood looking at the former Rockwood Asylum, now the renamed Ontario Hospital. It positively loomed. It stood tall, built in the grey limestone that seemed to be the building choice for all the municipal buildings in Kingston, probably because the entire city lay on top of it. Convict labour from the conveniently located Kingston Penitentiary was used to quarry a lot of the limestone. The hospital windows were large but barred, and Ruth could see shadows moving behind them. The front door looked huge and solid. Was it locked? She wasn't sure. The whole place gave her chills.

She'd been researching the hospital before she left for her placement. They'd changed the name when the term asylum went out of fashion. But the patients hadn't changed much. They were patients and prisoners with mental illness, shipped there from all over Ontario. Like her former patients at the TB Sanatorium, they would be mostly long-term residents. Unlike her former patients, they likely weren't as open to fun.

Or so Ruth suspected. She just wished her placement was over. Psychiatry scared her, especially after seeing her brother Billy so sick with severe depression when he came back from the war. Though he'd mostly recovered, there were many who never did.

Ruth wasn't sure now if she'd been smart to come at this time. She'd be without her classmates. The other students at the OH were a mix of girls from KGH, Hotel Dieu, and Queen's University schools of nursing, plus the psychiatric nursing school class running the place. None of them knew her. And she still dressed as a first year, which made her stand out even more. Most of the students on placement there were in their second year, had won their caps already. Ruth wondered if they wore caps in the OH. It seemed, as Jocelyn had told her last year in the San, that they'd just be in the way.

Sighing, Ruth turned toward Leahurst, her residence for her twelve-week placement. "It can't be that bad," she told herself. "After all, Betty survived it last year." She squared her shoulders and walked up the limestone stairs to her residence.

"Oh, there you are," a senior nurse said, as soon as she'd stepped in the door, shutting the cold winter winds out. "Hurry up! I have to go on shift soon. Why are you so late?"

Ruth scurried to keep up with the nurse as she raced up the stairs and along the hallway on the third floor. "Here you go. I'm sorry, it's the smallest room, but we are all chock-a-block. Bathroom is downstairs and down the hallway. Don't forget to sign up for your time in the bath. It gets quite mad around here, especially on Friday and Saturday nights. My counsel to you is to wait and wash late on those nights, after everyone else has gone out."

Ruth tried to insert a comment, didn't get far. Her mouth just opened before the nurse started up again.

"We have our own laundry here, but some girls prefer to stick with the Chinese one downtown. It's up to you. If you use that laundry, the pickup is twice a week, on Tuesdays and Fridays. Be sure you have your name sewn on absolutely *everything* or it'll for sure get lost. Now what else?"

"Food?" Ruth managed to squeak out.

"Oh, yes. Meals at the hospital. Not with the inmates, thank goodness. We have our own dining hall. It goes in shifts — most of the time we eat just before we go on or after we leave. We are never to eat with the medical staff. They have their own special cafeteria. As do the patients. And of course we have a tiny kitchen here. Sometimes there are snacks on the wards, depending on where you are. Do you know where you are yet?"

Ruth shook her head.

"Well, I'll bet they start you on a locked ward. Most of we OH students have already done a lot of time on them, so it gives us a bit of a break. Not that you can do much in twelve weeks. Just ask at the front desk when you go in, they'll send you in the right direction."

She regarded Ruth critically. "Remember, no bobby pins, no earrings, no necklaces or anything they can get a grab of." She looked at her watch. "Oh God, I've got to fly. They'll be expecting me in five minutes. Luckily, we are just across the street. I'm Doris Slaunwhite, by the way. Second-year in the OH set. Get settled and we can catch up later. I'm your official residence mentor, I guess."

She raced out of the door, leaving Ruth staring after her, open-mouthed.

She looked around her room. It *was* tiny, looking more like a converted closet than an actual bedroom. She was on her own, though, which could be good. Or lonely. Still, there was a smallish window that let in some light, and if she peered through it, she could see the lake through the trees. They were right by the coastline. The water looked like steel.

Sighing, Ruth started to unpack, not that she had much. Her makeup case was light, mainly filled with Woolite bottles, Rinso, hand cream, and tooth powder. Lipstick was a major no-no, and though she had some squirrelled away, she thought it best to leave it at the nursing residence near KGH. No point in stirring things up here, she thought. She was still getting over last year's misadventures.

Ruth hung up her uniforms and stockings in the tiny closet, cut at an angle to the roof. Fortunately, her uniforms, when hung, cleared the floor. Barely. She sorted out her freshly cleaned cuffs and apron and attached the cuffs to her uniform. They always took so long to get right. Soon a cap, she thought.

After unpacking, she sat on her bed and wrote her first note to Mary. She missed being able to chat with Mary like she had when they were at the San together. They saw each other when they could, but both of their schedules were so busy it made it hard to catch up. They'd resorted to writing notes to each other.

> Hello, Miss! How goes it on med-surg? Seen any exciting things yet? Are there any nice staff? You must be sure to let me know so I can look them up when I get there!
>
> I'm just settling in to my room here — got a whirlwind tour by a senior nurse who didn't even tell me her name until she was leaving. Doris Slaunwhite — do you remember her? She seems sensible, but I miss laughing with you. When can we get together for a catch up?
>
> I've just got to run cross to the OH to figure out my assignment, will pop this in the mail as I go.

She sealed the note in an envelope, stuck on a stamp, and as she headed out the door, dropped it in the "mail OUT box".

They'd have to get back to sending things inter-hospital mail. Stamps were expensive.

She wrapped her cape around herself again and stepped out into the wind, pushing against it for the short distance to the hospital entrance. As she crossed the street, she thought she could see people staring at her from the windows. Could she hear voices? Or was that just the wind? Surely not screams?

Shaking her head, she told herself to give up all the nonsense. She leaned in and pulled open the big front doors.

Historical Note

ROCKWOOD HISTORY

In 1859, the Rockwood Asylum opened in Kingston (Portsmouth). The name was later changed to Rockwood Hospital, and then in 1920 to Ontario Hospital — Kingston. Over the course of its earlier years, a gymnasium was added, then libraries, etc. in order to better serve the patients. During and after the Second World War, the hospital was understaffed due to the war, but by 1959, new buildings were added and the original asylum became known as the Penrose building, which housed people with disabilities. In the 1960s, a music department was added, as well as a unit for children and adolescents. In 1965, the name changed again to the Kingston Psychiatric Hospital. In March 2001, the hospital was placed under the authority of the Providence Continuing Care Centre's Governing Board. Its name was changed a final time to Mental Health Services, and the original asylum building, which had been closed since 1997, remains empty as of 2020.[*]

---

[*] Museum of Healthcare at Kingston,
https://mhc.andornot.net/en/permalink/artifact11497

THREE

Nobody likes me everyone hates me

Ruth bit her lip so hard she was sure it was going to bleed. Things were not going well. All she could think of were her disastrous challenges the previous year at the TB Sanatorium. She hoped and prayed it wouldn't be the same here.

Just once she'd like to feel competent starting out, anywhere. Heaven knows she had little enough support about this when she was growing up. "Jack of all trades, master of none," was all she ever heard at home.

The sinking self-doubt began when she was 'welcomed' onto her floor. Being locked onto the ward with people who might have criminal backgrounds was scary in itself. After all, the hospital used to provide care only for prisoners from Kingston Penitentiary who were mentally ill. They'd gradually been shifted out to allow more space for 'normal' mental patients, especially all those damaged by the war, but Ruth was sure there'd still be murderers amongst them. It wasn't reassuring to hear the metal doors slam shut, hear the clanging of the heavy keys in the lock.

And then there was the head nurse, Miss Myrna Thomas. She was a graduate of the psychiatric nursing school and Ruth could tell she found all the students rotating in and out a royal pain. The atmosphere was distinctly chilly as she toured Ruth around the ward, shaking her keys in her apron pocket. Doris, the nurse assigned to mentor her, was nowhere to be found. It turned out she didn't even work on Ruth's ward.

The patients were intimidating, too. Most of them were men, and that set off her fear left over from the previous year, when she was attacked by a patient at the Sanatorium. One man sat in a corner of the sunroom, rocking and humming. Another came right up to Ruth and stared into her face from an inch away. Another just sat. A few played cards, but even they made open mouths and fisheyes at Ruth like she was an alien species.

The tour ended quickly, after being taken around the bathrooms and the utility rooms. "Always keep these locked," said the head nurse. "There are sharp and dangerous things in there."

As if Ruth didn't know that! They walked into the sunroom.

"Go sit with Mrs. Matthews and play cards with her. You know Gin Rummy, of course?"

Ruth quailed. She hated playing cards and was terrible at it. But off she went to sit by the patient and try.

The patient, Elizabeth Matthews, sat, unmoving, with the cards in front of her. "I hear you like cards," began Ruth, trying to sound cheerful.

Mrs. Matthews said nothing.

"What shall we play? Maybe Hearts? Euchre?" She picked up the deck and shuffled it, started dealing out cards. "Let's play Hearts. I know that one," Ruth added. She dealt out the cards.

Mrs. Matthews didn't move to pick up her cards. She didn't move, period. Ruth laid her hand down.

"Maybe you'd just like a pleasant chat? I'm Miss Maclean. I'm new here. I'm so looking forward to getting to know you and the rest of the people here." Ruth gestured at the sunroom full of patients. "Have you made any friends here? Have you been here long?"

Mrs. Matthews turned her head then, and looked open-mouthed at Ruth, who found her gaze sliding away.

~

"She stared for at least a full minute," Ruth told Doris later, as they caught up over tea. "It was like being watched under a microscope. Or like in *Alice in Wonderland*."

"Did she ever pick up her cards?"

"No! She finished staring, looked away, and just picked at her nightie."

"What happened then?"

"Miss Thomas came over and asked how it was going."

That was even worse, Ruth remembered. "Oh, we're just getting acquainted," she had said to the head nurse. "We haven't started playing cards yet."

"Then," she told Doris, in tones of utter indignation. "The entire room burst into laughs. Apparently, Mrs. Matthews never moves, or talks, and would never ever play cards. She's a minister's daughter. It was all a joke to make me feel awkward." Ruth shook her head. "I was so embarrassed, but worse, I could see it bothered her!"

Elizabeth Matthews had heard the laughter, turned and stared at Ruth again, then stood and walked out of the sunroom like someone in a dream.

"I followed her. I felt so bad. But she went to her room, lay down on her bed, and turned away from me. I felt awful for her."

"Did she ever speak?"

"No," said Ruth. "I sat there for about fifteen minutes, watching her not move, and then thought I should have a look at her chart. Had I made her shut down like that?"

"Unlikely."

"No, that's when I found out she has been all but catatonic since she came in. Poor thing got sick after her babies. Her husband — he's a banker — he apparently isn't sympathetic at all. He comes in to visit and ends up yelling at her."

"How sad."

"And the patients and staff! They were terrible. One orderly told me they sometimes put her facing the corner of the sunroom for fun and she just stands there until someone comes to get her. Made me furious."

It had. Ruth heard the tale, the orderlies laughing and snorting, and put her head into the chart. It turned out Mrs. Matthews had two children, with slight depression after the first, and more acute symptoms after the second.

"Her husband is fed up. He's signed her up for electroconvulsive therapy. You've seen them do that, right?"

"Yes," said Doris soberly. "It's better than the insulin shock therapy, but ..."

"I'm supposed to go along with her soon. She was due tomorrow so she could have a 'quiet weekend' afterwards. But her husband usually comes in on Sundays. Will she be okay by then? He sounds mean."

Doris stirred her tea. "I'm glad to not be assigned to that floor. I've done some shifts there. That head nurse can have a judgey streak. I'm so sorry you got placed there! Especially after last year."

Ruth had given Doris an outline of her precarious adventures at the Sanatorium. Doris had been satisfyingly shocked.

"I know," wailed Ruth. "Why me?"

Doris laughed. "Maybe you should come to church with me. Try that magic for a change. Seems like yours isn't working!"

Ruth winced. She could just imagine her father's response if she, a Presbyterian minister's daughter, went to a Catholic Mass.

"Father would kill me," she said. "But you've given me an idea. She's a minister's daughter, too. I wonder if she'd like me to pray with her?"

"Can't hurt," said Doris. "Oh no, I've got to run! I'm due on in half an hour!" She leapt up and dashed out, upsetting her tea. "I'll get the next one," she called over her shoulder, as Ruth mopped things up.

Historical Note

DEALING WITH POST-PARTUM DEPRESSION

Doctor S Weir Mitchell ordered her to "live as domestic life as possible. Have your child with you all the time." (be it remarked that if I did but dress the baby it left me shaking and crying — certainly far from a healthy companionship for her, to say nothing of the effect on me.) "Lie down for an hour after each meal. Have but two hours intellectual life a day. And never touch pen, brush or pencil as long as you live." [*]

[*] Jeffrey L. Geller and Maxine Harris, *Women of the asylum: Voices from behind the walls*, 1840-1945. Anchor books, New York, 1994. p. xix

FOUR

Getting organized

The next day, Alison McGill, a senior nurse on the floor, took Ruth under her wing a bit more.

"Forgive us for yesterday. We'd just had a patient die, a long-term one, and we were all operating on half a heart. I'm so sorry if we seemed to drop you right into things. And I was away on insulin treatments all day. I'll be able to help you out more today."

Ruth tried a smile. "Oh, that's fine, Miss McGill. I had a chance to look around." And see some of the ways the patients are treated, too, she thought.

"So today, I'm going to show you our charting. It's mainly by exception. Are you used to that?"

"Oh yes, in the TB San people were there for a long time, so we often wrote 'same as yesterday' or 'walked the halls today.'"

"Yes, that's it. Just writing down what you see that differs from the day before. And medications, too, of course. We do take vital signs, but not every day unless the patient is sick with a physical disease. Look into the dayroom. What would you chart there?"

Ruth looked out into the room, trying to really see it. Patients were playing cards, spinning slowly around, rocking, tearing up paper. Some of them yelled out at nothing. "I'm not sure, not knowing how they were before. I'd probably want to remark about the paper-tearing. Is that a new behaviour? And are all the men playing cards the same ones who played the day before? Sometimes in the San, that was how you'd know the men were feeling sicker. They wouldn't show up for the card games."

Alison looked at her, smiling. "Very good, Miss Maclean. I can see you've had some practice evaluating patients in a non-medical way. But let me point something out. See that fellow over in the chair in the corner?"

"Yes," said Ruth. "He looks down in the dumps."

"He is. That's our dear Leonard Wiley. He's feeling sad because we took his sceptre away from him."

"His sceptre?"

Alison grinned. "He thinks he is the king of Belgium. He likes to walk about holding a stick, pretending it's a sceptre. Paranoid delusional. It's all fine and good until he starts using it as a weapon. We had to take it away earlier. Now we have to watch him, because any minute …"

"Who has taken away my sceptre," Leonard bellowed, right on cue. "What vile revolutionaries attacked me while I was asleep? I'll have your heads!"

Leonard stood, waving his arms threateningly at the men playing cards, who ignored him. He blustered some more, but when he saw the orderlies sauntering in from all sides, he sat back down. "I know you," he muttered. "You are coming to put me in jail. But I'm NOT GOING TO GO!" He looked over at the nursing station window. "You can't take away my right to rule." He paused, peered in closer through the window. "What fair maiden is this?"

"Oh, oh," said Alison. "Step away from the window."

"What's up?"

"With every fresh rotation, he thinks he's meeting his new queen. It's tiresome, actually. Now he'll start following you around pledging love until we hit him over the head with a big dose of Luminal."

"Really?" Ruth could feel dread running in icy rivulets all over her body. She'd just managed to get rid of TB patient George, who also had plans for her she wasn't involved in willingly.

"Has he …? He won't …" she gasped out.

Alison looked at her, shrugged. "No, he's harmless overall. Might try and kiss you or get you to walk around with him arm in arm. My advice is to be like those men there and just ignore him. If it gets too much, we've got the meds ready."

"Still," Ruth said.

"Oh, don't be a scaredy cat. We'll keep an eye out for you, won't we, Dan?" She turned to one of the orderlies, who stretched, made his hand into a fist, pushed it into his other hand.

"That's what we're here for."

"Meanwhile, let me show you how everything else works. This is the med room. It's always locked. All of our sharps and every pill, even baby Aspirin, gets stored in here. Never ever leave it open, even when you are inside. Close the door after you and be sure it's locked."

Everything seems to need to be closed and locked here, thought Ruth. How does anyone get any work done with all the locking and unlocking?

She demonstrated unlocking the door, and soon she and Ruth were squashed into a small, windowless space, surrounded by pills and syringes and vials. "The thing is, a lot of our patients are here because they really don't want to live anymore, so it's more about keeping them safe than worrying about what they will do to us. Overdoses are terrible. One time, one patient was palming her sedation meds for weeks, then took them all at night. By the time we found her, she was too far gone to save."

"How awful!" Ruth said. "It must be terrible to feel so sad. And aren't they afraid of God? Don't they have family that will look after them, give them something to live for?"

Alison looked at her pityingly. "Sometimes it is God or the family that causes their problems! Look at that dear Mrs. Matthews! Her husband is so mean! I wouldn't want to go home to him, either, even with two little babies looking for me."

"Really?"

Alison shook her head. "I shouldn't have said anything. But watch when he comes in for a visit. You can tell she's afraid of him."

She gestured to all the drugs lined up. "You should have the opportunity to give most of these while you are here. It's good for experience. Until you've tried it, you can't possibly imagine how hard it is to give a needle to someone who has been on injections for years and years. It destroys the tissue, makes it hard as leather. Here, we're probably going to need to give a dose to his majesty. Why don't you draw it up and get it ready? Here's the Kardex. You can see where all the drugs are listed. Did they use them at the San?"

"Oh yes, Kardexes seem to be everywhere."

"Good. Never know what knowledge you students will bring with you in terms of experience. The gals from Hotel Dieu seem to have a completely different approach than you KGH women, and we've always done it a different way, too. I'm glad they are giving you longer in your psych rotation, though. There's no way you could understand things in six weeks."

Ruth nodded, meanwhile mentally counting the days until she was off the ward and would never have to step through those locked doors again. And this being locked in the med room was terrifying, too. She also wondered how much of the placement change had to do with short staffing. There weren't many nurses on the ward. That seemed to be a constant for Ruth's placements, anyway.

"Ok. I hear him getting riled up. Can you draw it up? We'll use a 21-gauge needle for him since his tissue is so tough. Get one out of the drawer, will you?"

Ruth picked up the needle and, hands shaking, screwed it onto the syringe, drew up the medication, pressed the plunger so a little fluid came out.

"See, you've got it just fine. It's an unusually large dose, which you'll know once you have time to look at the medications we use here. Now let me get the orderlies to get him ready. You stay here, my Queen." Alison grinned and left, closing the door behind her. "Remember to lock it. I'll knock."

Feeling more paranoid than the patients, she locked the door. It gave her a chance to catch her breath. This was already a horrible rotation. She felt incompetent, frightened, and stupid. At least in the last place, she hadn't had to lock herself away from the patients.

Alison knocked on the door. "They're getting him ready. Come on out."

She could hear Leonard bellowing as she stepped out to the nursing station, the needle carefully held on a little tray. The orderlies had put him in the bed in his room and were holding him flat so she could reach his exposed buttocks. Aiming the needle as she'd been taught, she had to reevaluate as he writhed and protested until he saw her. "Oh, my Queen! You can do what you want back there."

She stabbed the needle in, but it bounced out! Trying again, she applied more pressure, afraid of hurting him, but it didn't seem to bother him at all. She pushed it into his flesh, checked for blood by withdrawing slightly, injected the solution, then pulled out the needle. He relaxed almost immediately.

As they walked away, Alison whispered to her, "Most of that is psychosomatic. It takes a while for the drug to work its way into his bloodstream with his tissues like that. That's why he has such a huge dose."

Reaching the nursing station, Alison turned to her. "Well, time to rinse out that syringe, and we have a whole load of needles and syringes that need cleaning. Over to you. I'll show you the autoclave once you get them washed in the solution. And we do boil the needles on the ward here. Again, be careful to lock the doors behind you. You don't want someone to spill the hot water by accident."

Ruth felt her shoulders slump as she stepped in to do even more grunt work. How was she going to learn about how to look after patients when she was on scrubbing duty? And, after she was done with the needles, she was sent to clean and sterilize bedpans and urinals, more of the same.

FIVE

Smells

After a few more shifts of cleaning bits and bobs, Ruth was sent by the head nurse to observe Mrs. Matthews' ECT treatment. "You take her, Miss Maclean. You've met her and it would be a good experience for you to see the treatment."

Ruth quailed but knew there was no point in arguing. She dreaded seeing the procedure, about which she'd heard so much. The treatment room was in a different section of the building, and she had to push the stretcher, loaded with her patient, along a long hallway under a few of the new fluorescent lights that flickered in a malignant way. The stretcher refused to steer properly, so she kept having to stop and set its squeaky wheels straight or send poor Mrs. Matthews careening into a wall. Fortunately, the nurses upstairs had given the patient some sort of sedative, and she appeared to be sleeping.

She woke up, though, when she was pushed into the room. She started a high keening "nonono" moaning that sent chills up Ruth's spine. Meantime, the smell. What was that smell? It seemed to be a blend of urine, feces, and acrid sweat. Ruth wanted to dash about and clean any soiled corners, but the room itself looked spotless, even the aged linoleum. The smell seemed to be airborne, left over from a previous patient, perhaps. There was a grumpy-looking doctor and a nurse standing waiting for her.

"Over here, Nurse," commanded the doctor. When she struggled with the rebellious stretcher, he got impatient and grabbed it himself, almost tipping it over. Ruth hung on like grim death to keep it balanced and fortunately Mrs. Matthews wasn't spilled onto the floor.

They transferred her onto the bed for the ECT and tucked a small pillow under her back. Ruth wondered if they had to ground the bed, thinking back to her high school science experiments. Mrs. Matthews struggled briefly but the doctor, who hadn't bothered to introduce himself, leaned over her and said, very close to her face, "Now, Mrs. Matthews, I discussed this with your husband and we both feel this is the way to go. I'm sure you will feel much happier once we're done the full series."

The other nurse strapped Mrs. Matthews onto the bed with rubber straps that held her arms and legs tight, and then the final one over her brow, holding her head in place. Mrs. Matthews' eyes opened wide then, panicking, but there wasn't much she could do, all tied down. Ruth took her hand, hoping to soothe her, but she pulled it away as much as she could.

"It's better just to do this quickly," said the other nurse. "She'll be calmer afterwards. And it doesn't hurt. You stand back now."

The doctor squirted some jelly substance onto Mrs. Matthews' temples and fastened a strange-looking headband with padded disks on each side on her head. He adjusted the disks so they nestled into her temples, and pulled the device tight. The headband was wired onto a machine that looked a bit like a small X-ray machine, with dials and readouts. The nurse placed a rubber mouth guard in Mrs. Matthews' mouth. Everyone stepped away and then the doctor fiddled with the machine dials, paused, and flipped the switch.

Mrs. Matthews immediately went into a grand mal seizure, spasming and jerking against the restraints. The doctor flipped the switch back, and everything started to return to normal, though the patient continued to seize for a few seconds more.

"There," said the doctor, "That was a good one." He faced Ruth. "Sending the electrical pulse through the brain helps … jolt … the depression out." He guffawed at his joke. "Seriously, it does seem to help our most depressed patients. Currently, it's our best treatment for depression. Just unfortunate it doesn't work as well for schizophrenia," he muttered to himself. He turned back to Ruth, who was frozen in stunned silence. "She'll be much better, you'll see. And if not," he continued, "we can always try a higher current, or a longer series. Have you read up about ECT, Nurse?"

Ruth shook her head. "I've had a brief look, but I just got notice to come here the other day."

The doctor frowned. "Why they don't just use the students from the school on site here, I'll never know. You must be one of the six-weekers, right?"

Ruth tried to object, but the doctor spoke right over her.

"As if anyone could understand anything about mental illness in such a short time."

The other nurse nodded agreement. "Miss Maclean, I notice you are wearing your name tag. We don't wear them here. Patients could grab them, intentionally or unintentionally." She smiled briefly. "I'm Nurse Skinner." She bent to remove the headband off Mrs. Matthews, pulled out the mouth guard. "Can you help me undo these straps? We have another five patients to get through this morning."

Ruth sprang in to help, undoing the clasps.

"We'll take her back to the ward in a few minutes and she'll have a lovely rest. You can stay with her, I hope? We usually stay with the patient until they are fully awake. Just be sure to keep her on her side in case she aspirates. She shouldn't, but it's a risk. Please remind her she'll come back for another treatment in two days."

Ruth nodded, but wondered if she'd know when Mrs. Matthews would be awake. She was so unresponsive even when sitting up. And what would she be like? What would that shock have done to her?

She wheeled the patient back to the ward. As they went down the hallway, they passed some patients waiting for the ECT room. It seemed a popular treatment, thought Ruth. But surely it must cause some damage, those shocks? Or did the brain recover fully, just be re-jigged? She made a mental note to ask the senior nurse when she had a moment.

She tagged an orderly to help her transfer Mrs. Matthews back to her bed and quickly took her vital signs. Her heartbeat was fast, her blood pressure down. She still seemed fast asleep. Ruth placed her on her side and tucked her in, then took the chart over to a table in the room and wrote down what she observed. Looking over at her patient, and revisiting the seizure she'd had, she suddenly felt close to tears. It must've hurt, she thought. Something like that can't just happen and everything be fine afterwards. What if it made her worse?

Gulping back her tears, she leaned out into the hallway and called the orderly back. "Could you stay with her for a minute? I need the washroom."

He nodded and came into the room, sitting heavily on a vacant bed. "Hurry, now. I've got a guy in solitary, but they'll be letting him out any minute and I need to be there then. Don't want him to get any more bad ideas." He smirked.

"Thanks," said Ruth, rushing out and wondering what the patient in solitary had done to send him there. Some of these patients were scary. It wasn't their fault, Ruth told herself. They didn't know where they were half the time, or even who they were, right?

SIX

Reaction

──────────

Ruth curled into a corner of the stairwell, arms wrapped around her chest, trying to stop her sobs. She couldn't hold them in, and her face was becoming decidedly tear streaked. She knew that would lead to questions, so she kept gulping, hoping to get control. Breathing in, deep and slow, like her father had showed her to do before she did the readings at church, she tried to calm herself. She felt so sorry for the people trapped here. She couldn't understand how they stood it, their minds so detached, and then the ECT treatment seemed so barbaric. All those spasms. It was a wonder Mrs. Matthews' legs hadn't snapped. She'd read that they often did. Her heart filled with pity.

Cigarette smoke! Someone was in the stairwell with her, and sneaking a smoke! They'd been told not to do that, ever since the huge fire that had burned down the Queen's Student Union in September. The fire department blamed it on someone smoking in the stairwell. Since then, it was absolutely forbidden here, given the challenge that it would be to get all the patients out in good order in an emergency. That said, everyone smoked everywhere else, so Ruth had to wonder who would need to sneak a smoke in here. Unless it was another student. Students weren't allowed to smoke while on duty. She sniffled hastily and wiped her face with her handkerchief, not really much use, as it was soaking wet with tears.

"Here, take mine." A deep voice spoke above her head, and a hand holding a fresh one and some wafting cigarette smoke followed it down. A man stepped down to sit beside her, and Ruth startled.

"Who are you? What are you doing here? Don't you know you shouldn't be smoking in the stairwells?"

The man, a youngish, tall, annoyingly handsome fellow, looked around, furtive. "Don't tell, will you? I just had to get off the ward for a minute. My patient is attacking me, and my supervisor isn't helping. I'm Richard Hartman, by the way. Medical resident and seriously reconsidering my life choices."

Ruth smiled, her eyes still watery. "Nurse Maclean," she said. "First year nursing, and with you on the life choice thing." She stood up. "I'd better go. They'll be looking for me."

"Where's your placement?"

"2B ward. The locked one on the second floor."

"Wow. That's a tough group of patients. I had to visit with one schizophrenic patient for a week and he didn't even speak to me once. Today I'm one floor down, manic depression. Also locked, but occasionally very exciting. They do speak. My patient today is in a manic phase and tells me repeatedly she can see triangles in my face. Points them out with her sharp fingernails. Difficult not to flinch."

Ruth's eyes opened wide. She dabbed at them with the handkerchief.

"But you've been crying. What happened?"

She shrugged. "I don't know. I had to get away for a bit. My patient just had ECT."

Dr. Hartman whistled. "Hard to watch, isn't it? I just saw my first one yesterday. Were they given curare?"

"No, just morphine. It was awful. The worst thing is when I took her back to the room, it didn't seem to have done anything but knock her out. I told an orderly I needed to go to the washroom and ran. I'm supposed to wait until she wakes up, but she's catatonic! How am I supposed to evaluate that?"

Dr. Hartman nodded. "Well, she may wake up and surprise you. The treatments seem to work in depressives. It's so much better if they sedate them, though. The first treatments used to break legs and arms with the seizures."

"I read that," said Ruth, her face a mask of horror.

"Well, we're managing things better and better. They say. Sometimes. Can you ask your professor to let you off? Just until you recover a bit."

"Oh, I wouldn't dare ask for that. I'm here on my own. It's a long story."

"Well, maybe we can go for a walk one day and you can catch me up on that story, Nurse Maclean. It seems to me we could have a good chat about our respective choices."

"Maybe," said Ruth, her voice chilly. She knew all about cozy walks from her placement the year before. "I've got to get back. I don't dare get caught crying." She started up the stairs. "And don't you tell anyone about this, or I'll rat on you in one hot second for smoking in the stairwell."

Dr. Hartman winced. "You wouldn't! They'll give me hell … forgive me … heck. I'm already on probation for talking back. If they find out I'm smoking on duty, they'll throw me out. Look, I'll keep your secret if you keep mine." He waved his hand frantically about, dispelling the cigarette smoke. "Want some?" He offered her the cigarette. "It's calming."

"No," said Ruth. She knew she'd be out on her uniformed bottom if anyone saw her smoking on placement. She turned to go, giving her eyes a final wipe with the hanky. Turning, she said, "Here, this is yours ..." But Dr. Hartman had gone, leaving nothing but a faint trail of smoke behind him. She sniffed at her uniform to make sure there was no smell of smoke before laughing at herself. The entire ward was filled with smoke all the time. She'd barely noticed it the first few days she was on the ward, she was so scared, but the patients had an allotment of cigarettes to be smoked under careful supervision, and someone seemed to be puffing all the time. Staff were supposed to keep their smoking for off the ward to prevent any risk of the patients stealing them. And students were reprimanded if they smelled of smoke.

When she got back to the ward, she slid carefully down the side of the hall, hoping not to be seen, and into the room with her patient. The orderly, who'd been reading a book, said, "Good timing. They're just letting my guy out of confinement. He's finally stopped yelling at everyone." He peered at Ruth. "You haven't been off somewhere crying, have you? You newbie students. No guts."

"No," Ruth said, sniffing. "It's the cigarette smoke. Makes me tear up sometimes. Just needed to get away for a bit."

"I hear you. Me, I never have to buy smokes anymore. Get all my juice just breathing the air in here. Anyway, you're on. She's been asleep, nothing new to report. You might need to change her sheets, though. I think she's wet."

Ruth felt sadness creep over her again. Mrs. Matthews was such a pretty, sweet-looking woman. It seemed like all they were doing was tormenting her.

Mrs. Matthews whimpered. Ruth went over to her bedside, leaned down. "I'm here, Mrs. Matthews. How are you feeling?

Can I get you anything? Some water?" She filled a cup and held it out to her.

The patient rolled over and sat up, took the cup from Ruth's hand. Ruth stared, amazed. That was more independent movement than she'd seen from her to date.

Mrs. Matthews cleared her throat. "You were there with me. For the treatment."

"Yes. Do you remember it?"

"No. Just you. You were kind."

Ruth felt tears starting again. She swallowed.

"So sleepy."

Ruth nodded. "We'll get you right back in bed so you can rest. But first, I think we need to change your things."

"I wet myself? Ohhhhhh ...." Mrs. Matthews' head dropped onto her chest, and she began crying.

"Now, now, don't fret. I think it happens a lot after the treatment. I'm sure you'll be right as rain after this. Let's get you freshened up." Ruth gathered sheets and a fresh nightgown to change everything, meanwhile thrashing herself for her turn of phrase. "Right as rain, indeed," she told herself angrily. "Might as well say, damp as a pond!"

In a few minutes, Mrs. Matthews was all tidy and dry and tucked back in bed. She turned on her side, curled up, but this time facing out into the room. Ruth pulled the blankets up over her shoulder. "Have a good rest. I'll be back to get you up for lunch."

Mrs. Matthews nodded. As Ruth was leaving, she called out. "Nurse?"

Ruth turned back. "Yes, Mrs. Matthews? Do you need anything?"

"No," she said. "Just, thank you."

～

"And then she smiled!" Ruth said to Doris Slaunwhite when they met that evening after their shifts were done. "It was amazing!"

Doris smiled, too, but raised a cautionary hand. "It often takes several treatments before the depression resolves. Don't be surprised if she goes back into catatonia a few times between treatments. And remember, she likely won't have a solid memory of things. She may not recognize you when you go back. Just be prepared. They usually treat them every couple of days for several weeks."

Ruth sighed, flattened.

"It all sounds like good progress, though. Better than when we were treating schizophrenics ten times in a row until they couldn't see straight. Glad some things are changing. Maybe she'll be able to get back to her babies," Doris added, raising her voice to sound cheerful.

"And her husband."

"Yeah." They both slumped. "Maybe he'll be nicer, too. Toast and peanut butter?"

"Please!"

Historical Note

ELECTROCONVULSIVE THERAPY (ECT)

In 1937 two Italian psychiatrists experimented with ECT on a patient. The story goes that they pondered over just how many volts to ZAP the poor sod with, and for how long, until they settled on 55 volts for 2/10 of a second. The patient was not anesthetized or sedated prior to being fried. He underwent a major grand epileptic convulsion, then sat up, looked around at the doctors and said, 'what the fuck are you arseholes trying to do?' This was a Very Good Thing. Surprisingly. The patient hadn't spoken a word of sense in weeks. Calling his doctors arseholes was a major step forward.

What happens nowadays during ECT is that the patient is given a general anesthetic and a muscle relaxant. Previously, as described above, there was no anesthetic. Electrodes are placed on the temples and an electric current is passed across the brain for three or four seconds. The effect is to set off a controlled epileptic seizure. The only visible effect is a slight tremor that runs through the limbs. Compared to earlier times this tremor is greatly reduced by the muscle relaxant. The patient wakes later, occasionally suffering from a slight headache or confusion. Or that is the general way of things. But is not always as straightforward as that. The most common additional side effects are nausea, muscle cramps and cardiac or respiratory problems in patients with tendencies to those conditions. The most distressing adverse effect for many people is short term memory loss. This occurs more frequently at the time of the ECT course and sometimes for a few weeks after. There may be some loss of past memories too.*

---

* Dennis O'Donnell, *The Locked Ward. Memoirs of a psychiatric orderly*. Jonathan Cape, London, 2012. p. 88

SEVEN

Bath time

It was the middle of her second week, and Ruth was starting to get a grip on what the hospital was like, how it functioned. She'd grown used to entering the main building through the hidden entry behind the front door, and walking through miles of hallways and downstairs to her student locker to leave her cape and outdoor clothes. She'd learned the routine of the dining hall where the nurses got their meals. There were four cafeterias and nurses were only welcome in one. Two were reserved for patients and the last was only for the doctors and medical students. The nurses often gossiped about what was served in the doctors' dining hall, as nursing students received the same food as the patients. They didn't think the docs would put up with that.

Ruth's ward was in the active treatment section. Some patients on the open wing on the other side of the floor were allowed to run the laundry machines, work in the library, or help with cleaning. The locked ward patients were kept separate or accompanied whenever they were moved around the hospital.

She'd also watched several ECT treatments with Mrs. Matthews. It seemed a bit as if she was getting better, but on the day in between treatments, she'd slow down again. Today, Ruth was to observe a water treatment. She followed a senior nurse who neglected to introduce herself (again! Ruth wondered why no one did that on the wards here!) and brought in Leonard Wiley, who was shouting about his rights, the divine right of kings, about the strange subjects he saw around the place.

Ruth tried to be comforting. "Please relax, sir. It's just me, Nurse Maclean ..." She left a space for the other nurse to introduce herself, but that didn't happen. "We're going to give you a lovely warm bath."

She helped the other nameless nurse run the water into the deep tub.

"If you look here, Nurse, we are going to run warm water continually into the tub here and drain it out there. The patient will be wrapped and suspended to prevent drowning, and we will keep a close watch on his temperature. I usually rub some petroleum jelly on them afterwards as the skin gets dried out, but he's too agitated to put on any now. Let's get him in."

And then, with no more ceremony than unwrapping a turkey, Mr. Wiley was stripped and re-wrapped in a cloth suspender. They lowered him into the water, while all the while he called out, "Nurse Maclean, Nurse Maclean, help me help me, they're drowning me."

After they lowered him into the water, they attached the canvas cover that sealed in the warmth and the water. "We'll turn up the current now," said the nurse. The water started to make waves.

"Ahhh," said Mr. Wiley. "That's better."

The nurse turned to Ruth. "You'd never know it, but often the patients come up and ask for this to calm themselves down. I think it might be rather pleasant, myself. At least the warm baths."

"Lots of room in here, Nurse," Mr. Wiley said, leering.

They turned their backs on him and walked to the corner of the room.

"On the other hand, the cold ones are not for the timid. I can feel myself shrinking when I'm watching one. But it does seem to make the more obnoxious behaviour stop. Now, Miss Maclean, you'll have to sit here to be sure he doesn't sink under. There's an emergency buzzer on the wall there if you need help."

"I just sit here? For how long?"

"Usual time is three hours."

Ruth gulped.

"I know, hard to stay awake. But at least it's warm in here. Since the oil restrictions started from the US, the rest of the hospital is often freezing! I wish they'd get rid of those. I mean, the war's been over for a while now. If you fall asleep, the supervisor will crush you. So, you can chat, read, walk around to keep your blood circulating. There are a few books over there, and sometimes the patients like us to read to them. Or there are a bunch of bandages to roll, should all else fail."

Ruth grimaced.

"Look, we all must do this. At least you are only looking after one person. It gets to be a pain when there are four or more."

"What do you do if they have to …" Ruth gestured at the patient's lower region.

"It's a man, dearie. Give him a urinal. Women, you have to take out of the tub and race them to the toilet quickly before they get cold. A lot of bother. Get them to void before you put them in. Or sometimes they just pee in the water. Be grateful we are starting you off easy. Oh, and don't forget to bring him something to drink now and then. The tubs are dehydrating."

The morning passed excruciatingly slowly. Mr. Wiley promptly fell asleep, so couldn't chat, leaving Ruth feeling alone and trapped. She looked through the books. The Bible, of course, a Dickens novel, which seemed unwise given the patients were living in Dickensian situations, and Anne of Green Gables. She grudgingly picked up Anne, a book she'd read multiple times when she was growing up. Next time, she vowed, she'd bring some of her study books.

The hours prescribed passed, and Ruth was rolling bandages and fighting sleep when the senior nurse came in to help take the patient out of the bath.

They pulled him out and quickly towelled him off, redressed him, put on his slippers. The nurse turned to Ruth and said, "So, you've seen how we do this. Next time, it's all on your own."

"But surely that can't be safe?" she asked, as they walked the tired man back to his ward.

"If you are lucky, you can get one of those nurses' aides they've started to train to help you, or an orderly. The nurses are far too busy."

"Nurses' aides?" Ruth had seen some people in unfamiliar green uniforms in the dining hall but was too shy to ask.

"Yes, new program. It's all about saving money. They can train them faster and control the pay. Makes me furious. We had to fight so hard to get our nursing program accepted as equal to yours, and now we are undercutting it."

Ruth walked Mr. Wiley back to his room. Mr. Wiley settled in well under his bedcovers, almost purring. "Thank you, Nurse. I shall make you an attendant in court for this."

Ruth tucked him in tight after checking his vitals and then went to record the treatment.

"How did it go with his majesty?" an orderly, Bob, asked. "He doesn't like men to look after his baths. Thinks we are knights come to kill him. He behaved for you?"

"Like a kitten. He says I can have a position in his court." Ruth smiled as she charted. Maybe some of this could be fun.

She changed her mind when she arrived on the ward the next day. Mr. Wiley was storming around, demanding to know who had stolen his crown. When he saw Ruth, he charged right up to her. She was expecting a positive greeting, so was startled when he stopped less than a hand's breadth in front of her and started shouting. "It was you! You took it off when I had my bath. Where is it, you hussy? I'll have your head for this."

Bob was on again and came up behind Mr. Wiley to restrain him. "Short time in court, eh?"

Ruth caught her breath. It was so hard to get used to people running right up to you and shouting. Too much like home, she thought, and laughed to herself. At least she didn't have to get on her knees and recite verses, she thought.

Mr. Wiley remained agitated most of the day, despite medication, until the nurses had a brilliant idea. They created a crown of paper and tape and handed it to Ruth. "Here. Tell him you have found it and return it to his majesty."

Ruth took it into Mr. Wiley's room in some fear and trepidation. Would the paper crown fool him? She wondered if there were any crowns anywhere left over from Halloween.

Mr. Wiley sat up, glaring.

"Your majesty," said Ruth, feeling utterly absurd. "Here is your crown. I must have misplaced it earlier."

To her amazement, Mr. Wiley picked it up, ran his fingers around it, touched the dots where the nurses had drawn on jewels with ink. "Look after it better next time," he said, perching it on his head. It slid down a bit sideways and Ruth had to stop herself from laughing, it looked so ridiculous, but Mr. Wiley seemed content. He walked out of the room and into the sunroom, bowing to his subjects.

When Ruth got back to the nursing station, they were all falling about laughing. Miss Thomas stopped them. "Miss Maclean, this is a key lesson for you. Remember, it serves no

point to challenge a patient's delusions. It will just cause problems
and make them troubled as they try to rationalize the real world
with theirs. Far better to go along until they can identify the real
world themselves." She sighed. "Mr. Wiley is due for ECT next
week. I'm going to miss the king."

"Will he forget about being the king?" Ruth asked.

"Sometimes, for days at a time. It doesn't seem to work long
term, however. I'm afraid we will have to try other treatments."

TRAINING NURSES' AIDES

The Kingston Training Centre is located on the second storey of a fine stone building ... The address is 321 Queen Street.

Uniforms are provided. The design has been carefully selected and the uniform is made to measure.

It consists of an apple green one-piece dress, over which is worn a white apron designed on princess lines. Brown shoes and stockings are worn. At the end of the six-month course, the trainee receives a cap. It is white with piping. After graduation and as long as she is employed in this type of work, it is hoped that the nursing assistant will continue to wear this distinctive uniform.

During the first three months, the trainees receive lectures in nursing and in the structure and function of the human body. There is also instruction in nutrition, personal hygiene, ethics, and housekeeping. Much is required of the teaching staff in the way of individual help, drill, and use of visual aids. The trainees' experience is broadened by planned trips to a dairy, library, day nursery, and visits to special hospitals.

The program for clinical experience consists of three months in a hospital for the chronically ill and three months in a general or children's hospital.

The Training Centres are open five days a week from 8:30 to 4:30 p.m. Trainees in the hospital are on duty eight hours a day, six days a week. They spend about one week on afternoon and night shift each, in order to acquaint themselves with the twenty-four-hour period of duty.

In the September 1947 class, more than one hundred young women entered training to become nursing assistants.[*]

---

[*] *Canadian Nurse,* Nov 1947

EIGHT

Diagnosis skills

In between trying to learn the various treatments at the hospital and studying the various diseases of the brain, Ruth was awash in long-distance wedding planning for her sister Meg. They'd set the date for November 23. The family wanted it to be done before the busy Advent Sundays began, and Meg wanted it after Princess Elizabeth's wedding. "I can't compete with the Princess!" said Meg, in indignant tones, when their father had begged for an earlier date.

There were telephone calls and telegrams, and Ruth spent every clear moment running around town with Betty or Mary, organizing gloves and hats and decorations for the big day. Though the hunts were exhausting, at least it gave time for the three friends to catch up and share horror stories about their various student placements. The wedding service would be held at her father's church, an hour and a half's drive away in Cloyne, of course, but the reception was still being planned. Financially, they were tight, though Billy's veteran's pay was helping with some special items, and Meg and her mother and some ladies from the church would bake the cake with donated supplies. Ruth spent her time between shifts making bows and garlands out of ribbon. She'd take them up for the day.

On the ward, everyone was teasing her. "Why aren't you the one getting married, Miss Maclean? She's your little sister, isn't she?"

Even Dr. Hartman, her doctor friend (as she started daring to call him in her head after running into him often around the hospital), came around to tease. "We've lost so many nurses to marriage after the war. Sure hope you aren't planning to do that!"

"No chance," said Ruth. "Besides, who would want to leave this?" She gestured to her soaking uniform. She'd just some back from another bath treatment and the patient had been quite agitated.

He winked at her and was just at the point of leaving when Ruth remembered something. "Dr. Hartman?"

He turned around. Her heart did a little flippy thing. There was something about him …

"I wanted to ask you about this patient. Could you come with me?"

He looked at her, startled. Ruth chewed her lip. She'd done it again, addressed a doctor directly. She needed to stop doing that! Only speak when spoken to … Fortunately, he eventually smiled and followed her.

They ignored the catcalls from the patients as they went down the hallway into a side room. The agitated patient, calm now, was lying wrapped up securely in warm blankets.

"May we have a look at your feet?" Ruth asked.

"No," the patient said. "They are my feet, and they have told me no."

"Will I have to put them back in the bath, then?" Ruth stood at the end of the bed, arms crossed.

The patient struggled, kicking, but she was wrapped tight and couldn't go far. Her kicking loosened the blankets at her feet and Ruth pulled them up. The bottoms of her feet were covered with red lines, stripes, small marks where something sharp must have pierced them.

Dr. Hartman leaned over them briefly, pressed on a couple. The patient, soothed by the presence of a good-looking doctor, let him, saying only, "Oooh, doctor, that tickles."

"Thank you for letting me see your feet," Dr. Hartman said, tucking in the blankets again. "Now you have a good rest."

"I will, doctor." She stuck out her tongue at Ruth.

They walked out into the hallway.

"Well spotted, Miss Maclean. She's been cutting."

"What?"

"She's been cutting herself. It's something patients do, especially women, when they are working up to committing suicide. I've just been reading about this."

"Surely she doesn't think she can kill herself by stabbing her toes? And how is she doing it in here, I wonder?" Ruth tilted her head in puzzlement.

"Well, some other patients do it to get a feeling of control. When you put her in the bath, the fresh ones must have stung like the dickens. We'll have to keep a close eye on her. I'll let the attending know. We might need to count her cutlery for a while."

"Has she done all of that since she got here?"

"I doubt it. Some of them look quite old. She's been here for how long?"

"Just two days. Her husband brought her in."

"Another husband, eh? Seems to be a trend." Dr. Hartman frowned. "Discontented husbands."

"She hears voices, seems to leave reality. I think she can really use some help."

"Ok. I'll have a look at her chart later. I've got to run —

there's a therapy session starting and I must be there — but I need a smoke first." Dr. Hartman paused. "Again, well spotted. Others might not have noticed."

Ruth felt a little warm glow. Perhaps too much of a warm glow, simply from the compliment. But then he'd rested his hand on her shoulder as he left, and that spot was warm for hours.

She tucked the patient in again, using the techniques she'd learned from the senior nurses. It held the patients tight, almost like swaddling a baby. It seemed to soothe most of them.

The head nurse came in to check her work. Initially frowning, she left in a more moderate mood. "Well, it seems as if you've learned something at least since you arrived."

"Thank you, Miss Thomas. Did Dr. Hartman speak to you?"

"Yes. We will keep a watch now. You should regularly search her area, and the patient herself, for sharp objects. How is Mrs. Matthews? Have you managed any progress there?"

Ruth shook her head. After the first few ECT treatments, Mrs. Matthews had shut down again. Ruth wondered if it was the visit from her husband that did that, but didn't want to say so. Miss Thomas seemed to dance in attendance on Mr. Matthews, and Ruth wasn't sure why.

"Come with me," Miss Thomas commanded. Ruth shuffled along behind her, not sure why the tone of voice had changed to one that sounded like she was going to get a dressing down. They entered the head nurse's office, and Miss Thomas shut the door. Ruth felt a stab of fear. What now?

"That was a good catch on your patient," she began, "but you should have contacted me directly, rather than going to the doctor on your own. There are chains of command, something I gather you've had problems with before. In the future …"

"Yes, Miss Thomas. I'll be sure to keep that in mind."

"You've interrupted me."

Ruth shut her mouth, looked at the floor. When would she learn to listen and only speak when asked?

"I know some of this is because of your enthusiasm for nursing, so I can forgive it somewhat. But you must learn your place. For this afternoon, I am putting you on dayroom duty. Please make sure it is clean and there are no behavioural issues while you are there."

"But my patients …"

"I imagine we can find someone else to watch them for this time period. Off you go, and no more backtalking, or I'll give you latrine duty. Oh, by the way, while you are in the dayroom, give it a good dusting. Just ensure none of the patients takes the mop."

How was she to do that? Ruth wondered. Often, because they were so short-staffed, the patients helped with the cleaning. How was she to tell them that this time that would not be allowed?

Sure enough, as soon as she stepped into the dayroom with the mop, three patients came up to help.

"Thank you, but I have to do it this time," she started to explain.

"She doesn't think you can do it," shouted one man.

"That's not it at all. You do a wonderful job. It's just your day off," she told them. "You can relax and supervise. Tell me where I've missed a spot."

They took to that task with great enthusiasm and Ruth was kept busy whipping the mop here and there as they shouted directions until the room shone. When she finally could return the mop to the utility room, she was exhausted. She must have walked that dayroom over fifty times. At least watching her pirouette with the mop kept the patients entertained.

She went back to the dayroom and sat with one table of patients playing Euchre. Looking back over her shoulder into the nursing station, she noticed Miss Thomas watching her, an approving, or at least not angry, look on her face. One test passed, she thought. Only a thousand more to go.

By the time she returned to the residence, she had regained some energy. Good thing too, as she had a plump letter waiting for her from Meg, with a dozen more requests. She vowed to elope if she ever got married. All this fuss was ridiculous.

NINE

Night shift

Ruth sat in her bedroom, looking out of the window, trying desperately to remember why she wanted to be a nurse. The psych hospital was doing her in. She had another nine weeks to plow through before she was released. She told Mary, over coffee on one of their hunts for Meg's supplies, "I'm afraid I'll end up as one of the residents if I'm there much longer. They're beginning to seem normal. Except at night, in my dreams, that is."

Mary, as was her wont, said, "Just say a prayer now and then. God approves of you doing this or you wouldn't have made it through last year. So, buck up. He's on your side."

Ruth was skeptical. Given that at least one patient had delusions HE was God until they put him into the cold bath, she was doubting her belief in any sort of God, let alone a helpful one. That patient would scream blessings as he was first put in, then slip into more and more inappropriate language, swearing, calling on Satan. Neither being came to help him.

Eventually he'd fall asleep, that is if the joking orderlies would let him.

But today was her first time on the night shift. She was scared. No, terrified. It would happen that it was also a full moon, and only one day from Halloween.

The orderlies had spent the past week regaling her with tales of patient deaths and ghosts just to get her spun around. They went on and on about the director, William Metcalf, who had been killed by a patient in 1885. "They say he still walks the grounds," orderly Jim said as he followed her, drawling in a deep voice. "Sometimes you can even see him, but most of the time you just hear his footsteps, and then a scream …"

So, she was a bit creeped out. To add insult to injury, her mentor Alison was off sick, and she was having to do the shift on her own, with only one nurse supervisor and the joking orderlies to help.

Flu season had started, and the isolation wards had filled up. The orderlies were busy taking sick patients from the wards over to Beechgrove to segregate them from the healthy patients, so she knew they wouldn't be much help. She hoped one would stay on the ward with her.

"At least most of the patients will be asleep," she told herself, gripping her blue prayer book tightly in her hand. "They can't possibly all be awake all night."

The supervisor said she would come by to watch her give any medications, and she could always hit the panic button in the nursing station, but Ruth's legs were quivering as she walked across the street to start her shift. It didn't help that the trees were scratching against one another and making unhappy noises, or that the lake seemed agitated under the full moon.

She grabbed a cup of coffee from the cafeteria and, tossing it back, headed up the stairs to her floor. The door locking behind her seemed even heavier than usual. Would she ever get out again?

In report, the charge nurse tried to reassure her. "Now, Miss

Maclean, we've given all of them that can have it a sleeping preparation. Mrs. Matthews is fatigued from her ECT today, so she should sleep. Mr. Smith is likewise worn out from his insulin treatment. He may wake up hungry and it is fine to bring him some toast and tea. Just be sure the tea isn't too hot. He has sometimes been a bit agitated when he wakes up."

Ruth tried to hide her shaking legs. She crossed them over each other, getting a stern look from the charge nurse, but at this point, she didn't care.

"You may have an issue with Miss Beauchamp. She often gets a little wild when the moon is full. I've left a syringe filled with Luminal in the medication room in case she gets out of hand. Actually, thinking about it, I'll get someone to give it to her before I go. The rest of them should be asleep, but you know you've got Jim and Bob here to help you if you need a strong arm. And the safety buzzer should bring the supervisor. Just a word to the wise. She may not be that quick in coming. She's older, tends to fall asleep on nights."

Jim, standing behind the charge nurse, tilted his hand up in a 'drinking' mime. Ruth's heart sank. So, she was to be left to the tender ministries of the two laughing orderlies and a drunken supervisor. Great. She thought wistfully back to the quiet evenings on the TB wards, where coughing was the primary concern.

"Oh, last thing. Dr. Ferguson wants temperature checks during the night. He's worried the entire ward will come down with the flu. Be sure to wash carefully between patients, and if I were you, I'd start the vitals right now so you can catch them when they are awake."

She stood. "Best of British luck," she said. Ruth winced. Did she know you only said that when you expected things to go badly? The charge nurse swept out of the nursing station, stopping briefly to tell Leonard Wiley to return to bed.

Ruth, agitated, ran her hands through her hair, messing it up. She didn't care. If she made it through this shift, she was going to take herself to the beauty salon and get it all trimmed as a celebration. Then she groaned. She was on the first shift of four!

"May as well get started," Bob said. "I'll come with you, just in case."

"Thanks." Ruth took a deep breath. "Let's go."

The first round wasn't so bad. Most of the patients were asleep. Ruth managed to get a temperature on some of them, and Mr. Smith took his tea and toast with no aggressiveness. They tidied up the dayroom and had just returned to the nursing station when the howling started.

"What is that?" Ruth turned white. Even Bob looked alarmed.

"No hope but to go look for the howler," he said, though Ruth got the feeling he would rather not.

"Where's Jim, anyway? Is he playing a trick on us?

"Don't think so, miss. I think he was taking Mr. Jacques to Beechgrove."

"So, there's just the two of us?"

"Unless you count the ghosts!" Bob grinned.

Ruth waved at him to pretend to slap him. "Oh, for heaven's sake!"

"Literally," said Bob.

Ruth growled. "Let's go, then, see what is going on."

They left the nursing station, carefully locking it behind them, and started walking down the long dim hallway. The lights were turned down to help the occupants sleep, but Ruth now wished for a super bright one to shine in all the corners.

The howling led them down the hall to the final room.

Bob flung open the door and shone his flashlight in. There, in the corner, was a new patient to Ruth. He was curled into a twitching ball and covered with brownish goo.

"Shit," said Bob.

Ruth looked at him reprovingly.

"Well, I mean …"

"I'll get some towels and a new set of sheets. Can you look after him for a bit? Do you think he needs medication? What's his name?" Ruth was running off at the mouth, both scared and trying to sound efficient. The result was slightly hysterical.

"Catch your breath," said Bob. "Well, maybe not in here. I'm holding my breath, myself. You might want to buzz the supervisor just to get an assessment."

"Right," said Ruth. "Thanks." She ran off down the hallway back to the nursing station, heart in her mouth. It took her a bit of a while to manage the keys, but soon she was in the station and called the hospital switchboard to leave a message for the supervisor. She hoped she'd arrive soon. In the meantime, she dug through the charts to get information about the patient. A new one, admitted this afternoon. Why hadn't the charge nurse warned her? Annoyed, she read, "Agitated, query psychotic due to syphilis."

"Oh, dear Lord," Ruth muttered. She knew there were a few others in the hospital with tertiary syphilis. It didn't seem like a cheery diagnosis. She'd heard they were terminal, restrained with drugs and other things until they died. Horrible way to go. This fellow they were trying to heal with that new malaria treatment, at least. His name was Charlie Brooks. Only forty-three. What a sin.

She heard a bang on the window of the nursing station and looked up, hoping to see the nursing supervisor. Instead, it was Jim, laughing at her startled expression.

"Go help Bob," Ruth yelled through the glass. "Last room, new patient. You need sheets and towels."

Jim made a face but went to comply.

Ruth returned to her reading of the chart. The doctor had

ordered benzodiazepines for this patient if he became agitated. "Well," thought Ruth, "check." She went into the medication room to see if the dose was there, but no. He had nothing in his medication box. Ruth stomped her feet. Why hadn't the day nurses set up anything? They must have forgotten about this patient totally. How could she get hold of the night pharmacist? Ruth grabbed a syringe and pulled up some plain saline. Maybe she could persuade the patient it was medication until the supervisor arrived. She only hoped she wouldn't have to inject it.

Another banging on the nursing station door brought her out of the medication room. Standing at the door were Bob, Jim, and the 'patient', now with a wide grin and dressed in his orderly uniform. The penny dropped and Ruth knew what was up. She swung open the door.

"What's all this? And are you ready for your medication?" Ruth turned toward the medication room. "It's all drawn up."

"Now wait a minute, Miss Maclean," said the 'patient,' as Ruth came back into the station, syringe in hand. "It was just meant to be a bit of fun. Bob and Jim here …"

"Now, if you'll bend over this chair here, we'll get you seen to right away. Can you hold onto him, please?"

Ruth was so serious that the orderlies didn't know what to make of her. Bob said, "It was just a joke." There was a pause, everyone frozen in place.

Ruth put the syringe back into the med room and came back into the station. She tried to speak bravely. "Look, lads. I grew up with quite a few brothers and one quite tricky sister. It'll take a lot more than some chocolate pudding to scare me." She sat down, hoping that would hide the trembling she was feeling.

"Did you call the supervisor?"

"Yes, I sure did. I imagine she won't be that pleased with how you've decided to spend your time. You created a whole chart! I couldn't believe the other nurses would forget to tell me anything!" She finally laughed, and the relieved orderlies joined in. "You'd better get the room tidied up. I'll get rid of the evidence here."

"You're a brick," Jim said. "We just wanted to welcome you to the team."

"Ha. I feel so welcomed. Go mop up before the supervisor gets here."

She tore the chart up and tossed it in the trash. She was furious, but also, in a way, cheered. They thought highly enough of her to pull this elaborate trick on her. Smiling, she stepped out of the nursing station, locked it behind her, and walked down the hall on her next set of rounds. As she walked, she heard a set of footfalls, echoing hers.

"Okay, boys. That's enough fun for tonight." There was no response. She swirled around to find the source of the steps. There was no one there …

TEN

Halloween

Coming onto the ward Halloween night, Ruth wasn't in her best form. She'd spent the day running around town for Meg, and she hadn't slept well after her frights the night before. Ruth hadn't found time to wonder about the ghostly sounds because she had to run around soothing patients until her shift ended, but she'd listened hard for them through the night and thought they were there again. When she told the other nurses about it, the ones who had been there longest all said they'd heard them too — soft footsteps in the hall when no one was about.

"He seems to prefer the locked wards," said one, shivering.

"Oh, stop it. There's no such things as ghosts," said another.

"Maybe we need to draw a salt circle or something? Get some holy water?"

Ruth laughed with the rest but went to bed, wondering just what she'd heard. She knew all the patients had been in bed, and the orderlies in the nursing station. Wind, she told herself. Changing temperature.

Still, nothing for it but to work through the shift. Yawning mightily, she dragged upstairs to her ward, knocked, and was let in. "You're in luck," said Bob. "There's another nurse on tonight."

"Oh, good!" Even one more body would feel more secure.

In the nursing station, the evening nurse was giving report. "Lost a few more because of the flu," she was saying.

"Lost?" Ruth asked, shocked.

"Oh, just over the road. They're getting pretty full over there. Can't wait until this outbreak is over. They keep transferring patients here to clear staff. We had five admissions today."

"Oh great," said the other night nurse. "I'm here with a probie and these two lunkheads? On Halloween? Do you know how to do anything? Anything at all?" she demanded of Ruth.

"Yes. I worked for a full year at the San before coming here."

"They should send you over to flu central, then. You've got all that infection prevention stuff down. I can handle here. I'm going to call the supervisor and see if they need you over there."

Ruth sagged. Spending the night trying to avoid the flu with a bunch of patients all unsettled from being moved away from their normal place and wild about the night did not sound fun at all.

The nurse got off the phone, shaking her head. "Imagine that! She says she'll keep you in mind, but you should stay here. I think they don't want you to catch anything. Not that I imagine you are any use here." She gave a vast sigh. "You can call me Miss Thorne. If you have to call me, which I hope you don't. Why don't you get started on the vitals the doctor is requiring."

"I'd be glad to," said Ruth. "Could I hear shift report so I know about the new patients?"

Another enormous sigh. "I suppose. Won't make much difference in what you do. Though I suppose it's good if you know who is incontinent."

Ruth gritted her teeth, but at least she could hear who were in the rooms. She didn't relish walking in on sleeping patients with unknown mental illnesses. She'd seen enough from the agitated schizophrenics to be wary of that. After report, she gathered up equipment and headed out to do the rounds. Bob slid along beside her.

"Everyone seems awfully quiet for Halloween. Maybe they're all sick. I'll come with you in case anyone gets riled up. Or if you need to change them. Easier with two."

Ruth smiled her gratitude and they started. Maybe it was having Bob with her, or maybe everyone was just tired from all the excitement of being moved, but the new patients were fairly biddable, and they got the rounds done in record time. Ruth was just charting the results when Miss Thorne came back onto the ward, reeking of cigarette smoke. An older man walked with her, the two of them laughing loudly enough to wake the patients.

Ruth made a face, but Bob gestured with his hand flat, pushing towards the floor. He shook his head. "Don't say anything," he whispered. "That's the night pharmacist. We've got to stay on his good side. He restocks our supplies. If he gets mad, we wait a long time for everything."

Ruth nodded. "I wondered when they restocked. I haven't met him before." She headed over to say hello, but Bob grabbed her arm.

"Let's go check on everyone. Best not to be around when there's flirting goin' on."

As they walked along, shining flashlights carefully into rooms, Bob revealed the story. "Those two been going together for years," he explained. "Taking smoke breaks together since I got put on this ward. Longer ones lately."

Ruth nodded, walked into a room where the patient had kicked off their blankets. It was King Leonard, having some sort of dream of conquest. They tidied him up, and as they left, Bob added, "Thing is, though, he's married. Has a bunch of kids.

And …" he lowered his voice. "I don't think having all that access to morphine has helped him much. Did you see his eyes?"

Ruth didn't know what to think. She didn't like gossip, but she did like the fact that Bob was friendly enough with her to tell her stories.

"We'd better get back," she said, just as they heard a shout.

"Miss Maclean! Where are you?" Miss Thorne called out. "These students," she said to the pharmacist. "Can never count on them to do anything," she added when she saw Ruth and Bob come down the hall, "Always flirting with the orderlies. Honestly."

"Just finished our rounds," said Ruth, firmly. "May I get by you? I need to chart." She squeezed by the giggling couple and sat to record the vital signs.

"We're just going to do the count." Miss Thorne said. "Coming in?" She gestured to the pharmacist, who crowded into the medication room behind her. They locked the door behind them, leaving Ruth and Bob in the nursing station.

More squeals, and Ruth was getting fed up with overhearing them when she heard a sound from the ward. Getting up quickly, she headed out to see who was crying.

It was Mrs. Matthews. She was wrapped up in her blankets, sobbing like her heart was breaking. Ruth tiptoed in, gently put her hand on her shoulder. "Mrs. Matthews? Can I get you anything?"

"No," she gulped, swallowed a sob. "I'm just missing my babies. I can't even remember what their faces look like."

"Oh, that's terrible. It's probably a short-term thing from your treatment. Maybe we can get your husband to bring in photos, at least. And you're getting better. Soon you'll be able to go home and see them."

Mrs. Matthews was silent.

"Can I get you anything to help you sleep? Some warm milk, maybe?"

"No. I'm better now. Thank you." The woman turned away, pulling her blankets over her head. It was obvious the conversation, therapeutic or not, was over.

So was Ruth's run of nights. It turned out she was booked for other things that would give her a break.

ELEVEN

Canvassing for TB

The 'break' involved getting dressed up in all of her warmest gear. She and many other students had been released from ward duties to help with a mass free X-ray canvass. Tuberculosis was still rampant in Kingston and area and the city gathered over 800 volunteer canvassers to get everyone signed up for a free X-ray.

Miss Thomas hadn't been thrilled when Ruth told her she'd signed up, but all the nursing schools were doing it, so she had to accept it. Ruth just hoped she didn't have to make up the time. She headed over to the nursing residence to meet Betty and get their assignment area. It turned out they had to go back to Portsmouth Village to canvass.

"Drat. I was hoping for the base," Betty pouted.

"Well, let's do this quickly and maybe we can pick up another area that seems more exciting."

"Sure. Let's catch a bus, okay? It's brr cold out."

They wrapped their capes snugly around themselves and ran out just as the bus was heading by. It was packed, many of the riders carrying the pouches with the information about the canvass.

Ruth thought it would be easy, just drop off the card and tell people to sign up for the X-ray, but at the doors, they ran into some odd reactions.

"I'm not havin' that done. Would fry my insides. And we don't got no TB here, anyhow." The woman saying all this coughed mightily at the end of the sentence and the girls stepped back out of range.

Ruth spoke up. "I've been X-rayed two times already and I'm fine. It's really very safe. And we've worked at the TB San, and you really don't want to leave TB untreated. It's a horrible disease." She looked at the woman so earnestly that she gave in and took the card.

"I'm not sayin' I'm gonna call, mind. But I'll think on it."

"Remember all the people around town you see living with the outcome. It's not pretty and we have drugs to treat it now."

"I hear ya. Run along now."

The next house, Betty was in front.

"Hello, me beauties," said the man who answered the door. "I didn't know they'd be sending out the pretty ones to canvass. Do you want to come in? It's so cold out today. That wind would take the skin off a moose."

Betty and Ruth looked at each other. "No, thank you," said Betty. "We have a lot of people to visit today. Can't stop for long. We're just bringing you information about the free X-ray you can book to screen for tuberculosis. Had you heard about it?"

"Yup. Was in t'paper."

"Well, here's where to call to book your appointment." Betty handed him the card. The man looked at it and tore it up into tiny pieces, tossing them into the breeze.

"So you go along for this 'free X-ray', right? And then they find something in your lungs and you're out of a job. It ain't goin' to happen. I'll bet less than half of the people you talk to will bother to go."

"But TB is all over the city! It's a terrible disease, but we have drugs that work on it now, and if we catch it early …"

"T'is all a huge plot to get us out of our jobs. We've been talking down't the Port. None of us want it. Bosses is always looking for a reason to throw us out, hire cheaper help."

"Some employers here are making it a condition of employment that you get the X-ray, and treatment if needed. You surely don't want to spread it to your workmates?" Ruth was starting to feel red easing up from her collar. Why do people resist things that will keep them healthy? "And you're unionized, aren't you?"

"Yup."

"Well, then they can't fire you for being sick, can they? They can only fire you if you don't comply with the order."

"Humph."

"Here, here's another card. Think about it and ask your boss or your union leader?"

"Fine. Goodbye, girls." He turned and went inside, slamming the door.

"I get the distinct feeling they don't like to argue with us, even if they refuse to go," said Betty, pulling her cape tighter around herself. "It was seriously tempting to go inside with that man, though. I could use a cuppa."

"We still have these two blocks to do, then maybe a treat, right? I don't want to be doing this after dark."

"Right you are. Who's up, you or me?"

"I'll take the next one," Ruth said. "Let's run."

They ran, laughing, around the block and onto the next street, where cottages jumbled together like broken teeth. "This is where all the prisoner's families live, isn't it?" Betty whispered in Ruth's ear.

"Well, the prison is right over there, after all. Convenient, I suppose." The Kingston Pen loomed large and dark, the guards in the towers pacing around.

At least the canvassing went better among these families. There was a TB outbreak in the prison and the families were scared they also had caught it. "Can I get wee Jimmy X-rayed? Is he too little?" asked one harried mother. "He's got the most godawful cough. Keeps everyone up all night."

"Definitely," said Ruth. "Shouldn't you take him to the doctor?"

"Who can afford that?"

Ruth frowned. It suddenly occurred to her that even if they found TB, people might not be able to pay for treatment. "Well, call this number and get booked in soon, and at least someone will have a look at him."

"It's free, right?"

"Yes. Totally free." She made a mental note to ask about coverage for the medications.

"Okay. I'll do all 'f us."

"That's great!" Ruth smiled at wee Jimmy, who clung to his mother's skirt. He looked pale and tired. "It's great fun, Jimmy! It's a big machine that makes all sorts of funny noises and it doesn't hurt the tiniest bit. I'll bet they are giving out candies, too."

"Can we go, mum?" Jimmy pulled on her skirt, suddenly eager.

His mother laughed, and for a moment Ruth could see a glimmer of hope in her eyes. "We'll call right this minute, eh? We gotta walk to the phone. Put your coat and hat on. There's a good boy." She turned to the girls. "Thanks. I hope we gets some help. It's hard when we're just living on income from the prison."

"I'll bet it's tough! Good luck!" Ruth left, dragging Betty behind her.

"Can't we do anything for her? I've got a bit of money." Betty was digging in her coat pocket.

"Stop it, Betty. This entire street is in the same state. We can't look after everyone."

"But that little boy … what a cutie pie!"

"I'll bet there are even more down the street. Let's go."

Sitting in the Portsmouth Tavern, the local pub, after passing out all their cards, Ruth and Betty sipped their tea and rubbed their feet.

"You'd think walking wouldn't be hard after all our walking on the wards!"

"Yes, but we don't wear boots in the hospitals, thank heavens." Ruth waggled her toes experimentally. "I think I've got frostbite in my toes. I need better boots! Ooh, they are burning!"

"That's it. Tea isn't doing it for us. Maybe we could have a wee dram of something?"

"You go ahead. I'm playing everything very safe after last year."

"Can't say as I blame you." Betty raised her hand and immediately four men came over to them.

"What can I get you, sweetheart?" asked one.

Looking at the line-up of grinning men, Betty reconsidered. "Actually, I think we'd better get back. Need to be on the wards, you see."

Two men stood. "Can we give you a drive? Our car is just outside."

The girls fled. "Honestly, what is it about these men? They are all hanging about, waiting to pounce. It's so annoying." Ruth stomped up the street.

"Long war," said Betty.

"Were they this bad before the war?"

"I honestly can't remember. Now, though, it's like being surrounded by sharks. Exciting to flirt with, but they always want to bite."

"Chomp!" Ruth laughed. "Did you see that fellow's teeth? We'd never recover."

Historical Note

TUBERCULOSIS PREVENTION

A Division of Tuberculosis Prevention was created in the Ontario Department of Health in 1934, and the programs to monitor and control the spread of tuberculosis were increased. An important element in these efforts included the Tuberculosis Case Register, which was a sophisticated paper-based information system, with colour-coded forms, index cards, tabs, and other administrative tools to systematically collect, organize, analyze, and document comprehensive data about cases of tuberculosis in the province.

The local Boards of Health were the keepers of the tuberculosis case registers, which correlated information from family physicians, sanatoria, hospitals, clinics, laboratories and public health nurses about each case in their area. Special standardized forms were to be used for each reporting process and very specific instructions were provided for completing them.

Summary information from the register was sent to the Division of Tuberculosis Prevention and the Provincial Medical Officer of Health. Public health nurses visited each case and maintained files on the family and other contacts. This system allowed the tracking of all cases so they could be treated and followed up, and also identified contacts for testing and treatment where necessary.

The Division also encouraged and supported communities in providing free mass X-ray surveys of their entire population. It published a detailed instructional report on how to organize the survey, with sections on publicity, door-to-door canvassing to obtain appointments, operation and set-up of the X-ray space, and of course, samples of the necessary forms and paperwork. The mass surveys aimed to reach 82 percent of the people in an area, and it was estimated that 800 people could be X-rayed in a day with one X-ray machine, to be borrowed from the Division.[*]

---

[*] Medical Records at the Archives of Ontario — Tuberculosis Records. https://www.archives.gov.on.ca/en/explore/online/health_records/tuberculosis.aspx

TWELVE

Princess Elizabeth's wedding

The rest of the month was spent on evening and day shifts, with bath treatments, ECTs and dodging the flu. On Nov 20th, Ruth was sound asleep, dreaming of big pillows and comforters, when she heard a sudden thundering of feet down the stairs. Rolling over, she saw it was only five in the morning. "Honestly! Is there a fire or something?" she muttered to herself.

"Ruth! Are you coming?" one of her housemates shouted. "The wedding, remember?"

Ruth pulled her pillow over her head, groaning. It seemed like she'd just sunk into her bed after her evening shift. Five hours would not be enough sleep for her today. But the Princess was getting married! She sat up with a grunt, wrapped her blanket around herself, and ran downstairs.

Everyone was in the social room, planted close to the radio. The BBC was broadcasting the wedding all over the world, and CKWS had picked up the feed. Already they could hear the plummy sounds of a high-class British accent, explaining what was happening.

"Oh, wouldn't it be great if we could see it!" whispered Doris.

"I know," said another girl. "I hear she had to use coupons for her gown. Everyone sent in their coupons, but she could only use her own. I'd love to see how she managed. I'll bet it's beautiful."

"Shhhh!" said a third. "I can't hear!"

The room sat in reverential silence as the BBC explained everything that was going on. "Can you hear those crowds?" whispered the chatty girl. "Oh, I wish I was there!"

"Shhhhh!" the whole room said. The chatty girl shrunk into herself, blushing.

The plummy voice described the Princess's gown. "It was designed by Norman Hartwell, inspired by Botticelli's painting, Primavera. It is made of duchesse satin, ordered from Winterthur in Scotland. It is decorated with orange blossoms and other flowers done in embroidery and applique, enhanced by ten thousand seed pearls.

"Ooh, my fingers are aching just thinking of that!" whispered Ruth.

"It has a 13-foot silk tulle train, attached at the shoulders and embroidered in pearl, crystal and transparent appliqué tulle embroidery drawn by Hartnell, produced at Lullingstone Castle in Kent and woven by Warner and Sons," said the voice, interfered with from time to time by appreciative 'oohs' by the girls, followed by shushes.

The wedding went on and on and on, with all the girls in the room imitating swooning as the vows were said. "So romantic!" one said. "She said she'd obey him!"

"She's going to be Queen. The Queen shouldn't have to obey anyone," said Ruth.

"Shhhh!" said everyone else.

Finally, the service was over, and the radio reported the cheering crowd outside the church and all over the Mall.

"Oh, it can't be over already!" cried one student who had been lying in front of the radio and sighing loudly throughout.

Ruth and Doris exchanged glances. They were ready for breakfast.

One of the older nurses said, "I hear the Brits are sending film of the ceremony over so we can watch it in the theatre."

"Really?" the sighing one said. "I'm going to take that day off! We should all go see it together!"

Again Ruth and Doris exchanged another amused look. "I think not," Doris whispered to Ruth. "All that sighing would block out the film!"

They stood up and wandered into the kitchen, where Doris filled the kettle, and Ruth pulled the loaf of Canada Bread out of the breadbox and cut some slices. "Toast?" she asked.

"Please. Let me grab the peanut butter."

They sat, calmly munching, while the party continued in the social room. A few others drifted in and followed their example.

"A little bit of royalty is enough for me," said Doris. "I love the Princess, and all, but the cost! I'm glad the Brits have something to celebrate, though. It's been a long war for them."

"Everyone donated to them. Food from everywhere. Even Canada sent flour, apparently. I hear the cake is nine feet high. I'd love to see that!" Ruth crunched her toast. "Did you hear they are going to be firing the guns in Ottawa in celebration? I wonder if there are crowds gathering there?"

"Well, the pubs in town here are all dressed up in royal colours. I think they even have special drinks and meals. Fred and I might head downtown to check them out," said Cindy, a senior nurse. "I'll bet there will be fireworks later."

"Well, I'm on evenings, so I'll guess I'll have to miss them," said Ruth.

"Fireworks always set the patients off. Good luck tonight," said Doris.

"Oh great. I'm off to catch another hour of sleep then. I'll need to be in tip-top form!"

"Have a good nap," several voices chorused.

Ruth hauled her quilt up to her third-floor room, for once glad to be away from the melee downstairs. They'd probably be celebrating all day, she thought, and she needed just a teensy bit more sleep.

An hour later, she dragged herself up again and readied herself for her shift. Arriving on the ward, she was surprised to hear the radio on, still broadcasting about the wedding. King Leonard was in full paper regalia, telling everyone that his invitation had obviously been lost in the mail. The orderlies were playing along.

"Did you listen to the wedding?" asked Alison.

"Oh yes, the entire house was up and sitting by the radio. Here too?"

"Well, it's been hard to hear sometimes. Everyone got so excited. But I didn't feel I should make them miss it."

The other nurse, Anne, chimed in. "We've had to medicate quite a few of them. They needed to calm down, especially with the king romping about. I think it's time for his shot now, too." She went into the medication room to draw it up.

"Oh thanks," Ruth said. "I appreciate you getting them all settled for me."

"Well, that's before the gun firing at Fort Henry. I understand the Army guys plan a salute. If you can, put some music on to distract everyone. Cannon fire is still alarming to most of the soldiers here."

"I bet it is. Don't they think of that?" Ruth frowned.

"It is our sovereign, I suppose. She really did her part during the war. And the guys over there do so like to march around. They are doing the firing after dark, so it will seem more exciting."

"Fantastic," said Ruth, plopping herself down in a chair. "What's been happening other than that?"

Alison started running through her report. "Of course you've heard about the king. He's been so excited he'll probably sleep the night through. Mrs. Matthews is still pretty out of it after her treatment yesterday. None today, as everyone except us is off on a holiday. And we caught our cutting gal at it again, so we've medicated her and she's in restraints. We moved her table out of her room, so she'll have a harder time hiding things. She could probably use some gentle talking this afternoon. I think she's terrified."

That was the first patient Ruth checked, only to find her sound asleep. She went down the hall to speak with Mrs. Matthews. She was awake, but groggy.

"How are you feeling today?" Ruth asked her.

"I'm so confused. I kept hearing wedding music. And people cheering."

"Oh, didn't they tell you? They've been listening to the royal wedding. Princess Elizabeth just married Prince Philip."

"Really? I've been sleeping all day. Is it all over?"

"Yes, they are off to their honeymoon now."

"Oh, how wonderful. It reminds me of my wedding." Mrs. Matthews cried softly. "We were so in love. I don't know what happened …"

Ruth squeezed her hand, uncertain of how to respond. When she thought of it, she didn't know of many women who were happily married. It seemed expectations exceeded the reality of daily life, babies, worrying about finances. Her mother and father were happy, she believed, but she figured it was mainly because of her mother's hard work. Even Dorothy Dix, the nurses' favourite agony aunt from the Whig-Standard, told newly married people to "Take it easy" with each other, since marriage was a long-term commitment.

"I think we are having some celebration cake for dessert tonight." Ruth bent down to look into Mrs. Matthews' eyes. "Wouldn't you like to get up and join us?"

"Maybe. Can you come back?"

"Sure thing," said Ruth. "I'll just do my rounds and then come back to you. I'm looking forward to some cake myself!"

Mrs. Matthews smiled. "Makes a change from Jello and applesauce," she murmured, making Ruth laugh out loud. Most of the desserts in the OH were made to be safe if thrown and good for putting ground up pills into. Cake was extremely rare.

"Well, you'll just have to get up then. I'll bring you some towels so you can get started."

Ruth did so and then started her rounds. Why the day nurses hadn't washed and dressed Mrs. Matthews she didn't know, but she felt sorry she'd missed all the excitement. Heaven knew there was little enough joy in the hospital most days.

THIRTEEN

Sister Meg's wedding

The shifts crept by in slow progression. Winter was coming, freezing the lake, sending the birds from the sky. Ruth still couldn't get a reply from a schizophrenic patient she'd been assigned. Mrs. Matthews went in and out, depending on if it was a shock day. Her husband refused to bring in photos of his children, saying they would make her too upset. The ward nurses were turning against him, but for some reason, the head nurse still kowtowed to him every chance she got.

Finally, Meg's big wedding day arrived. Ruth couldn't believe the preparations were almost over. Ruth and her friends had already packed up all the ribbons and roses she'd made and the gloves and bits and pieces she'd bought from Stacey's, and as soon as she got off her night shift, she ran to Leahurst to lay her dress across the top of her bag. She didn't want it to be all crushed — she'd splurged on an actual fancy dress after years of holding back. It worried her to be seen spending some money. She was sure her father would lecture her. But she was Meg's Maid of Honour, and she thought she should at least look decent. Plus, there was a little part of her that wanted to show off for the people back home. She even bought new shoes. The girls at Leahurst had all helped her stretch them out, and she practiced walking in the high heels. They felt odd and so light after days in her solid nursing shoes.

The men arrived at seven-thirty sharp, when the morning fog still hadn't crept out of the streets. Ruth's brother Billy lived at the Veterans' home, as did his friend Jerry. Both were recovering from their war injuries. Jerry had suffered a terrible bout of tuberculosis, while Billy ended up a double amputee. They both had jobs with the Veterans' home and so had housing there. They filled the lengthy ride north to Cloyne with jolly stories of veteran misbehaviour from the Legion. Billy had been busy coaching the soccer team all fall and was looking forward to a break.

"I wouldn't count on it," Jerry said. "I just saw our duties list. They have you serving in the bar."

"Really? Tabernac, as you'd say. I was hoping for a rest."

"Don't talk to me. They are making me un serveur. I'll be running around all over the place."

"Yeah, you're whining about that?" Billy waved at his amputated legs, and they both laughed.

Ruth relaxed into her seat. She was afraid Billy would blow up about his disability, but it seemed they joked about it all the time.

The weather was dreadful. Drizzling rain and frozen patches on the road made driving challenging. Ruth tried to doze but the windshield wipers kept shrieking whenever they hit a dry space and then had to be turned off and on and off and on in between the screaming. One of them threatened to peel off. Everyone in the car silently wished for regular rain, or none. The misting was annoying. Fog kept crawling across the road, too, sometimes making it disappear. Jerry drove slower and slower.

Jerry saw her looking at him in the mirror. He shrugged. "It's not our car, eh. I must baby it. It's the Legion's and I hope they'll loan it to us encore."

"Yes, but …" Ruth turned to look out of the window, to watch the pine trees crawl slowly by. Time was going by faster than the car. Finally, they reached Kaladar, over halfway there.

"I'm so excited," Ruth said, trying to build enthusiasm despite the gruesome weather. "Did you hear? They were able to book a room at the Salmond Resort."

"Won't it be freezing? Haven't they shut it down for the season?"

"Apparently Father did the funeral for one of the family and they were impressed, so they've opened up the hall. I've never been in there, have you?"

"Wow. How many people did Meg invite? Wasn't it going to be a small, in the house kind of thing?" Billy frowned. "I don't know about letting everyone see me … like this …"

Jerry put his hand on Billy's for a moment, then pulled it back to manage the car through the winding roads.

"You can always wear my dress, Billy," said Ruth, quickly realizing she shouldn't have. "Or one of Mother's quilts. I just meant to distract attention," she added, a bit abashed.

"No. He is a hero, and they should see him as one."

"Jerry …" Billy wrung his hands. "Hero or fool, eh, Jerry? Hard to tell."

Ruth tousled Billy's hair. "C'mon boys, we all know you are heroes! Didn't you go to the Armistice Day celebration and get feted like the rest of the men? What would we have done without you all?"

"Hey, where were you that day, Ruth? I didn't see you anywhere."

Ruth wriggled down in the seat. She'd been there, but with a coterie of patients. She hadn't wanted to bring them up to Billy. "I was working, Billy, I told you."

"Yeah, yeah, probably sleeping in."

Ruth barked a sarcastic laugh. She couldn't remember when she'd last slept in, with work and running about for Meg. "I forget what that's like. Tell you one thing, I'll be glad when this wedding is over. It'll be nice to have a day off now and then that isn't taken up with wedding preparations. My suitcase is crammed full!"

"We're almost there. Everyone smarten yourselves up." Billy said. "We've got to look good for the neighbours."

They pulled into the driveway and were immediately mobbed by children.

"Can we go for a ride?" they chorused.

"Who's that?" James, their bubbly 5-year-old brother, pointed at Jerry.

"It's our friend, Jerry," said Ruth.

Jerry pulled Billy's wheelchair out of the car and opened it up. "It's so good they gave this chair to you, Billy."

"I'll say. Can you imagine dragging the wicker one up here? It wouldn't even fit in the car."

Ruth agreed. The veterans had been the first to get the new folding wheelchairs early that year, and it changed Billy's life. He could get out and about, away from the Legion Hall.

"Thank heavens, you're finally here!" Meg came running down the stairs. "We've got to go decorate the church. People are already arriving."

It went to highlight how boring life in Cloyne could be in the in-between season that people were already massing about. Neighbour children were climbing on the car, squelching about in the puddles.

"Where's Mother?"

"She's over at the resort. Maybe Billy, you and Jerry could go over and help her? I need Ruth here."

"Bien sur," Jerry swiftly transferred the wheelchair back into the car, and added a child or two. "We're off."

"Don't forget to come back. And don't eat all the food! We've been cooking for days!"

The rest of the day flew by with last-minute preparations, getting dressed, and setting up the church. There was an unusually large crowd fluttering about. Meg's to-be husband Wayne had lots of family and friends of family, and many parishioners also wanted to join in. There were even some old friends from the Maclean's former parish in Napanee, who had known Meg and the family from babyhood. It all made for a big, noisy group that only hushed when the service started and little Thomas, James, and Sara at last trotted down the aisle, sprinkling the paper roses Ruth had made. Sara got fed up with walking slowly and dumped her basket in a pile, running up to the front to hug her father. Thomas went back, responsible boy that he was, and picked it up, spreading the roses more effectively. There were appreciative ooohs from the congregation.

Ruth smiled at Meg and started walking up the aisle. Everyone made eyes at her dress, and she felt glad she'd bought it. But Meg was the star. She shone despite the grey day, her happiness radiating to replace the absent sunbeams. Ruth saw her father wipe his eyes before putting on his serious minister face.

Wayne, for his part, was frozen, his face stunned, mouth open. Meg, when she took his hand, shook it a bit, trying to unfreeze him.

"You look great," he whispered at last. The whole church heard and smiled.

Reverend Maclean started the lengthy marriage service, filled as it was with beautiful words. Ruth tried to listen, but she was so tired, so tired. Dozing in the car hadn't helped.

"From the pristine purity of the Garden of Eden, two divine institutions have been passed on to the generations of mankind. One of these is the Sabbath, which comes to us regularly week by week, often (though unfortunately not today) introduced by gorgeous sunset colours." The congregation laughed as they dripped, soaked from their travel to the church.

Reverend Maclean continued, "The other is the marriage institution, which ushers two young people into the love and blessings of a home and into an eternal companionship.

"God is calling these young people into a life of service here on earth. Ere many days have passed, they will be busy preaching the gospel. There they will devote their lives to the proclamation of the love and kindness of the Lord, who means so much to them."

Ruth squinted. She didn't think this was Meg's plan, but maybe she'd missed something. She looked at Meg, who winked at her, made a tiny shrug. Obviously, the remnants of a battle.

"Christ loves His people. He loves His church, and this love is held up to us as a model for the love that should characterize the homes of Christians. He says:

'Husbands, love your wives, even as Christ also loved the church, and gave Himself for it … So ought men also to love their wives as their own bodies. He that loveth his wife loveth himself …'

"For this cause shall a man leave his father and mother, and shall be joined unto his wife, and they two shall be one flesh. Into this holy estate of matrimony these two persons come now to be inseparably joined."

Ruth found herself fading in and out of her father's drone and her own daydreams. What did she want from life? Did she want marriage, a home, children? Would she ever be standing there, saying those "I do" words to someone who loved her? Would anyone ever love her with their body? She blushed, reproved herself for her thoughts. She had to pay attention.

Meg and Wayne had turned and were starting down the aisle. Had she missed the proclamations? Awful sister that she was, she had. She must have fallen asleep! She hurried to catch up as they walked down the aisle. The best man took her arm, and it was only then that she realized it was Chuck, the boy who'd wanted to marry her the year before. He grinned at her as they walked together, but she noticed he kept pulling back his hair with his left hand. Sure enough, it had a wedding band on it.

"You got married?" Ruth whispered.

"Yes. Some people don't want to make a fellow wait."

"Shouldn't you be walking with your wife?"

"Nah, she's too fat to fit in a dress. We're having a baby soon. Nope, I'm standing in for Billy — get it? Standing in? Since he can't?"

Ruth recoiled. She pulled her arm out of Chuck's and walked alone the rest of the way. What an awful, awful boy. Imagine! She'd almost ended up being married to him!

FOURTEEN

The reception

They all somehow arrived through the downpour to the Salmond Resort, a white clapboard building surrounded by single floor cottages. The main building, which had been opened for the festivities, had an enclosed front porch where guests stacked their coats. The main room was lit and warmed by an enormous fireplace and dozens of candles that Ruth's mother had run about lighting as soon as they arrived. Ruth tried to help.

"No, no, no! You don't want to get wax on that pretty dress. Billy, you come here and serve the punch. Ruth, these things over here aren't likely to spill."

Ruth looked at the dry pastries she'd been assigned to manage. "Oh for heaven's sake!" she said, and ran off to the kitchen of the resort to get an apron she'd seen hanging from the wall. She went back and found two more. Coming back, she draped one around herself and one each on Billy and Jerry.

"There. Now we can serve with abandon!"

It was a good thing, too, since the guests were crowding the food table. They all knew or had heard about her mother's cooking. Ruth looked around but didn't spot her mother. "Where did Mother go, children?" she asked the little ones.

"She went outside for fresh air, she said."

Ruth nodded. She could understand that for sure. It was already getting hot and close in the room, and they hadn't even started the music yet.

All of that was forgotten when the local fiddlers started up and the room swung into dancing. Meg and Wayne started off, and then Meg danced with their father, and Ruth with Wayne, and then everyone was up and circling, stamping feet, laughing and swooping between the table with the punch and the dance floor.

Jerry bowed before Ruth and soon they were dancing, and after that she barely had a chance to sit down. It seemed all the young men in the area wanted to dance with her now. Surely she hadn't changed that much?

"I hear you're moving home," said one lumpish lad, sweating heavily at her. "I guess you're done being a nurse, eh?"

Ruth clamped her lips shut.

The next fellow to take her out for a four-step had the same idea. "Did you see Chuck is married now? Bet you're glad not to marry him. And she's already having a baby."

Ruth said nothing.

"I wouldn't be like that — I wouldn't ask you to stop being you. I mean, at least not right away. You could nurse for a while. You look so pretty right now. I bet you look sexy in your uniform!" He squeezed her buttock and breathed moistly in her ear.

Ruth spun away from him and went to find Billy. "Can we leave now?"

"What's up?" he asked, slurring a bit. He'd been overseeing the punch and Ruth thought a fair bit of it had been overseen right into his mouth.

"Everyone keeps asking when I'm moving back and threatening to ask me to marry them."

"Well, you look awful pretty in that dress. They probably haven't seen anyone in such a fancy thing … well … ever."

"Oh, no!" Ruth cringed. "I just wanted to look properly dressed to be Meg's Maid of Honour. Is it too fancy? I can put the apron back on."

Billy laughed. "You look good," he said. "Nothing wrong with that. Doesn't help that Chuck is *very* married, either. The rest were all holding off until you two were settled. Didn't want to step on Chuck's toes."

"Ugh. What is this, some Jane Austen novel?"

"All I know is that a few of the boys keep sidling up to me and asking me all about you."

"Oh no. We've got to get out of here! Weddings make everyone so … romantic. It's sickening."

Billy shrugged. "Think of it as stockpiling against a cold winter. If you want to get away, you could always take the little ones home. They are getting quite overexcited, Father says."

Ruth looked around. Two of the little ones were racing between the dancers, tumbling into them. "Brilliant idea. Do you think Jerry could help me take them back in the car?"

"I'm sure he'd love to. Now, I must get back to that punch."

Ruth hit him on the arm. "Be careful, you. People have drowned …"

Laughing, Billy rolled off. People cleared the way for him and Ruth felt a hot white anger at the way they looked at him, all pityingly. It really was time to get away.

It took almost half an hour to round the racing, giggling children up and get them into the car. Ruth looked about to say goodbye to her mother and tell her she was leaving but couldn't find her. She tapped a smiling Meg on the shoulder in the middle of a dance and gave her a hug. "Congratulations, Meg and Wayne! I'm so happy for you! I'm going to take the kids home."

"Are you coming back?"

"I think I'll stay and get them settled. You have fun!"

Meg frowned, but nodded. "It would be good to give Mother a break."

"Have you seen her?"

"Not in the last little while. She's probably trying to keep the food going."

"Likely. I'll see you soon. Have a wonderful night!" Ruth winked at Meg and tugged on her arm. She leaned in to whisper in Meg's ear. "Don't frighten him away …"

Meg grinned and pushed her. When they were little and talking about the big event that would happen on their marriage night, Meg had always said she'd grab a big stick and chase the man away. "No man is ever doing that to me," she'd vowed.

Tonight, though, Ruth thought Meg looked excited, not fierce. She wondered how it would be. She hoped it, and the marriage, would go better for them than it seemed to have for some of her patients.

Ruth and Jerry started up the car, and they drove the short distance to the Maclean house. As the children piled out, the neighbour whispered to them from the front door. "Quiet you lot. Into bed, quietly, and I'll bring you a treat." The children all started walking on tippy toes and telling each other to 'shh' in loud whispers.

"Your mother's having a lie-down," the neighbour said to Ruth. "I brought her home a little while ago, made her a cuppa. She's just exhausted, poor thing. You'll stay with her?"

Ruth nodded, afraid if she answered she'd be held to a promise that she'd stay there forever.

A young stage-whisperer tiptoed back down the hall. "Treat?"

"Here," said the neighbour. "I saved some goodies from the reception."

"Thanks." Ruth turned to go upstairs to take the cookies to the waiting children. Jerry had already carried the babies upstairs, and she followed him.

"You seem to have a lovely young man there," the neighbour said, eyebrows raised.

"Yes, he is a real sweetheart," said Ruth, realizing quickly that everyone would get exactly the wrong impression. Well, she thought, perhaps that's for the best.

She knew Jerry was really sweet on Billy, and vice versa, but best to keep that to herself.

FIFTEEN

After the party

The next morning, Ruth came downstairs to the remainders from the reception. Quite a few men were snoring on the living room floor, apparently too drunk to drive themselves home. Several had bruises. She whispered to her mother, who was up, making gallons of coffee and pancake mix, "What happened?"

"Oh," she laughed. "Typical Cloyne party, don't you remember? It isn't finished until someone starts throwing chairs. Seems a few of them were on the receiving end. I gave them some ice when they came in, but they seem to be sleeping it off okay."

Ruth remembered her high school graduation party, where the folding chairs that were used in such gatherings had been flung here and there as the drunkenness progressed. She'd left early then, too, so hadn't seen the worst of it.

"Should I go check out the hall?"

"Oh, I think your father is over there now, smoothing things over. They knew what it could be like, and in truth, the fighting didn't start until very late. I think you may have caused some of it." Her mother smiled at her.

Ruth said, "What, me? Why?"

"Oh, you know boys. They couldn't understand why you didn't accept Chuck, why you wanted to be a nurse. They thought you should be more excited to see them. Some ugly things were said." Mrs. Maclean put up a hand as Ruth opened her mouth, face indignant. "Billy and Jerry said some things back, and then it all got wild, as these things do. Now, don't get upset. You're out of here today and you don't have to worry about what a bunch of yokels have to say. You are different, that's all. They can't grasp different."

"Are Billy and Jerry okay? They didn't get hurt, did they? Imagine attacking a man in a wheelchair! They should be ashamed."

"Oh, I think he held his own. Probably was good for him. If you look at that fellow in the corner, you can see some of the outcome." The man lay snoring, his front tooth conspicuously missing and a black eye expanding. "They're fine, just quite seriously hungover, I think. Didn't Meg look beautiful? I was so proud of her. And that Wayne, so handsome! And he is so much in love with her. It makes me happy."

Ruth, sensing that was the last she'd hear about the fights, turned to the safer topic of how beautiful everyone was, how happy Meg looked, and more, all while dashing about with cups of coffee and cool towels to the fellows waking up on the floor. Eventually Jerry and Billy surfaced, and she helped them gather their things and pack up the car. She couldn't wait to leave.

Ruth's sense of relief as she checked back into Leahurst was huge. Every time she went to Cloyne, she could feel the suction of her father wanting her to stay there. This time he'd barely spoken to her except to direct activities. It hurt. They'd never been close, but she remembered times when they'd be reading scripture together and laughing over the sillier bits or acting them out with the little ones. And she remembered last year when he came to the Sanatorium and prayed with the men, how warm and kind he'd seemed then. She knew she didn't meet his idea of what a proper woman should be, but she thought he'd come around a bit, especially after letting her go back to nursing school this year. Instead, he'd seemed more closed, angrier. Perhaps the wedding was too expensive, and he was worrying about money. Ruth vowed to send more money to her mother. Maybe he was horrified at what she was supposed to do as a nurse. Heaven knows she still was sometimes.

And yet he always was so warm with Billy. Of course, Billy had done his "duty," something at which Ruth was failing, according to their father. It was hard. Everyone was quiet on the drive back to Kingston, tired or hungover, so they hadn't talked about family things. Ruth was left with a wound and nothing to salve it. She ended up hugging Billy goodbye with unusual fierceness, surprising him.

"You okay, Ruth?" he'd asked, sleepily.

"Fine. Have a good rest, you two! And look after that hand."

Billy flexed his fist, showing Ruth it still worked fine. "Doubt we'll get a break. We'll likely have to get right to work."

"Me, too. Talk soon."

She tripped up the stairs and threw herself into her room. Night shift ahead, so she had a few hours to nap before getting all pressed and exact for inspection. She couldn't wait until she moved to day shifts again, but she had to make up for lost time first.

~

The ward was humming when she got there. There was a new patient who arrived with an angry face and scars on both wrists. The orderlies were in close supervision.

"That is Sgt. Turner," said the charge nurse, another student, this time from the Ontario Hospital program. Honestly, thought Ruth, it was impossible to keep all the students straight. They got rotated all over the hospital to fill empty spaces. No wonder the patients were confused. "We admitted him from the Dieu earlier. Suicide attempt."

"Wrists sliced the wrong way, of course!" another student snorted. "You have to cut up the wrists to really get a good result, not across. Not even bright enough to kill himself properly."

"Thank you for that insight," said the charge nurse, in tones of ice. "He's on suicide watch overnight, to be more fully assessed tomorrow morning. Are you up for this, Miss Maclean? Or should I call in another nurse from another ward?"

"Will the orderlies be here with me?" Ruth picked up the chart and started to read it.

"Yes, but Bob is pulling a double, and the other is a relief. Of course we're short-staffed again. They may be sleepy. You'll have to keep them focused, especially the relief guy."

"Are there any other nurses on with me?"

"Just a student, that one in the sunroom, from Queen's. She's finishing a half shift, leaving at midnight. Then you are on your own."

"Really?" Ruth felt sweat breaking out over her brow.

"Now, don't panic. We've had a few discharges today to the open floors so it shouldn't be too busy, and a lot of the patients are over in Beechgrove coughing on the poor souls there. Short staffing there, too. Wish we'd get some decent funding. It's tough learning and teaching and looking after the patients all at once. Oh, and the supervisor says she'll swing by as she can throughout the night."

"Great." Ruth was unimpressed. She'd yet to see a supervisor during any of her night shifts, even that first one she'd called for.

"Sgt. Turner is medicated with morphine for now. It cuts the pain and makes him sleepy as well. He can have another dose of medication if he seems restless. The orderlies have just put him to bed. He will need fifteen-minute bed checks if someone isn't in with him all the time."

Ruth breathed deep.

"My advice to you? Keep the orderlies moving, getting them to check on everyone, and that will keep you free for Mr. Turner."

"That sounds like a plan," said Ruth. "Then they won't fall asleep, and I can always call them if I need them."

The other nurse guffawed. "You'd better keep an eye on them though and be sure they aren't hiding somewhere, smoking. Or sleeping in one of the empty beds."

Oh, fabulous, thought Ruth.

"Let's do rounds then," said the charge nurse. "I don't usually bother, but it looks like you could use some help to get a grip on the inmates."

"Thanks." Ruth grabbed a pencil and her notepad, and they started around the rooms. Many of the patients were still in the dayroom. They were quietly playing cards or listening to the radio, but Ruth now knew that could change at any moment. They walked by the rooms where patients were either already asleep or recovering from treatments. Mrs. Matthews lay in her bed, turned to the wall. Ruth said hello, got no response.

"She's really not responded very well to the ECT," the charge nurse said.

One already in bed had been through the bath treatment, and there was one fellow recovering from an insulin shock treatment. He was deeply asleep.

"He's new, too — you'll have to check his blood sugar. Do you know how to start an IV?"

Ruth paled. "No. Will I have to?"

The nurse sighed. "I guess you'll have to call the supervisor if he goes low, then. Try to give him orange juice or a sugar tablet first. That usually does the trick. When we get back, call the supervisor and let her know about the situation."

The last room they went to was Sgt. Turner's. He was deeply asleep, snoring. A slight man in his early thirties, he was handsome enough. Curly brown hair, well-built if gaunter than he should be. How did that happen, Ruth wondered. We all had rationed food here, nothing special, but more than enough to live on. She wondered if he had TB, too.

"He was just remustered," explained the nurse. "Worked in signals. Was one of the men who liberated the camps. I don't recollect which one."

"Those concentration camps? How awful."

"From what I've heard, he lost it when he saw what it was like. He's been in hospital in England until just recently, when they thought him stable enough to transfer. I guess he wasn't." She gestured at his bandaged arms. As they left the room, she whispered, "Check those bandages. They used short ones, I think, but I've seen patients eat them or make them into a noose."

"Oh my goodness!"

"People can be pretty determined."

Ruth once again found herself wondering why she signed up for this. Then visions of the local Cloyne boys sweatily pressing up against her at the reception passed through her mind and she straightened up. "I'll … we'll be fine," she said. "Thank you for the rounds. I appreciate you spending the extra time."

The nurse smiled. "Glad to help. Have a good night. Oh, here are the keys."

Ruth took them with a feeling of trepidation, her hand shaking as she tried to insert them into the nursing station door. She fought the urge to go into the medication room and lock it behind her and let the devil take the hindmost.

SIXTEEN

Sgt. Turner

The first bit of the night was quiet, with most everyone asleep. Even Sgt. Turner was quiet. As she headed out on her 2AM rounds, Ruth could hear Sgt. Turner moaning. She entered his room and immediately turned on the light, in case he was having nightmares. She'd found that helped with her TB patients when they were having bad dreams.

"Go away," he moaned. "Turn that damn light out."

"Sgt. Turner? I'm Nurse Maclean."

"Why the hell should that matter? Why does anything matter? Why didn't they let me die?"

Ruth put her hand on his shoulder, but he shrugged it off.

"Are you comfortable?" she began.

"Am I *comfortable*? Are you insane? How can I be comfortable, knowing about … about … the men … the women … the children! I'll never be able to stop seeing them!"

Ruth was silent.

Sgt. Turner opened his eyes. "Do you know what they did?"

"A little," Ruth said. "We haven't heard the whole story in the news yet."

"You haven't been paying attention, then," he said, snorting with disgust. "All you Canadians, warm and safe from the war, not seeing anything …"

Ruth's blood rose in her cheeks. "Hey! My brother fought. He lost both his legs. And I used to nurse at the Veteran's Hospital. I've seen some things."

"Not these things."

To Ruth's astonishment, he began to cry softly, turning away from her towards the wall.

"No, you are right. I can't imagine what you've had to endure."

"Me? I had to endure nothing, nothing, do you hear me? The people in the camps … We should have bombed Germany right out of existence. They don't deserve to live."

"Sgt. Turner, is there anyone I can get for you? A priest? Anyone else?" Ruth had no idea how to deal with this level of agonizing grief. Helpless, she listened to him sob.

He stopped suddenly and looked at her, his gaze intense. "Yeah. Get me lots more drugs, enough to shut off these visions. Or something sharp. I need to die. I want it all to be over. I can't bear another day of knowing that human beings choose to do such things."

"But we also saved some of the people. Fought to stop the camps, the war. There is good in us." She quietly moved to ring the patient buzzer. She didn't know where this conversation would go, and she wanted support.

Sgt. Turner sat up suddenly, grabbing Ruth by the arm. In a second, he had a grip around her neck, pressing it tight. She felt her breath being cut off. "No, please …" she squeaked.

"Take me to the med room. You've got the keys, I can see that. Take me there, now. You need to give me a lot more medication."

He got out of bed and stumbled along the hall, dragging Ruth by the neck. Where were the damn orderlies?

They arrived at the nurse's station, and he grabbed the door handle, juggled it. It was locked, of course. "Open it," he commanded, shaking Ruth by the neck. "Open it, dammit!"

"I ... can't see ... which key to use," she said. "Let go of my neck."

He squeezed her neck tight one more time, making her gasp, and released her. "No tricks," he growled. He could barely stand, weaving from the medication he'd already been given. Ruth fumbled with the keys, trying one, then another.

"I'm sorry. I'm new. I don't know which key goes where."

Sgt. Turner pulled back his hand as if he was going to punch her, and she shrunk down. There was a sound down the hallway, and he turned to see what it was. Quick as a rabbit, Ruth inserted the key, turned it, and slid into the nursing station, shutting the door behind her. The man roared in rage and started hitting the window in the door with both fists. She could only hope it held and no other patients got hurt. She grabbed the phone and dialled the supervisor. No answer. Shaking, afraid of both the patient and the probability she'd be in massive trouble for doing it, she pressed the overhead alarm system. Within seconds, the sirens were wailing.

Sgt. Turner panicked, putting his hands over his ears and shrieking. Other patients started to come out of their rooms. "Oh no," Ruth cried. Now they'd all be in danger. She spun around the nursing station, trying to decide what to do. With trembling hands, she checked his Kardex. Yes, it had been long enough since his last morphine dose. Ruth unlocked the medication room. She wasn't allowed to draw up morphine yet without supervision, so the nurse on days had done it with her before she left.

She locked the med room behind herself and walked to the

nursing station door. The sirens overhead had stopped. No sign of the supervisor, though.

"Sgt. Turner! Sgt. Turner! You wanted more medication. I have some for you, but you need to calm down. Stop yelling." She repeated this all twice more, and finally the man looked at her with a calmer expression.

"Will it work?"

"It should."

"I want a really big dose. I want it all to end. Will you give it to me?"

"I have a shot for you. It should do the trick." She waved the syringe at him like he was a dog looking for a bone.

Sgt. Turner followed it with his head, then slumped. "Ok, Nurse. I'm ready."

Ruth took a deep breath. Did she dare open the door? Would he attack her? "You must stay calm, or I can't give it to you. Can you walk back to your room? I will meet you there." That way, at least, he couldn't break into the nursing station right away.

Sgt. Turner glared at her, then, defeated, headed back down the hall. Ruth waved at the other patients, sending them back to bed, and fortunately they turned, as if asleep already, and went into their rooms. Still no help was in sight. Where was everyone? Ruth's heart was racing, but she knew she had to settle him before he hurt someone.

After he'd gone down the hall a way, staggering, she carefully opened the nursing station door, shut and locked it, checked it twice. Tucking the keys way down in her pocket, she walked slowly down the hall, taking deep breaths to slow her heartbeat. As she went, she spotted a shadow behind her. Turning her head, she saw Bob just behind her. He put his finger to his lips to tell her to be quiet.

She reached Sgt. Turner's room. He had laid down on his

bed, and was pulling down his pyjama bottoms so she could inject him.

"Are you ready?" Ruth asked him softly.

"I'm ready," he said, the words coming out like a sigh. "Wait, wait. Would you pray with me?"

She carefully put the syringe and tray on the other side of the room by the sink and came over to the bedside. "Of course. What would you like to pray?"

"Just an Our Father, Nurse. To sort of introduce me, like." He laughed shortly. "Seeing as I'll be seeing him soon."

Ruth felt the pressure of her lie. The medication wouldn't kill him, just knock him out. She could only give him what had been ordered. He'd likely be furious when he woke up.

She held his hand, and they prayed. Sgt. Turner sighed, deep and long. "Thank you, Nurse. I'm ready now."

"A little poke now," Ruth said. She marked the site, injected the drug smoothly and swiftly. And no one here to see that, she grumbled. She still needed a check mark for her placement requirements.

"When will I feel it?" Sgt. Turner asked.

"Soon. Just relax, try to sleep."

"Will you stay with me, Nurse?"

Ruth didn't know. What if he didn't fall asleep and went into another rage? She looked over her shoulder at Bob. He nodded.

"I can stay for a while," Ruth said. "Just until you fall asleep."

Sgt. Turner grabbed her hand and held it tight, pulling Ruth over into an awkward position. She didn't dare move until she finally felt his grip loosen. Then she eased away from him and fled into the hall.

SEVENTEEN

Reports

Bob was at the nursing station, speaking on the phone. It was the supervisor, apparently, as Ruth heard when she eased into the room and flung herself onto a chair. She could barely lift her arms to pick up Sgt. Turner's chart. Her whole body was shuddering and wanted to be wrapped into a ball. Preferably somewhere else.

Bob hung up. "Well, you handled that well," he began.

"Where were you? Where's the other orderly? Where was the supervisor? He almost strangled me, forced me to open the door, tried to get at the drugs." She was shaking, her voice wobbly as the stress leaked out. She gulped back a sob. "He thinks I've killed him. I don't know what he'll do when he wakes up and finds out I didn't."

The orderly reached out a hand to her, pulled it back. "I was around. You seemed to be handling yourself well, and I thought he might get more violent if I approached him. Amazing move at the door, by the way. I dropped something in the hall to distract him, but you knew to take advantage. Where did you learn those skills?"

"Cloyne," Ruth laughed, breathlessly. "Post party wrestling. And my brother."

Bob looked over her, appraisingly. "Well, it was pretty impressive altogether. And you kept your head. I told the supervisor how well you did."

"Is that a good thing? Does this mean she'll never send me help when I call?"

Bob laughed. "Hell, they're never around when there's trouble. I was amazed she called back." He paused, rubbed his hands together. "Sorry you were attacked like that. That guy is fast. I was talking to Mrs. Matthews. She's in a heck of a mess. Thought she could use a bit of support."

Ruth felt panic overwhelming her. Would nothing go right this shift? "Oh no! What's happened there?"

"Her husband visited today. By God, if I get that bastard alone downtown one night, well, he wouldn't be walking in all pretty-like like he does. He never gives her a break."

"What did he do?"

"He said if she didn't get better right quick, he was going to put her in a longer-term care asylum and put the kids up for adoption."

"What? That's terrible!"

"And then he said he'd hold off if she'd take the insulin shock treatment. She didn't want it."

Ruth pulled Mrs. Matthews' chart off the shelf and opened it. Sure enough, the doctor had ordered seven "initial" rounds of insulin shock treatment, as she was "unresponsive to ECT." Under his order, the doctor had written, "As requested by husband."

"This is appalling," Ruth said. "She hasn't finished her ECT treatment and insulin shock is so scary."

"I know," said Bob, rubbing his bald head with his hands. "I hate them. They are hard on people — and then they get really fat after them. She's so pretty right now. Why do you suppose he wants to make her sick and fat?" He sighed. "I bet he has another filly around somewhere. Bastard. Oh, sorry, Miss Maclean!"

"I'm afraid I have to agree with that word, Bob." Slapping her hands on her thighs, Ruth stood. "Well, there's nothing we can do about that right now. Shall we do rounds? I need to check on the other patients and be sure they got back to bed safely. And of course I need to look in on our sergeant."

"Sure. I'll tag along in case he's restless."

"He shouldn't be. He's had enough morphine to knock out a horse."

They walked down the hall to Sgt. Turner's room, where he was snoring away peacefully. They watched him for a moment, in case he was pretending to be asleep, but it seemed he was really out for the count.

"I really don't want to be here when he wakes up," she whispered. "Should we restrain him?"

"With luck, that's the next shift's problem. And we can't put him in restraints without an order. We'll ask them to get one tomorrow."

They raced through the ward, checking on everyone, and found the other orderly asleep in one of the far rooms. Bob pounded on his shoulder. "Hey, wake up! Lazy bugger! This is what we get when they assign relief. Where do you usually work, anyway?"

"Outpatients," the orderly replied in a sleepy voice. His eyes were barely open. "I don't like this floor. Everyone's too weird up here. And no one talks to you."

"Well, wake up and help us with rounds. You do the vitals, and we'll pretend you were awake all night."

"Really?" The fellow leapt out of the bed, pulling it tidy. "You really won't tell? I'm sorry. New baby at home."

"Yeah, yeah, we hear that all the time. Either that or your grandmother just died. Get a move on."

"Do you even know his name?" Ruth asked as he ran off.

Bob made a dismissive movement with his hand. "Naw, but I'll find it out and see he's not assigned here again. Not right to leave you with no support."

"Thanks," said Ruth. "I am just a student."

"Yes, and they are working all you students hard. Not enough senior staff. You're doing good, though. Better than a lot of the girls. You don't scare easy."

"Just as long as our friend doesn't wake up."

"Be sure to mention that in report in the morning."

"I will." Ruth pushed her hand through her hair. It was still a mess from the tussle with Sgt. Turner. "Oh, I'd better fix this. What if the supervisor comes?" She quickly stood and fled the nursing station, headed for the washroom for staff. Gazing into the mirror, she was astonished to see she still looked the same. She thought for sure there would be grey strands in her brown hair after that fright. Her neck was reddened from his stranglehold. She prodded it with her fingers, but it didn't hurt. She wondered if it was going to bruise. What would the other nurses think?

She laughed once. Maybe they'd think she was out 'necking'. She shook her head. She could hardly wait for this shift to end.

EIGHTEEN

Betty

Ruth had the next day off and used it to meet up with Betty. She had so much to tell her! Betty got off shift at three and Ruth was there waiting at the nursing residence.

"Go get ready!" she called to her. "Time's a-wasting!"

Betty ran upstairs and in just a few moments she was down in her outside clothes, looking fabulous as always. She had the most delightful hats and gloves to go with every outfit.

"I hate going around with you," moaned Ruth. "You always make me look like a dog's breakfast."

"Don't be foolish. You look fine. Just maybe a bit pale. What's been happening, anyways?"

"Not here," Ruth said, looking around. "The walls have ears."

"Okay. Let's go for a walk down Princess Street. It's too windy by the lake and we can window shop as we go."

"Oh, if only we could really shop! I spent all my pay on Meg's wedding favours."

"How was that?"

Ruth regaled Betty with tales of a reception Cloyne-style as they walked toward Princess Street from the residence. They were both laughing by the time they hit the first cafe.

"Treats?" Betty asked, her head tilted.

"Yes, pretty please!" Ruth pulled open the door with great vigour and soon they were sipping hot cocoa and eating from a plate of cookies.

"I am so glad sugar isn't rationed here! It must be awful in Britain," said Betty. "So, what were you so urgent to tell me? How is your rotation going? I, personally, am so sick of sputum I could literally … be sick."

"But the patients there …"

"Oh yeah, they are usually nice, easy to look after. Except when they aren't. How did you stand it for a whole year? Heartbreaking when those young ones just up and die."

Ruth stirred her cocoa. It had been terribly sad. TB wasn't a nice disease. She remembered this one young man who was so charming that when his X-rays came back positive, at least six nurses ended up sobbing in the utility room.

"It's still better than my rotation. See this?" She pointed at her neck.

"Well, well, well, now what have we been up to?" Betty grinned. "Boy romps?"

"Not that. Last night, one of my patients," she leaned forward to whisper the rest, "grabbed me by the neck and forced me into the nursing station to get him more drugs." She took a sip of her cocoa. "He wanted me to give him enough to kill him."

"Really?" Betty's eyes were like hubcaps.

"He'd been to the …" she lowered her voice more. "the concentration camps. Couldn't deal with what he saw. Already tried suicide once."

"Oh my golly! How scary! What happened?"

"I was able to trick him and get into the nursing station and lock it until I could get him to calm down."

"Wow. You are amazing! Where was everyone?"

Ruth snorted. "One orderly was asleep and the supervisor was nowhere to be found. I even rang the alarm! No one came except for the good orderly, Bob, eventually. By that time, the patient was going back to his room waiting for 'the shot.'" Ruth shivered. "I'm so afraid that he'll want to hurt me when he wakes up and finds I didn't kill him!"

Betty sat back in her chair, thinking. "Gosh, Ruth, things just seem to keep happening to you! What did the supervisor say, if she ever got there?"

"Well, that was a good thing. Bob was really impressed by how I handled everything, so when she arrived — at shift change, of course — he had told her and everyone else about it. I think I'm going to get a commendation note on my report."

"Well, that's fantastic! I've never had any of those."

"Yes, but I still have to go back on the ward with this man. I'm terrified."

Betty shrugged. "What do you bet he doesn't even remember you? I'll bet he was drugged to his teeth, right? He'll probably just remember a brown-haired nurse. Hey, I've got an idea! We could buy you some hair dye today. Then he'll never recognize you! Haven't you always wanted to be blonde, like me?" She patted her curls.

"Great idea." Ruth rolled her eyes. "With my luck, I'll turn out all green, like Anne of Green Gables!"

Laughing, the two girls got up, paid their bills, and headed out into the winter afternoon.

"I hate winter," said Betty. "When I'm done, I'm going to move someplace warm to nurse."

"Silly girl. What would you do with all your sweet winter hats?"

They continued down the street, past Stacey's and Jackson Metivier, gazing enviously at the mannequins in the windows all decked out in finery.

"Are you going to any of the Christmas dances? I can't wait. I haven't had much chance to meet my boys, what with the placement at the San. Everyone looks at me like I'm carrying TB. And the supervisor is watching my every move."

"I don't know if I can go. I'm tight on money since Meg's wedding. Can't get a new dress or anything. And my old one doesn't fit with all the treats we've been eating." She patted her stomach ruefully. "You'd think I'd run it all off."

"Can't you wear the one you wore for the wedding?"

"No, I left it for Meg as a wedding gift. She can use it more than I can."

"We'll find you a different one. There's got to be a girl about your size in the dorm. You've got to come. All those luscious boys, all looking for a dance and a cuddle. Warms me right up."

"Yes, I remember. But maybe I don't want cuddling." Ruth thought of her doctor friend at the OH. Now if she could go with him, then she'd be up for some dancing. But what if he was like George, grabby and demanding?

"Ruth? Where'd you go? Are you still upset about George? He's gone, gone, gone. That was almost a year ago!"

"No," said Ruth, lying. She could still feel George's breath on her. "Sorry, thinking about tomorrow." She looked over at Betty, guilty.

Betty jumped up and down to warm her feet. "I'm freezing. Should we just pop over and get some new stockings and then head home?"

"Sounds about right to me. I start days tomorrow."

"That's a short shift turnaround."

"It is. They are terribly short-staffed. So many nurses left when the men came home. They are still catching up. And even the orderlies are doing double shifts."

"Wow. It wasn't that bad when I was there. Hey, are you getting along with the hospital students? They were a bit prissy when I was there."

Ruth shook her head. "I think they are in a better mood now that the placement is lengthened to twelve weeks. I think they felt really unappreciated when we just came in for a short time. They still hate the Queen's students who never work the late shifts, though."

On the walk back, Betty was her usual chatty about boys. Ruth listened and laughed but kept her mouth shut about Dr. Hartman. She didn't want to jinx anything. Or start anything. Would she ever get over her experience last year?

NINETEEN

Insulin shock

The next morning, Ruth stepped onto the ward, shaking in her ugly shoes, wondering if Sgt. Turner would be after her. Had he calmed down any? She almost ran into the nursing station, knocking on the door a little too fast.

"Are you okay?" The senior nurse, another new one to Ruth, peered at her. "If you are getting the flu, you should go home. Half our patients are over at Beechwood already."

"No, no, I'm fine. Just wondering … if …. Sgt. Turner is still here?"

"Yes. He's pretty heavily medicated, though. I understand you had a bit of a run-in with him the other night?"

"I did. He wanted me to kill him with drugs. I gave him a dose of morphine, knowing it would knock him out. He grabbed my neck …"

"Yes, I heard. Just in case he remembers you still, I'm assigning you to the insulin shock treatment ward. Mrs. Matthews is due a treatment. You'll be busy in there most of the day, so he won't have a chance to see you. We are looking into transferring him to another floor, just in case. He was pretty wild when he woke up."

"Oh no!" Ruth started shaking again.

"A few days of sleep and he'll likely not recall anything. His poor mind just needs a break from what he saw."

"As long as he doesn't break my neck on the way!" Ruth was furious. The nurse didn't seem to be taking the risk to her at all seriously.

The nurse coolly handed her Mrs. Matthews' chart. "You'll be working with Dr. Hartman today. Do you know him?"

Ruth hid a smile. Good things come to those who wait, but great things come to those who endure, she thought, recalling one of her father's favourite sayings. "That should be fine. We've met before." She felt happy thoughts percolating in her stomach. A whole day with Dr. Hartman? Perfect.

"He's done the procedure a couple of times before, so he should be able to guide you through what you have to do. He's under supervision, of course. I'd come along, but, as usual," she sighed, "we are short-handed. Half the Dieu students have the flu. And I so wish they would fund us as they should. I'm tired of always making do. We'll likely only get to bathe a few patients a week. And then Dr. Ferguson orders more insulin treatments! Ties up even more staff."

"Has she had a treatment already?"

"She had one yesterday, when you were off. They didn't give her enough insulin to cause a coma, so there will be a higher dose today. You'd better get over there — likely they are waiting for you."

Ruth nodded and left the nursing station, jumping when she heard a roar from Sgt. Turner's room. "Please, God, let him be transferred!" She quickened her steps.

~

The insulin shock room was down the hall in the treatment wing. Ruth had walked past it many times before and peered in, but this was her first time actually inside. There were three patients lying on the beds. She went immediately to Mrs. Matthews.

"How are you today?"

"I don't know!" she whispered as Ruth bent down to hear her. "I keep thinking I am getting better, but my husband doesn't think so." She closed her eyes for a moment. "I didn't want this treatment, but he's making me have it. He's getting tired of waiting for me to get better."

Ruth blinked. This was the most she'd ever heard from Mrs. Matthews since they met.

"Well, you are sounding ever so much better," she said, holding Mrs. Matthews' hand.

"Will you be here with me today?"

"Yes, I'll be here the whole time."

"Oh, I'm glad. You seem to understand."

Ruth straightened up, feeling a bit shiny. Her patient liked her! She felt her heart lift until she turned to see the nursing supervisor glowering at her from the doorway. Her heart sank again. Why did she only appear when she was doing something she shouldn't?

"Have you done the patient's vitals, nurse? When the doctor gets here, you won't have time. You'd better get right to it."

"Yes, ma'am," Ruth said, dashing to gather stethoscope and thermometers. She was listening for the blood pressure in the last patient, a heavyset man who barely seemed conscious when she felt a tap on her shoulder. Turning, she saw Dr. Hartman behind her, smiling.

"I was hoping I'd have a chance to work with you, Miss Maclean!"

Ruth smiled all over. Then reality intruded. "I hope I'll be a help to you, doctor. I've never worked with insulin shock treatments before."

He frowned, then said, "Well, I'm pretty new myself. I imagine we can muddle through. Why don't we start with this fellow? We already know what dose of insulin he needs. Can you start an IV?"

"No, I don't know how to yet."

Dr. Hartman shrugged, as if that didn't matter. "Well, you go draw up the insulin then, while I start it. I need the practice, anyway."

Ruth went to the medication fridge and took out the insulin, checked the order, then drew up the prescribed dose. Interestingly, there were none of the small insulin needles in the room, so she left the bigger needle she'd used to draw it up on the syringe. When she returned to the bedside, Dr. Hartman was waiting impatiently.

"Can't you do that any faster?"

"Could you check this for me? We have to have two people check the doses of insulin."

"Really? We docs never have to do that. Okay, let me look." He quickly looked at the dose, initialled beside Ruth's signature, then took the syringe. "We usually give this deep intramuscularly, unlike with regular insulin. I like to use the ventrogluteal site, especially with a large dose," he explained. "I imagine students can't do this, either."

"I've just started being able to do medications since I came here. I can do it if you watch me."

"Never mind. I'll do it. You do know what we are doing here, I hope?" He injected the insulin into the patient's hip area, then handed her the empty syringe.

"Oh, yes. We —" She was going to tell him what she knew, but he cut her off.

"Well, then wait and watch. I'm sorry, I don't mean to be

rude, but we have to get these people started. I have ward rounds to do." He wrote out orders for the other patients' insulin doses and Ruth drew them up, faster this time, and injected them.

As the insulin eased into the patients' bodies, they became sleepy, then restless. They started making faces and twitching, moaning, and their bodies jerked. The heavyset man started yelling, but quickly calmed down. The other two women were quiet, but sweated so much Ruth was kept busy with towels and cool cloths. In between, she took their blood pressure, pulse and temperature, becoming alarmed as their pulse rates and blood pressures rose. Temperatures were done axillary in case of seizure, and they were going up as well. By the time Dr. Hartman returned from his rounds, forty-five minutes later, she was close to panic. All the patients had sunk into stillness, and they didn't respond when Ruth checked them. They were breathing deeply and strangely, like patients did just before dying.

Suddenly, the man went into a full grand mal seizure. Ruth noticed she hadn't attached the straps on the bed to keep him from falling out. She quickly grabbed one end and gestured to Dr. Hartman to grab the other, and they got it buckled just in time.

"I'll do up the others," Ruth said, embarrassed that she'd messed up yet again.

"The others shouldn't seize. That's not really the aim, though with him, that's what the doctors want. We'll watch him for a few moments until he stops seizing and then we'll give him a bolus injection of glucose. I'll prepare one. You keep an eye on him, make sure he doesn't go too deeply into the coma."

Ruth, watching the man seize, had no idea how she'd identify if he had gone too low.

Dr. Hartman, seeing her confusion, handed her the record book. "See, here is what we are looking for. Did you not record any of this?"

"I didn't see that before. I've been keeping track on my own," she added, pulling a damp piece of paper out of her pocket. She'd listed the vital signs for the every-fifteen-minute checks she'd been doing.

"But you didn't record the start of coma, the neurological assessments … oh damn it. I am going to be in heaps of trouble."

When the patient finally stopped seizing, she quickly checked his vital signs. It felt like that was the only thing she knew how to do. His pulse was raising, and his blood pressure had risen as well.

"But, Doctor, I thought you had done this before."

"Don't blame me. You should have had some sort of orientation, anyway." He sighed. "I probably shouldn't have left you here while I did rounds. You're supposed to stay with the patient, but there is just so much work. We'll say he seized for seven minutes, since I was here at the start. Next time, you mark the coma or seizure period, right?"

"Yes, doctor." Her lower lip was trembling.

"You'll do better next time," he said, setting up the bolus. "I think I'll bring him back quickly. I need to pull back the others, and he did have a good seizure. He'll be dozy for the rest of the day, and your job will be to check his vitals every fifteen minutes for the first hour, then every half hour for the next four. At some point, you'll have to get a urine sample to make sure his blood sugar returned to normal. You can give him juice as he wants as long as he's awake. Got it?"

"You're writing the orders, right?"

"There are standing ones, but I'll be sure to put them in his chart."

"What was his diagnosis?"

"Paranoid schizophrenia. This seems to be helping his brain reset. It is really the only treatment for schizophrenia." The doctor intoned this information as if he was lecturing an undergraduate.

Ruth was turned away but made a face. Why was he lording it over her? Most annoying. "But these women? They are just diagnosed with depression. Does it help depression? I heard ECT was better for that."

Historical Note

HYPOGLYCAEMIC SHOCK (HC) THERAPY

- Insulin shock is given in a special ward. Afebrile patients, start treatment at 7 AM, NPO, doc and nurse supervising for full period of treatment (4 hours). Beds carefully selected so injury through the "excitement" of the patients can be kept at a minimum.
- Start with 20 units of insulin a day, can move up to 150-1000.
- Treatment given 6 days a week. Injections are deep IM.
- About 1 hour after injection, symptoms of hypoglycaemic shock start. Sleepy, perspiring, increased salivation, complaints of hunger and thirst.
- Next hour, patient drowsy, sleeps. Some try to get up, toss around, shout and yell.
- 3rd hour, HC comes on, patient unresponsive, can't be wakened. Face flushed, pulse accelerated, pupils dilated.

- 4th hour, pupils non-responsive, eyeballs turned to one side, pulse accelerates more, patient appears cyanotic. Spastic waves come on, pupils later contract.
- 5th hour Pulse slows down, respiration forceful. Leave for 15 minutes for first treatment, never more than an hour afterwards, deep coma no more than 20 minutes.
- When coma has lasted long enough, sugar solution given by mouth (if patient can swallow) or through nasal tube, or by IV (importance of keeping one vein healthy for IV)
- 50-60 comas done before cessation of treatment. Never more than 100 as risk of brain damage. Risk of prolonged coma.
- "Even a normal person under insulin shock therapy would act rather oddly."
- Awakening: reflexes, then motor function, then they respond to stimuli, lastly speech. Immediately after termination, patients appear relaxed, more in close contact with the real world. After a few hours they may return to psychotic signs and dream world. Over many treatments, hallucinations become fainter, etc.
- Ideal treatment for schizophrenia, especially paranoid and catatonic forms ...
- Generally use insulin therapy for schizophrenia, EST for depression.
- "When we have to deal with affective disorders, the convulsive treatments are the treatments of choice, but it is with real depression and the depression occasioned by the menopause that electric shock therapy is most effective."*

---

* *Canadian Nurse,* November 1947. p. 843

TWENTY

Who's to blame?

He didn't reply, just kept on drawing up glucose. "It's good we have an IV line," he said, eventually. "Otherwise, we have to get them sugar by gavage. I hate doing that." Seeing Ruth's puzzled look, he added, "When we give it by gavage, we pass a tube through the patient's nose down into the stomach and administer the glucose that way. I have trouble getting the tube down the right side — to the stomach or the lung. Easy to get things mixed up and cause a pneumonia." He pushed the glucose into the man's IV, watching to see if there was a reaction. He remained unconscious.

The two women also were still unconscious, but seemed to be breathing better. Dr. Hartman poked at them from time to time, testing their eye response to touch. "We'll leave them there for an hour or so. They did well," Dr. Hartman said. "And for this one," he indicated Mrs. Matthews, "on such a low dose. That's good. Less damage done. I wonder why it was so easy, though."

"Well, she doesn't eat very much. Maybe her blood sugar was already quite low?"

"Maybe."

"Why did you let the first man have a seizure, while the other ones were stopped at a coma?"

"We don't really want a seizure. The coma and unconsciousness are the things that are supposed to help. Seizures mean generally that we've given too much insulin too quickly."

"But …," Ruth gestured at the first patient.

"He's been here for a lot of treatments. The regular coma outcome wasn't helping as much as his doctor wanted, so they've upped the treatment."

"Isn't that dangerous?"

"Shh." He pulled Ruth over to the wall. "It is, but after this there's only lobotomy. The doctor thinks it's worth the risk. What kind of life does he have, anyway, trapped in here?"

"Does he know what is happening?"

Dr. Hartman shook his head. "I've seen him on the ward. He's barely awake, they have him drugged so heavily." He leaned over to write an order in a chart. "He's gained a lot of weight, too. All that glucose going directly in his veins."

"Do they all gain that much weight?" She looked over at Mrs. Matthews, now sleeping quietly.

"Most do. The insulin plays havoc with their system, and it means the glucose is even better absorbed than usual. That's why they are dopey when they are coming out of the coma. Their blood sugars are completely out of whack."

"Does it work, though?"

Dr. Hartman looked around and then bent in towards Ruth's ear, making her shiver as he whispered. "Everyone here who has had it seems to be fat and slow. I don't see the benefit, myself." He stood up, lecturing again. "We really have nothing else, especially for schizophrenia. I hear there are some medications in development, but who knows when we will get them here? Do you remember the delay with the streptomycin? I thought we'd never get it and so many with TB died waiting for it."

"I know," said Ruth. "Last year I was working in the Sanatorium."

"Wow, how was that? I've only seen TB patients in the main hospital, and they were pretty well gone, too sick to move."

"It was tough. Lots of young people affected after the war. All these sweet young men who had survived the hell of fighting, only to come home and be cut up and still die. Heartbreaking."

"Sweet young men, eh? Met any special ones?"

"No." Ruth spat out the word and went to check vitals. She could feel his eyes on her. Please, God, don't let him ask about my experiences over there. She wasn't keen on any cozy chats.

She went around the beds, checking vitals on the first patient. He hadn't awakened yet. "Dr. Hartman? Should he be awake by now, after the bolus?"

He came over, pulled up the patient's eyelids to check his pupils, rubbed his knuckle on the patient's chest bone. "This is supposed to be painful, but he's got so much fat on there I can barely find it. He's not responding well. Wake up!" he yelled. "Mr. Connor? It's time to wake up now!"

It was loud enough that Ruth looked over at the other patients to see if they were waking, but they lay as if dead.

"I'm going to give him another bolus of glucose." He drew up the solution and injected it, testing him for eye response afterwards. No improvement. He stood for a moment, thinking.

Ruth looked at him. "But maybe he's hyperglycemic now? He's had a lot of sugar over a short time."

"I know what I'm doing." Dr. Hartman paused. "But you may be right. I'll call the attending."

Several nervous minutes passed until Dr. Ferguson arrived. He stormed into the room, looking at the notebook entries and moving over to the patient briskly. "What have you given him?" He listened as Dr. Hartman recited his orders. The senior doctor pulled up the patient's eyelids, too. "Pupils still rotated to the side and dilated." He pulled out his reflex hammer. "Did you test for reflexes?"

"No," admitted the younger resident. "I … I lost my reflex hammer and there doesn't seem to be one here."

"Nurse! Find a reflex hammer! You shouldn't have started treatment without one. How will you assess the level of coma? My God. Students. They'll be the death of me!" He looked at the patient. "Let's hope the killing doesn't start here."

Ruth searched all the drawers in the room, but there was no hammer present. "I'll just run to central supply," she said as she left the room. She didn't want to be there for the stripping down her doctor was going to get.

In five minutes, she was back, two hammers in hand. Dr. Ferguson was testing the male patient's reflexes, tapping on his ankles and knees, folding his arm and testing the inside of his elbow. She handed one hammer to Dr. Hartman, and he followed along on the patient's other side.

"So, no reflexes," said the senior doctor. "What does that tell you?"

"Deep coma state?"

"Yes, as we would have expected with the dilated and fixed pupils. What could be the cause?"

"Well, that's my problem. It could be hyperglycaemia or hypoglycaemia. How do we decide what to do?"

"Did you take a blood sample?"

"No, not yet."

"For heaven's sake! Whyever not? Nurse! Draw some blood and take it to the lab right away."

Ruth froze. She'd never drawn blood, wasn't sure how to do it. The doctors stared at her and then Dr. Hartman went to gather the equipment. "She's a student. Probably hasn't learned how to draw blood yet. Have you?"

Ruth shook her head, miserable to have her deficiencies demonstrated.

"She could have catheterized him and tested his urine."

Ruth was going to say she didn't have an order, but thought better of it, especially as Dr. Ferguson was turning on Dr. Hartman, his face flushed.

"Didn't I see you doing rounds?" he whispered furiously. "Did you leave these patients alone, with a student nurse? What in God's name were you thinking?"

"I thought they'd be stable for a few minutes …"

"This," Dr. Ferguson stage-whispered again, "is a dangerous medical procedure. It needs to be carefully observed and problems like this need to be acted on immediately. You have been irresponsible and …" He gathered himself. "We'll discuss this later. First, let's try to bring this poor fellow back without any additional brain damage." He turned to Ruth. "Shouldn't you be checking vitals again? Do you know how to test reflexes? Oh, never mind. Run this down to the lab right away."

Ruth grabbed the vial and raced down to the basement, where the laboratories were located. Fortunately, they could test the blood right away and would call the room when the results were back. She ran back up, arriving half out of breath. The two doctors were arguing, but stopped when she arrived.

"Still no response," said Dr. Ferguson. "Give him some oxygen."

Ruth ran to get an oxygen mask and rolled the canister closer to the bed. Dr. Hartman turned it on and regulated the flow. Meanwhile, Ruth went to assess the other patients. They were still asleep, but Mrs. Matthews was twitching her arms and legs. "Thank God," she thought. What if they'd killed them all?

"You'd better hope he comes out of this," Dr. Ferguson added. "We get special grants to study insulin shock, and it won't look good on the record."

The phone rang and Dr. Ferguson answered it, grunting in response as he hung up.

"No wonder he's out. How much insulin did you give him again?"

"The amount we used last time to cause a seizure," said Dr. Hartman, his voice shaking.

"Humph. Flirting with that pretty nurse, no doubt. He needs more insulin, stat." He bent forward and scrawled a number on the chart, then went to gather the medication.

"Maybe we gave the wrong dose?" Hartman said, looking over at Ruth.

"I checked it with you," said Ruth. "We both examined the dose."

"Yes, but you drew it up," he retorted.

Ruth was livid that Dr. Hartman tried to put the blame on her. The shine was dimming a bit on her doctor. Maybe she'd go to those Christmas parties after all.

"Pay attention. Let's get the insulin into him and try to bring him back. We'll leave a bag of D5W running to try to stabilize his blood sugar. If we can."

Dr. Hartman did so quickly, only shaking a bit. Within a short while, the patient's eyelids flickered. The doctors tested everything again. "He's still quite deep. Let's watch for a bit while we test the other two. You check them, I'll watch," said Dr. Ferguson, mopping his forehead. It dawned on Ruth that Dr. Hartman shouldn't have been left alone in the ward, either, if things could go wrong so fast. No wonder Dr. Hartman seemed so tense. Probably he was being left unsupervised all the time, just like she was.

TWENTY-ONE

Floating

The rest of the shift went better. Eventually, all three patients woke up, but Ruth was shocked at how confused and weak they were. The doctors had discharged the patients from the room, leaving Ruth alone with them again until orderlies could come and pick them up. She wasn't pleased.

Mrs. Matthews almost fell on the way to the toilet. Ruth stayed with her to be sure she didn't fall to the floor in there, and while she urinated, she moaned. "I don't like this! I feel like I almost died. I don't want it."

Ruth said nothing but made soothing nurse noises and helped Mrs. Matthews back to her bed. "Maybe you'll feel better after a rest," she said, meanwhile planning to haul Mr. Matthews into a room and have some strong words with him. She growled in frustration. She couldn't do that, she knew. Nurses at her level were meant to be seen and not heard, maybe even not seen. They were supposed to float around like angels, silently doing what they were told. Still, she could write things in the nursing notes, couldn't she? That's what she'd do, record Mrs. Matthews' fears and reactions. She wrote vehemently in Mrs. Matthews chart, describing how she was speaking well before the treatment and was very frightened and weak after it. Feeling slightly better, she went around, tidying everyone up and getting them ready for transport.

She still had hours left on her shift, but when she called up to her floor to tell them Mrs. Matthews was ready to go back, she got another surprise. "They are short-staffed on one of the open floors, 1B. I thought it might be an excellent experience to see what it is like there, so I've said you'll go down and join them when you are done with the insulin treatments. You can take Mr. Connor with you. His room is there."

Oh great, thought Ruth, envisioning rebelling and fleeing the hospital entirely. She was exhausted from the insulin shock clinic drama and wished she could go along with Mrs. Matthews and offer encouragement, but now, nope, now another completely novel experience. After the other two patients were picked up to be returned to their floors, she called over to the ward to let them know she was bringing Mr. Connor back. He was much heavier than Mrs. Matthews and the steering was challenging, but just as she got to a sharp turn, an orderly she didn't know came up and met her. "Let me give you a hand with him," he said. He took control of the stretcher, and Ruth only had to steer.

Thank God for the orderlies! Ruth wasn't sure how she'd have managed anything in this placement without them. Usually cheerful, strong, and no nonsense, they were so good with the patients and everything else besides. Such excellent team members, most of the time. She wondered if there were as many in the regular hospital. On the short placements she'd had there, she hadn't seen very many, but she'd been afraid the whole time then and hadn't been looking at anything but her patient and the head nurse. She realized suddenly that she wasn't afraid, not so much anymore. Maybe after all the terrors of this placement, other things seemed less worrying. Or maybe she was just numb.

She helped the orderly transfer Mr. Connor onto his bed, astonished at the different feel the open ward had. There were pictures on the walls, the patients had personal items in their rooms, there were even plants. As she walked to the nursing station, she saw one of the patients watering a tall tropical plant in the corner of the sunroom. He looked up at her, smiled and waved.

Ruth stopped short in shock. He seemed almost normal. He tilted his head toward her as he shambled to the next plant, and she could see a scar on his head. Brain injury?

She introduced herself to the charge nurse, Miss Withers. "Welcome, Miss Maclean. I'm glad you could join us. We need some help with feeding and toileting."

Ruth nodded.

"We're a bit of a different crowd here. Raymond, the man with the plants, he's post-lobotomy. Sweet as anything, but can't remember anything for the life of him. We have three post-lobotomy patients here, all impaired more or less. We also have a few deaf patients. Because they can't hear, they haven't learned to speak or read. After several years, the lack of communication leaves them unable to care for themselves." She pointed out one patient, sitting at a table, face blank. "I hear there are advancements coming along, but I just wish we could afford more deaf-dumb schools. Or that there was more access to the Sir James Whitney School for the Deaf in Belleville. It seems wrong to just lock them up, but it is really up to their parents. Sometimes," she added in a warning tone, "they get frustrated. Watch their hands. They may hit or grab."

Ruth wasn't surprised. She'd want to hit out, too.

"One orderly will look after Mr. Connors. Can you give me a report on how the IST went?"

"Yes, of course." Ruth wasn't sure how much to tell. It had seemed like an unholy mess to her. She started, and Mrs.

Withers gently prodded her with questions about the length of his coma, the response time. When Ruth finished, the head nurse sighed.

"I expect there won't be much of his brain left after all that. Honestly. He was barely moving as it was. But 'ours is not to reason why.' Meantime, let's put you to work. If you could start with Miss Elliott here, would you do the toileting rounds and get everyone set up for dinner?"

Ruth looked over at Miss Elliott. She was a merry-looking girl dressed in an OH student uniform who pulled her into the supply room.

"It's not too bad on this ward," she whispered. "Most of them are old dears. Some men do try to hug you, but you can usually just say no. Where did you float from?"

Ruth told her, and Miss Elliott made a face. "Locked ward. I am so glad I didn't get placed there yet. Aren't you scared?"

"Sometimes." While they chatted, they were setting up a cart with washcloths and bowls. "Vitals?"

"Nope, we only have to do them in the morning, unless they are sick or unless they've had a treatment. So glad we don't have to monitor Mr. Connors. So much work! Okay, we'll start down here with the deaf patients. They are the hardest to do, so we may as well get them done first."

"I like your approach! Get the hardest things done first."

Miss Elliott laughed. "I'm really glad to have your help. Toileting some of them is a challenge."

Ruth found out why as they entered the first room. Four female patients were rocking and moaning animal-like sounds as they walked in. They looked up when they spotted the cart and started walking toward the girls. It felt a bit like a horror movie as they shuffled along, not speaking, just reaching with their hands. Ruth could feel pity overwhelming her.

"We'll start with Norma. She's always in need of the toilet, aren't you, Norma? She can walk okay but needs reminding about washing her hands and using tissue."

"Oh," said Ruth.

"Here, you take her in. I'll bring Brenda."

Ruth took Norma's arm and led her into the toilet. Norma immediately sat down and urinated. Ruth didn't even have time to help her pull down her undies, but she looked and realized she wasn't wearing any. She stood Norma up and stopped her as she was just about to gallop out of the toilet. She turned her towards the sink, turned on the water, helped her soap up her hands, wash them and dry them on a towel. "There, that's better, isn't it?" Ruth said, realizing too late that speaking was useless. She faced Norma and smiled. Norma reached up and touched Ruth's face, then pulled back her hand for a slap.

Ruth leaned back and she missed. Norma shuffled out of the toilet without looking back.

"Coulda warned me about the slapping," Ruth grumbled.

"Oh, did she go for you? She does that sometimes, but it's usually just a tap. Doesn't like it if you try to move her."

"Thanks. Next one need any special treatment?"

Miss Elliott laughed, tossing her head. "No, she's as good as gold, poor thing. Still so young — only thirty-five — and trapped here."

TWENTY-TWO

Lobotomized

As they went room to room, Ruth asked, "Do you really need to toilet everyone? They look self-managing."

"Some are. The usual depressed patients who are here for a 'tune-up' they call it — they can look after themselves most of the time. The deaf people, well, you saw, they need reminding. As do the lobotomy patients. The ones that do well after that surgery go home, usually. These are the ones who have ended up with serious damage. They don't know what they are doing. That fellow over at the plants, Raymond? He'll water them again and again and again if we don't take the watering can away from him. Then he forgets all about the plants and dusts until we stop that as well. Then he sits."

"Wow. My mother could use him at home!"

"I know! Everything here is so clean! Where is home for you?"

"I'm from Cloyne. Do you know it?"

"I do! I'm from Tamworth. It was so good to come to Kingston. So many things to do! Are you going to the Christmas dances at the base?"

"I wasn't going to, but now I think I will. If I can borrow a dress. My sister just got married and I spent all my pay on her."

"I only have brothers, fortunately."

"I have those, too."

"Nurses! Less chatter, more work!" Miss Withers was glaring at them from the nursing station.

Giggling, Miss Elliott pulled Ruth into the next ward. There were the lobotomized men, all frozen in place. "Come on, boys, time to get washed for dinner!" They stood as one and walked toward the toilet, lining up tidily to use it. Each of them used the toilet, washed their hands, dried them, and quietly left the room, heading for the dining table.

It was weird. Ruth almost preferred the more agitated patients on the locked ward. These people all seemed half dead. The next room was better, a group of women who were in for depression, said Miss Elliott. "Ladies, time for supper."

"I'm not hungry," whined one. "Leave me alone."

"Now Ellen, you know what the doctor said. You can't go home until you start eating properly. Let's go, we'll walk with you. Here's a new nurse, Miss Maclean. Would you like to meet her?"

She handed Ellen over to Ruth and went around the other beds.

"They make me eat," muttered Ellen. "I don't want to. I'll get fat."

"But you are so slim," responded Ruth. "And besides, you'd like to go home, wouldn't you?"

"Want to go home. Sick of this place. Smells."

"Well then. Where do you want to sit?" They'd arrived at the big table where all the patients gathered for meals.

"Anywhere but beside that guy. He pinches." Ruth looked over at a leering patient, who grinned wider and made a rude gesture her way.

"Tom! Stop that this instant, or you will eat alone in your

room, after your dinner has cooled." Mrs. Withers bore down on him like a ship in full sail. He cringed and sat down, chastened. The senior nurse came over to speak to Ruth, pulling her slightly away from the table. "Watch Ellen's eating. I think she's hiding food and not eating it. She's going to fade away."

"What do I do if she does?"

"Speak to her gently. Tell her to take just one mouthful. Sometimes that works. Best to sit beside her."

Ruth did so, and spent an exasperating time trying to get Ellen to eat one pea, one piece of meat, one potato. Eventually, she did, but it took so much pleading Ruth wished she could take Ellen home to her younger siblings. They needed no persuasion to eat their food. There wasn't enough around for that, and usually dinner was a free for all. The competition might cue Ellen to eat more. Eventually the meal was over, and Ruth could report that Ellen had eaten half a potato, two peas, and a mouthful of meat. When she went to chart it, Mrs. Withers said, "Well done! Now follow her to her room. Sometimes she makes herself throw up. Did you see her teeth? Eroded by stomach fluid. Better hurry."

Ruth ran to Ellen's room to find Ellen lying on her bed. "Why not come to the social room, Ellen? Maybe we could play cards? Listen to the radio?"

"No."

"I could really use your help," Ruth said, desperate to make some sort of connection. "I never learned how to play Euchre and it's all anyone seems to do here. Do you know how to play?"

Ellen rolled over, peered at her from under her hair. "You can't play Euchre? Who doesn't know how to play that?"

"I know. I'm so embarrassed. Could you teach me?"

Ellen glared. "I like to nap after dinner."

"It won't take too long. It's a short game, isn't it?"

"Not if you play for money." Ellen's eyes glinted. "You got money?"

"Oh no," laughed Ruth. "I'm a nursing student. We're all poor."

Ellen grunted, turned away.

Ruth leaned over. "Oh, come on. It'll be fun. You can show everyone how much better you are at it than I am."

Muttering to herself, Ellen sat up, pulled on her housecoat and slid her feet into slippers. "Well, come on, then. I don't have all day."

"Right."

"We've got to be careful who we ask to make up the four. Some of them are real sharks. There's Lucy and Cindy. They'll be kind to you, maybe." She grinned a greasy grin. It made Ruth uncomfortable, but she was committed now. They sat at the card table and one of the other ladies got the deck and cut the cards. Ellen shuffled them like a Mississippi gambler.

Miss Elliott came by. "You're brave, Miss Maclean! These gals are pros!"

"I'm just here to learn," Ruth said. "They'll be nice, right?"

Thirty minutes later, the rest of the table stood up and left. Ruth was alone, shuffling the cards slowly. She'd lost, and lost, and lost.

Ellen came back with a glass of water. "Hey, Nursie, you didn't do too badly. You'll learn. It's just naptime."

Ruth smiled, relieved. Miss Elliott came over. "Okay, here we go again. Toileting and hygiene all over. Shall we go together?"

"Oh yes, please, I don't know the patients that well."

As they walked along, got the patients with lobotomies sorted and into bed, Ruth couldn't help but ask. "Why did they have that done? It seems like it causes more damage than they already had."

"Well, you didn't see them before. Mr. Smith over there used to get so mad he could throw his bed against the wall. He spent some time on your floor until the surgery. Now he's gentle, just forgetful. Jim with the plants was a long-term, violent schizophrenic, terrified, hearing voices, poor man."

"And what about the deaf patients?"

"Those are the ones I really feel sorry for. Their parents put them into an institution at birth. No one spoke to them or even tried to work with them. It's a crime. I don't know why they wouldn't have been sent to the deaf school. Now it's too late, of course. Some of them are in their fifties."

When they'd finished their rounds, Mrs. Withers thanked Ruth. "You've been a great asset here today, Miss Maclean. You can come back anytime."

Ruth wasn't sure she wanted to come back. She didn't know if she'd be able to work around the sadness and pity she felt for many of the patients. It seemed like so many of them had no chance to get better. On the active treatment floor, patients had interventions almost every day. It felt like progress, even if it wasn't.

Historical Note

LOBOTOMY

"The defrontalized element, deprived of one of the principal centres of psychic life, recovers his equilibrium at the price of intellectual impoverishment, but it is better for him to have a simplified intellect, capable of elementary acts, than an intellect where reigns the disorder of subtle syntheses. Society can accommodate itself to the most humble labourer, but it justifiably distrusts the mad thinker."*

---

* H. Cushing, quoted in Walter Freeman and James W Watts, *Psychosurgery In the Treatment of Mental Disorders and Intractable Pain*. Charles C Thomas, Springfield IL, 1950. p. xvii

TWENTY-THREE

Freeman's technique

The next time she was on her ward, the supervisor was waiting for her. Rats, thought Ruth, what have I done now?

"Miss Maclean?"

"Yes, Miss."

"I heard about your good work yesterday on the open ward. They said you were asking about lobotomies?"

"Yes …" Ruth shuffled her feet, "Yes, Miss."

"Well, as a reward for your good work, and, frankly, to keep you away from Sgt. Turner for another day, I've arranged for you to observe the procedure today in the OR."

Ruth felt queasy. The TB surgeries were bad enough, watching young men be chopped up and tugged apart. She wasn't sure how she'd feel about seeing someone cut into the brain.

"Come along. This isn't an opportunity many students get to have. I know you helped in surgery at the San, so you know how to behave in an operating room. And we have a special doctor here who does a quicker procedure than usual."

Ruth trotted along behind the supervisor, who went on. "Because it's a special procedure, you'll be observing from the seats. There will be a few other students there as well, mainly residents and medical students, though a senior nurse has crept in here and there." She grinned. "I can't wait to see it myself. No need to shave the skull, no suture line to keep clean. Amazing." Ruth desperately wanted to ask about the procedure, but this supervisor was very much of the thinking that nursing students should be invisible, so she held her tongue and extended her eyeballs. So to speak.

When they entered the operating room, Ruth was astonished to see that the area was not being kept sterile. People were crowding around the patient, pushing to see. She saw Dr. Hartman standing across the room. He made a little wave to her and when she went over, he nudged her in front of him. "I can see fine over you," he whispered. "And you should be able to see well from here." They were standing right behind the patient's head.

"As you all know," said the surgeon in tones of great seriousness, "We have been using leucotomy, or lobotomy, as the treatment of choice when all other treatments have failed. Until now, it was major surgery, and although done under local anesthetic, was quite alarming to the patient. We needed them awake as we drilled into the head to allow the surgeon to get into the appropriate brain area. Now we have an option. This can help make leucotomy a procedure to be tried first, rather than putting the patient through years of failed treatments. It's quick, painless, and leaves no scar. I hope you have read the seminal work by Dr. Freeman about the types of lobotomy surgery and the outcomes we can expect."

Nods around the room.

"So, given that this patient has only recently become seriously depressed, what would be your recommendation of surgery type?"

"Radical is what's recommended for depression, isn't it?" said one keen medical student. Ruth hadn't seen him around.

"Don't we want to minimize the damage first, try to keep things as small as possible?" asked another.

The surgeon looked at the new student. "Correct. We can always go back in if we need to later. We want to minimize the side effects of the surgery while still relieving troublesome symptoms."

Ruth looked down. The patient, a pretty young woman, was lying wide-eyed on the stretcher.

"So," continued the surgeon, "which type of approach would you recommend?"

"Um …," continued the second student, "I haven't seen it done, but I've heard great things about the transorbital lobotomy. Is that what you'd suggest?"

"I've seen pictures. Sounds horrible." One of the senior nurses shivered and wrapped her arms around herself.

"If you are likely to faint, either step back or leave the room," said the surgeon. "That is the procedure we will be doing today. I've recently taken training with the famous Dr. Freeman of the United States, who has performed hundreds of these procedures to good effect. We won't even have to shave your head," he added to the patient, who smiled faintly. "We use an unusual treatment for anesthesia to make the operation even less dangerous. Doctor, could you bring over the ECT machine?"

A resident rolled over the machine. "Each of you students, please take hold of the patient's limbs. Just to protect you," he reassured the patient. "Now, we'll give a series of brief shocks until the patient is asleep. You won't feel a thing, dear, and it's much safer than putting you out with drugs," he added. Ruth was impressed that he spoke to the patient, but perhaps it was a performance for the students and others. She rarely had experienced the doctors saying much before procedures. They were always running too fast between patients.

"Now, let's get started. First, the series of shocks. Hold her gently, please." He turned on the machine, the lights dimmed a bit in the room, and then the patient went into a seizure. He waited until she stopped seizing, then shocked her again. Waited, and then a third time. "One benefit of this kind of anesthesia is that they remember nothing about the start of the procedure, so don't know to be frightened if we must do it again. Also, it is safe in debilitated patients who can't handle regular anesthesia."

"But doesn't the shock cause issues as well?" One resident stood back from the leg he was holding, where obvious bruises were already forming.

"I told you to hold her gently, you idiot. Step back." He pointed to another resident. "Time for the procedure. You, clever boy, you come and help me hold the instruments." The student stepped forward and was given a small hammer.

The surgeon opened a case and took out one of two instruments that looked just like an ice pick. "We've done hundreds of these, and it is a much safer operation than the larger procedures. The pick will go in through mostly empty space behind the eye until we can reach the connections between the frontal lobe and the thalamus, where emotions come from. We'll use this additional tool," he pulled out a two-piece bendy object with a sharp knife that came out of the end, "to sever the connections. This is the leucotome. Severing the connections allows the mind to be lightened from destructive emotions. She may still feel them, but they won't matter to her anymore."

Two nurses left the room. One medical student, face grey, pushed to the back of the crowd.

"You okay?" whispered Dr. Hartman, squeezing her upper arms.

"Fine," Ruth replied, though she was trying to hide the horror she felt.

"Right, here we go. Can I get a couple of you students to come and hold her arms and legs, just in case she wakes up?" Two keeners came forward. Ruth was quite happy to stay where she was, with the warm comfort of Dr. Hartman behind her.

It seemed to be over in a moment. The surgeon bent forward, pulled up the patient's eyelid, slipped the ice pick into her tear duct, and thumped it with the hammer. The pick slid in easily.

"The skull is very thin here. Now, we just need to push it in for five centimetres …" He pulled out the pick and pushed the leucotome into the tear duct. Angling it around the eye socket, he explained, "I'll push this in a bit farther. As I rotate this, I'll be cutting the connections with the knife at the tip. This is a time to be very careful, as there are blood vessels nearby. Haven't hit one yet," he boasted.

A bit of wiggling later, and he pulled the instrument out. "That should do it. Now for the other side." He pressed on the patient's eye. "I'm applying pressure just in case of some bleeding. Can someone take over? I'd like to do the other side."

Ruth felt her hand being pulled over and pressed on the patient's eye. She almost threw up, but gulped back whatever was coming. Thank heavens she'd only had a slice of toast that morning.

The second eye was done the same quick way as the first, with new instruments. "You will note we did not need to cleanse or drape the area. Tear ducts are usually sterile and there is no risk of infection. However, sometimes on withdrawal, we contact the eyelashes, which is why we need two sets of instruments. There may be some infection in the hairs around the eye. Best to start fresh."

In no time at all, he finished and pressed on the other eyeball. The room burst into applause. "But the best thing," the surgeon added, "Is that the patient feels nothing at all. She may not even think she's had the surgery." They lifted their hands off her eyeballs.

The patient moaned but slowly wakened.

"We'll check her out right now. Hello! How are you feeling?"

The patient's voice. "I'm fine. A little sleepy."

"Do you know where you are?"

"I think I'm in the hospital, though it looks like a party here, with all of you."

"These people all wanted to come and see you getting better. Is that fine?"

"Yes, that's fine."

"Do you know what day it is?"

"Tuesday?"

"That's correct. Do you know who I am?"

"The surgeon? I don't remember your name ..." Her voice trailed off, uncertain.

"No, of course you wouldn't. We just met a few moments ago." He grinned, turning to share it with the watchers.

"Are you going to do the surgery now? Because I don't think I need it. I feel better."

The surgeon laughed, a hearty, room-filling guffaw. Ruth restrained herself from kicking him.

"We're all done, my dear. And now it's time for you to head back to your ward to rest and recover. Perhaps this nurse can keep you company." He patted Ruth's shoulder.

Ruth cringed. In again to a spot where she knew nothing. What was post-op care for a transorbital lobotomy, anyway? She barely had time to look around for Dr. Hartman as the room emptied quickly, all the students talking loudly to each other, heading for the cafeteria. Apparently, there were snacks.

TWENTY-FOUR

Post-op

Ruth followed her patient, Mrs. Walters, back to her room on the open floor she'd worked on before. The orderlies wheeling the stretcher vanished as soon as they helped put her in bed.

The charge nurse came into the room. "And you are?"

"Miss Maclean, from 2E. KGH nursing student."

"Ah. I'd heard they were sending someone back from the OR. I'm the head nurse here, Miss Preston. Are you able to special Mrs. Walters? Because we could really use you here." The charge nurse, Miss Preston, looked absolutely weary and pleased to see Ruth. "I'll call your floor and see if they can do without you today."

Ruth paused. "But I don't know how to look after someone after a lobotomy."

"I'll be back with the orders after I check with your floor. We can go over them together. We haven't had this type of lobotomy done here before. In the meantime, just take her vitals and get her settled in."

Ruth gathered a blood pressure cuff, thermometer, and

stethoscope from the utility room and headed back to the patient. Mrs. Walters was sitting quietly on her bed, looking at nothing.

"Hello, Mrs. Walters. I'm Miss Maclean. How are you feeling now, after your procedure?"

"Oh, I haven't had it yet. They are coming any moment to take me to the operating room."

Ruth blanched. How could the woman not remember an ice pick going into her eyes? She was certain she'd never forget it if it happened to her. Thinking back to her training about dealing with delusional patients, she knew enough not to challenge her about it.

"Could I just check how you are doing? Take your temperature and blood pressure? You know, like we always do." Ruth smiled. "At least I'm not waking you up for it."

"Of course, Miss," said Mrs. Walters. "And call me Jean? I don't like being so formal all the time. It makes it scary to be here, though that doesn't seem so bad now."

She obediently held out her arm, opened her mouth for the thermometer, and sat still while Ruth took the measurements. Her blood pressure was low, her temperature and pulse were up. As Ruth folded up the blood pressure cuff, Mrs. Walters stood, and urine poured out of her onto the floor. She sat down again, faintly smiling.

"Oh, I'll get that cleaned up," Ruth helped her lie back on the bed after checking to see if her gown had gotten wet. "Here, you just lie here for a minute so you don't slip."

"Is there water on the floor?"

Ruth gawped again. Miss Preston arrived at that moment. "Hi, Miss Maclean, you're cleared to stay. Oh, she was incontinent, was she? That's really common with lobotomy patients. It usually gets better in a day or two. I had hoped with the gentler procedure it would be better."

Ruth called Miss Preston over and whispered, "She doesn't know she's had any procedure, or that she's voided."

"Yes," Miss Preston said. "That's also typical. Let's look over the orders over here after you get that cleaned up."

Ruth quickly mopped up the floor, using the mop conveniently located in the hall nearby. They must have expected this to happen. It would have been nice to have a warning, she thought. Why does no one tell me things?

"Did they take her for an X-ray yet? Well, we'd better get her ready for that. They'll take her down to check for bleeding or other injury. Here are the rest of the orders. We're to position her in bed with the head raised thirty degrees, unless her blood pressure drops below 100."

"It's only 110 now. I'll keep an eye on it."

"Good. We have to take her vitals every hour for 24 hours, toilet her every two hours. She had an enema before the procedure, so she should be good for that until tomorrow. We'll need to get her up to be sure she doesn't just stay in place. The doctor says every two hours, so I guess we'll walk her around when we take her to the toilet. She has orders for medications if she has pain or nausea. Sounds just about the same as for the regular lobotomy, but at least we don't have to keep her from pulling at her bandages."

"Do we do anything for her eyes?" Ruth couldn't believe they still looked only a bit red, though that was rapidly changing.

"Just look for bleeding. We can put a cool compress on them if they are sore, I suppose. Are your eyes sore?" she asked the patient.

"My eyes?" She felt them. "They feel a bit puffy, but not sore. Why would they be puffy?"

"Do you remember why you are here?"

"Oh yes, I'm here for surgery on my brain to make me happier."

"Do you still feel worried?"

"No, not at all." She ran her hands over her scalp. "But did they do the surgery? I don't feel any bandage."

Miss Preston took her hand. "We did a special new procedure on you. That way, we didn't have to cut your hair."

Mrs. Walters ran her hands through her hair again. "Oh, I'm so glad. I love my hair."

"Well, now you rest for a moment or two. I'll check if we can take her to X-ray now. Best to do before she has to urinate again."

"Don't leave me," said Mrs. Walters.

"Miss Maclean will be right here with you. Are you feeling all right?"

"Just a little …" She leaned over and vomited, spraying the floor. Ruth ran to get a cloth for her face and the mop for the floor. Looking after her was going to be a challenge. She'd just finished cleaning everything up when an orderly arrived with a stretcher.

"I'll take her down to X-ray. You take a break. It's a long day with these patients."

Ruth smiled at him. She desperately needed the toilet herself! She dashed off and accomplished that and got the bed freshened up before her patient returned. After that, it was an endless round of taking vitals, toileting, mopping up, and repeating explanations. She watched as blue-black bruises formed around Mrs. Walter's eyes, and applied compresses to no effect until the patient told her to stop. She looked like she'd been in a fight. Altogether, it was exhausting.

Mid-afternoon, the doctor came by. He was carrying sunglasses.

"And how is our patient?"

"Hello, doctor. Are you going to do my procedure now?"

"How are you feeling?" Ruth noticed he didn't challenge Mrs. Walters, either.

"I feel so much better for some reason. It must be this comfortable bed." She ran her hands over the bedspread.

"And are you still feeling worried? Do you think something bad may happen?"

"Oh, doctor, why would I think that? No, I am perfectly content. Is my husband coming in soon?"

"Do you want to see him?"

"Oh yes, please. I miss him."

"That's fine. We'll call him to come in as soon as he can."

"Thank you, doctor." Mrs. Walters lay back with a happy sigh. The doctor beckoned Ruth to follow him.

"You were observing this morning, yes?"

"Yes." Ruth didn't trust herself to say more. She was still squirming with horror at the ice picks.

"Well, you can see the results. This woman was so anxious she was hiding in the closet for days, threatening her husband with a hammer whenever he would come near. All of that is gone. And with such a simple procedure! It's a miracle, really. Normally they'd be shaved from ear to ear, and their skull drilled. This is so much easier on everyone. I must go report this to the head of the hospital. With this, we should be able to do dozens of procedures every day if we need to." He swept off, his step bouncing with his success. Suddenly, he turned back. He handed Ruth the sunglasses. "Here. Please put these on the patient. I notice there's some bruising, and it's easier for everyone if we tell the patient her eyes may be sensitive to light for a while, rather than have everyone see the bruises and think she is hurt. Especially the patient."

As Ruth headed back into the room only to see another incident of incontinence, she grumbled, "I hope they hire more nurses if they do more of these!"

There was a knock on the doorjamb, and Dr. Hartman was there. "I wanted to see the results for myself," he said with a smile. "May I come in?"

"Oh yes," said Mrs. Walters. "You're that handsome doctor. I saw you earlier."

"I love your sunglasses," Dr. Hartman said.

"I do, too — aren't they stylish? The doctor says I need them since my eyes might not like the light."

Ruth laughed. "Just let me tidy her up and check her blood pressure. It's time, and it's been running low." Sure enough, it had dipped to 90/50. "We just have to put the head of your bed down for a moment," she said.

Dr. Hartman helped her lower the head, then had to ask. "Do you know where you are?"

"Yes, in the hospital. They are going to take me for my procedure any minute now."

"But you had your procedure this morning! Don't you remember?"

She ran her hand over her head. "No, there's no bandage. You must be mistaken." She lay back, a peaceful smile on her face.

"Well, I see you have an excellent nurse to look after you," he added. Ruth blushed. He called Ruth over to the side of the room. "I'd love to have a chat with you over coffee about this whole thing. Would you be free after your shift? I'm eager to know how the post-op course goes, but I've got to get back to my ward."

Ruth felt her heart give a little jump. "Of course, doctor. I'd be glad to go over the treatment."

Dr. Hartman spun on his foot and hurried out.

"Those young men! They move so quickly!"

"And we should, too," said Ruth. "Up for another walk?"

TWENTY-FIVE

Coffee with Dr. Hartman

"We seem to keep running into each other," Dr. Hartman said, after he carried two coffees over to the table in the cafeteria.

"We do." Ruth gazed around. This was the only time she'd seen the doctor's cafeteria, and she wouldn't have come in at all except for Dr. Hartman's invitation and the fact the room was empty.

"So, how is our patient?"

"Exhausting. I know the surgeon was saying he would like to do lots more of these, but they'd better get more nurses on board. Just keeping ahead of the incontinence and nausea is a lot, and then she started running a high fever just before I left, so that added an extra layer of management to bring it down. Her eyes are all black and blue, too. Thank heavens she doesn't seem too fussed about anything."

"Is she still confused?"

"Yes, but peacefully so. You know how when you confront patients with dementia, they become angry? Everyone keeps telling her she's had her procedure, and she just smiles sweetly and says she hasn't."

"Bizarre. At least with the regular lobotomy, they have the physical evidence."

"Apparently the confusion will be worse tomorrow because of swelling in the brain. I never thought I'd say it, but I'll be glad to go back to my old ward."

"How much longer is your placement?" Dr. Hartman sat back, his coffee done.

"You drank that coffee awful fast!" She sipped hers. "I'm here until the end of January."

"Residents have to drink fast. Especially if you need to sneak out for a smoke." He grinned. His eyes sparkled. "I'm so glad you are here for a while longer. I enjoy working with you. And I wouldn't mind getting to know you better."

Ruth looked down, not wanting to show her eyes. She wasn't sure she trusted him yet. She turned her coffee mug back and forth, back and forth. "So, how much longer are you here?"

"I've got another two months or so, depending on my reports. Then I have to figure out where to head next."

"Where do you think you'll go?"

"I'm really not sure. Lots of options. I just have to pick where I want to work, what I want to specialize in. Surgery. Medicine. General practice. I've even thought about going north."

"North? Where north?"

"Way, way north. Frobisher Bay."

"Brr." Ruth shivered.

"Well, it would be nicer if I had someone warm to come with me."

Ruth blushed. Such cheek! "I should get back. We really aren't supposed to be in this cafeteria. It's only for doctors. I snuck in because no one else was here."

"Would you be perhaps more comfortable having a coffee with me or a walk outside the hospital?"

"A coffee outside the hospital might be nice," said Ruth in a small voice. Her heart was pounding so loudly she was sure her whole body was vibrating. But she wasn't going on a walk with any man unescorted. Not after last year.

"Done. What are you up to tomorrow? I'm off."

"So am I," said Ruth. "Thank heavens. I'm tuckered out."

Dr. Hartman laughed. "Not surprised. I came by later in the day and saw you dancing with the mop again."

"I had just taken her to the toilet! And then she stops in the middle of the floor and lets go again. I should have kept her there longer, I guess. She'd stay in the toilet forever if I didn't move her. And she urinates so frequently there's no point in putting her in diapers."

Dr. Hartman made a sympathetic grimace. "So, tomorrow?"

"How about Morrison's for lunch?" Ruth suggested. Lots of people, she thought. Nothing bad can happen. And she knew the waiters and owners at Morrison's. They loved nursing students and would make sure she'd come to no harm.

"You're on. 12:30, Morrison's."

"See you then." Ruth stood up quickly and fled. She'd seen a gaggle of medical personnel heading into the cafeteria.

Ruth tossed and turned all night. She kept dreaming of Mrs. Walter's face, slack when not being spoken to, a shy smile when she was. It was hard for Ruth to picture her trying to hurt anyone with a hammer. And all day long, she still didn't grasp that she'd had the surgery done.

And then the image of Dr. Hartman's face would slip in, and her stomach became all excited butterflies and giggles. She told herself firmly to get control of herself, but it wasn't helping. She wasn't sure why she'd been so bold to invite him for lunch except that lunch would give them things to do with their hands. Or something. She was second-guessing herself endlessly as she wandered through her dreams. She hoped their lunch either went well, and they became closer friends, or went so badly she never wanted to speak to him again. It was hellish being hung between the options.

The next morning, she raced to get into the washroom before everyone else, so she'd have time to set her hair. As she was putting in the curlers, Doris poked her head in, fresh from nights. "You're off today, aren't you?"

"Yes. I'm going out, though."

"Am I sensing a date? The whole hospital was talking about you and Dr. Hartman having coffee after your shift."

"Oh phooey. Why can't people mind their own business? We were reviewing the lobotomy case," said Ruth. "He wanted to know how she was doing."

"And then?"

"Oh, all right. We're meeting for lunch today. Just a quick one, nothing serious or anything like that." She fussed with a bobby pin to hide her nervous smile.

"Hmm," said Doris with a grin. "Everyone knows he's sweet on you, you know. Just take it slow." Ruth had told Doris about her disastrous last year.

"Fingers crossed it's a pleasant time," she said. "I don't want a repeat of last year's adventures. And I'm not looking for anyone. I am … completely … focused on getting my nursing certificate."

Doris laughed. "Sure, sure. Just keep telling yourself that." She leaned forward and stage-whispered, "Have fun. He's a dreamboat!"

Ruth shivered with anticipation. She couldn't say it out loud, but she thought him dreamy, too.

Lunch was everything she'd hoped. Richard asked her to use his first name, spoke to her like an equal, asked her advice, told her about medical school and his family and his plans. Ruth was quieter about her family. She remembered all the drama with George last year, when he'd pretended to speak to her father and demand her hand in marriage. That entire experience left her frightened and traumatized. And no wonder, after he'd attacked her.

Richard was different, and she found herself having to avoid looking at his lips. It made talk awkward, but she couldn't look at them without wanting to touch them, have them touch her. She focused on his nose.

Lunch went on until the dinner hour, and they laughed as the waitress somewhat impatiently brought them a supper menu. "I suppose I'd better get back," Ruth said. "They'll be wondering where I am."

"Me, too, though I think they watch us less closely. I'm so sorry, I've taken up your whole day off."

Ruth looked at him from under her eyelashes. "I'm not regretting it."

"Good, neither am I. Can I walk you home?"

"I usually take the bus when it is after dark." The sun set so early these winter days. She hadn't even noticed it happening.

"Good plan. May I bus you home?"

She squirmed. Should she? Was he safe? Mind you, the buses were pretty full this time of night. "I suppose."

He looked at her, peering at her as she tilted her head away. "Did I say something wrong?"

She sighed. "No. Just a bad experience last year. Makes me wary."

Richard thumped the table, making Ruth jump. "A soldier?"

"A patient. And a soldier."

"I have heard way too many stories about that sort of thing. It makes me furious. The police should be on top of it, and they don't seem to care." In a softer voice, he asked, "Did he … hurt you?"

Ruth flushed, then laughed. "No, fortunately I grew up with an older brother, who taught me a mess of nasty fight moves. But it sure scared me."

"I'll bet." He took her hands in his. "I am not like that. I can get a note from my parents, if that would help. They like me a lot." He paused. "Please take a chance and trust me a little. And nasty fight moves? I'll be extra careful."

A few minutes passed. Finally, Ruth squeezed his hands. "Let's catch that bus." She jumped up, and Richard helped her into her cape, wrapping it around her warmly.

"Let's go."

TWENTY-SIX

Catching up with Mary

After that first lunch, it seemed like Ruth and Richard kept running into each other, both at the hospital and out in the town. Kingston was getting all decorated for Christmas, the shop windows fluttering with ribbons and fancy packages. It was like everyone was trying to pretend the hardships of the war were over. Every time Ruth would walk down Princess Street, admiring the window displays, there would be Richard, walking up.

They would meet and end up going for a warm drink or a meal, and their off-duty hours got quickly absorbed in each other. Richard was always a perfect gentleman, rarely even holding her hand, and Ruth started to wonder if he had any interest in her at all. Maybe he was just looking for a colleague. When they walked together, he'd tuck her arm in his, "in case it was slippery", he'd say, and though Ruth thrilled at the warmth of his arm and the feel of his greatcoat, it never went any further than that. When they'd get back to Leahurst, he'd kiss her on the cheek goodbye and dash off. It was getting worrying, and Ruth spent quite a lot of time studying herself in the mirror, brushing her teeth, smelling under her arms. Then she felt foolish and pretended it didn't matter if he liked her.

It didn't help that right while all of this was happening, she was having one of the worst sessions of her monthlies that she'd ever experienced. Life became a series of exciting escapes from staining her uniform. The girls at Leahurst, ever sympathetic, brought her extra pads and wintergreen tea, but Ruth felt icky and smelly, and a little grateful Richard stood well back.

But only a little bit.

She would head up to study and within moments would slip into a daydream about him, one involving little white picket fences and roses growing along a trellis. She'd slipped into one of those one afternoon when Doris came up behind her and tapped her on the shoulder.

"Wha?" Ruth said, spinning around. "Oh, Doris, you scared me!"

"Were you asleep? I wasn't very quiet coming up here."

"No, just distracted ..."

"And I know why! That handsome doctor you've been seen everywhere with! Listen, your friend Mary, from the Dieu? She's downstairs wanting to see you. Are you free?"

"Oh yes," said Ruth, shrinking a bit with guilt. She hadn't corresponded with Mary in days and days. She closed her book and scampered down the stairs.

"Mary! I'm so sorry I've been so absent!"

Mary hugged her, and all was forgiven. "I've been crazy busy, too. It's hard to keep on top of surgery. There's so much to learn!" Mary only had one more term until graduation, and her workload had increased. She was working on the surgical floor and had regaled Ruth with stories of all sorts of tubes and pumps and bandages.

"I can imagine! Do you have time for a visit? I can make something warm to drink."

"Ooh, a cup of tea would be wonderful after my walk here." Mary shivered.

"You are making me feel guilty again. We must make better plans to meet up. I've been terrible at keeping in touch."

They walked into the kitchen and Ruth put on the kettle, pulled out some teacups.

"You have. Especially since I have to compete with that fellow you are seeing."

Ruth blushed. "We're not 'seeing each other', officially. We just seem to walk around the same places."

"Hmm. I remain unconvinced. But tell me, how is it going on psych? Are you feeling better about things? Your last letter had me worried."

Ruth poured the tea, offered milk and sugar, which both turned down. "Too many treats," said Mary. "My uniform is getting snug!"

"I can't wait until walking is pleasant again. I try to walk, but it's so cold I refuse to go far. Shall we sit in front of the fire?"

They took their cups to the social room. Ruth continued, "I'm still finding this rotation difficult, Mary. I can't seem to stop feeling sorry for the patients. Half of them are trapped because of their illnesses, the others trapped because of the treatments we are giving them. And some of those treatments seem horrible!"

"Well, it could be worse." Mary made a face like she was smelling something awful. "They could be dying with infected wounds. Ick. Sometimes I can't eat anything for days, though you'd never guess it." She patted her stomach. "The other day, it took three nurses to clean this one patient's wound. We kept having to leave the room to clear our sinuses, and another nurse would come in. The patient never guessed, thank heavens, probably thought we were all the same nurse under our masks. I guess they used to burn rope under the beds of people with gangrene. I can't imagine the smoke would smell any worse than that wound did."

"You're right," laughed Ruth. "It could be worse! Thanks for the truly terrible comparison. Now I simply cannot wait for my surgical rotation! Thank you so very much."

Mary giggled. "Well, it's at least interesting. And the stories are great to bring up if you are in a boring conversation. Everyone stops talking and goes away. Almost as good as TB stories." She frowned. "Unfortunately, like here, it seems there's only so much we can do for patients. That patient with the smelly wound didn't make it."

Ruth sighed. "Seems the way everywhere. I wish we'd get some new medications or treatments to help. It was so wonderful at the San when the meds came in, and suddenly people could hope to get better."

"I remember. It was wonderful seeing them smile. Are the other nurses here still good to work with? I found them really nice."

"Oh yes, they are, most of them. They've been so kind to me. And they are wonderful with the patients. I've learned a lot. The orderlies are great, too."

"Oh yes, they sure are. There are some in the general wards, too, but not as many."

Ruth leaned forward, poked the fire, and asked, "Did you ever think of staying here to work? Despite the sadness, I mean."

"You know what? I have thought of that. What about you? It seems a good place to work, despite all the short-handedness and the … 'supervisors'… who never supervise," she added in a stage whisper. "Do you think they might be hiring?"

"I wondered why you were pumping me for information! I know they are eager for more staff. The problem is if they can afford them. They've just been training up a load of nurses' assistants who would cost less, I imagine."

"Shoot. Well, I suppose there's no need to fret about it until we're done. I've just been wondering where to have my final placement. We can choose among a couple of places. All I know is that I never want to work maternity ever again. And I'd really love a position here in Kingston when I graduate."

Ruth poured Mary another cup of tea. A twinkle in her eye, she said, "Oh, but didn't I tell you? They're putting a maternity ward in the hospital here."

"No! Really? Say it isn't so!" Mary fell back in her seat in shock. "Why ever would they do that?"

"Well, they don't like to transfer the patients. They are hard to manage in the regular hospital. And maternity is a real money spinner, Mary," Ruth went on, but looking at Mary's face, she couldn't keep it up. "No, you silly, I'm just pulling your leg. Can you imagine? It would be literal madness. Who would yell the loudest?"

Mary pummelled Ruth with a pillow until they were both laughing so hard other nurses came into the room. "Hey, Mary! Nice to see you again. Are you coming back to us?" asked one senior nurse, who had stopped in for tea. "I sure hope so." She turned to the other nurses. "She's fun, this one. And you two are friends? What a pair. I claim them for my floor!"

Ruth and Mary laughed along with the group. Soon there were a dozen conversations going on at once. By the time Ruth crept away back to her books, she felt more connected than she had in years. Who cares if Richard doesn't want me, thought Ruth. I have such lovely friends here!

But when she got back to her room and opened her books, there was that image again, a cozy brick house, Richard coming home to her waiting arms.

"Oh, give it up," she told herself crossly. "Study the brain!"

TWENTY-SEVEN

Tragedy

The call came through at midnight, causing a fluttering in the residence. Normally calls weren't put through at that hour. The on-duty nurse answered it and ran to wake Ruth. When Ruth came downstairs, Muriel Peters, the switchboard operator at the Ontario Hospital and a friend to all the students, was on the line.

"Miss Maclean? Do you have someplace you can sit? Is there anyone with you?"

Ruth, panicking, looked around. The student nurse from the OH on phone duty was back behind her desk. Ruth waved at her to come over.

"I am. And yes, one of the other students is here." She didn't know the student. Must be a newbie, she thought. They hadn't even really met. So many students flowing through here, especially in flu season.

"Miss Maclean, I am calling with bad news. Your father left a message this evening on the switchboard. We've been trying to find out if you were on. I'm not sure why he didn't at first call

Leahurst directly. Miss Maclean, your mother … I'm so sorry. She passed away this evening."

"What? How? I just saw her at my sister's wedding, and she seemed fine! This can't be true!" Ruth could hear her voice climbing in volume and pitch and the student came closer, sensing disaster.

"Again, I'm so sorry. Your father is asking if you can come home. The funeral is in two days."

"What? No. It can't be. This cannot be true. He's playing a trick. He's always wanted me to come home …"

As the minutes passed and Mrs. Peters said soothing things, Ruth started thinking about how her mother had looked at her sister's wedding — bright and smiling, but almost transparent. And she'd left early, claiming she wanted to check on the youngest children, even though they had a couple from the church watching over them. At the time, Ruth thought she just wanted to go home to let the young ones have a fun party and fallen asleep settling the baby.

Ruth finally put the phone down, barely able to breathe. The memories of dancing and laughing at the reception came back to her, tinged with grey. Why hadn't she noticed anything? What kind of nurse was she? She leaned forward, trying to stop the moan that wanted to come out. Her hands were already wet with tears. The OH student put her hand on Ruth's knee. "Can I help?"

"I've got to call the supervisor. Do you know who is on?" Ruth said.

"At this time of night?" The student's eyes widened.

"Yes. Do you have her number?"

The call was brief and slightly hostile at first. She'd woken the supervisor and that was never a good idea, but she was able to arrange for time off. She paused, gulped, and called her home.

She'd wanted to get things settled before she had to talk to her family.

Meg answered, thank heavens.

"Meg — tell me it isn't true!"

"Isn't it awful, Ruth?" Meg was sobbing through the phone, her voice clotted. "She was just here, laughing, and now she's gone. The doctor thinks she had a heart attack or a stroke or something. You'd know more."

Ruth doubted it. When would she be able to use her nursing skills for anything but watching horrors happen around her? When would she be able to act to prevent them? She shook her head, her throat closing over with tears. The OH student quietly put a glass of water by her elbow.

"How can I get home?" she asked once she could speak again.

"Jerry is driving up with Billy. They said they'd pick you up tomorrow morning at seven. The funeral isn't until the next day but we're having a wake and that will start at noon tomorrow. You can come, right?"

"I can. I asked the supervisor and got some time off. They aren't very generous about it, though, so I must come back right after the funeral."

"Oh no, do you? I've missed you so much! Everyone is so sad. We need you! I wish you could stay longer."

"I wish I could, too," Ruth lied. The less time she spent in Cloyne with her smothering family, the better. She wanted to slap her father for making her mother pregnant so many times. Surely that was what had killed her. That and the exhaustion from looking after the family and the Parish. "I'll see you tomorrow."

The Veteran's home had that car the men could use, so Ruth assumed that's what they'd be taking to Cloyne. They'd used it to get to Meg's wedding — not even three weeks before. How could she have missed that her mother was ill?

She packed quietly, trying not to cry, but she'd put in a sock and remember how her mother had shown her how to darn it. A shirt that her mother had passed down. A skirt she'd sewn for her. Finally, she had to just sit and sob into her pillow until it was soaking wet and crushed. How ever was she going to manage without her mother? Her mother, who had arranged for her to come to nursing school, encouraged her to continue, and made it all possible.

Suddenly, a chill swept down her back. Her father was going to demand she come back and look after the children, she just knew it. And how could she refuse with them obviously being in need, with her father left to do all the housework and childcare as well as his parish work? Meg could help look after them for a while, but she might start having a family of her own and she would want to spend some time with her new husband. The family was planning to move onto Wayne's farm with all the children as there was so much more room, and Meg could help with the family then, but that hadn't happened yet. Everyone wanted to give Meg and Wayne some private time after their wedding, so the big move wasn't due to happen for a month or so.

No! She had to stand firm, at least until she finished school. There was no point in stopping now, she'd tell him. Better to wait until she qualified and then she'd come back, she'd say, fingers crossed behind her back. Ruth had no desire to ever move back to Cloyne. She sat up, mentally strengthening her spine. That's it, she told herself. No more weakness, or he'll certainly take advantage of it. She'd lived the past year in an anxious state, waiting for him to pull her back, and she would not go through that again.

The next morning, she was ready and waiting as the car pulled up. She said soft helloes to Jerry and her brother, so as not to wake her fellow students, and crowded in the car beside the wheelchair. They were all quiet until they started out on Highway 2. It was empty this time of the day except for milk delivery carts, and they drove along quickly.

"How are you doing?" Billy asked, his voice low.

"So sudden." Ruth wiped her nose. Tears just kept on flowing, no matter what she did.

"I know! What do you think happened?"

"Got to be exhaustion. I should have caught it at the wedding! I feel awful."

"You're just a beginning nurse. Take it easy on yourself. You caught lots of things when we were in the San, remember."

"Yes, but Mother …." She couldn't say any more.

There was a long silent time, interspersed with sniffling.

"Ruth," said Billy, "You know he's going to try to make you stay, right?"

Ruth gulped back a sob.

"We'll keep on trying to prevent that, if we can. You need to finish your course. You're already a good nurse."

"Oh, Billy. I wish I believed that. I'm having such an awkward time on the psych ward. Everyone they give me on my ward just won't respond, and it's so desperately sad."

"Maybe they need a soccer game," laughed Jerry. He and Ruth had formed soccer leagues at the San to pull Billy out of his depression. It worked for him and many others, and the games still went on. Billy coached them.

"They won't let me do much of anything. They keep floating me around to observe. And clean up messes."

"When do you finish there?"

"Another six weeks now. I can't wait. I just hope I get a decent evaluation, get my cap, and can move on. I can't stop now!"

"Mother wouldn't let you!"

The rest of the trip they spent sharing shared memories of their mother. Ruth ranted about all the children, told Billy about what happened when he was away at war. Billy told Jerry the old stories about when he and Ruth were small and how they'd worked together to decorate the church for Christmas, the Nativity plays, the domineering churchgoers that had made faces at them whenever they breathed. And the fun of hiking around their home in Cloyne, making forts in the forest. All that was behind Billy now.

Ruth didn't mention the medical student she'd been allowing herself to dream a little bit about. She couldn't leave school and lose him, too.

TWENTY-EIGHT

Arriving home

As they pulled the car into the driveway, Ruth could already hear the crying. Howling, almost. It was like all the other children were crying at once. Suddenly she heard her father yell, hoarsely. The children quieted.

"Nothing has changed, then," said Billy.

Ruth hesitated before opening the door. She could feel the fear starting. Fear of her father without the soothing influence of her mother. He wasn't a kind man towards his family. He always had exacting requirements, and they'd only gotten stricter as the family grew. But then she remembered his compassion for the soldiers in the San. Which father would she find today?

"We better face the music. It's only going to get worse if we dawdle."

Ruth raised her chin and opened the car door. The children ran outside and mobbed her, crying again and rubbing their noses on her skirt. Meg smiled at them from the doorway, though her eyes were red and swollen.

"Billy," said Reverend Maclean. "Good to see you, Son." He spotted Jerry hanging back, after having pushed Billy's wheelchair into the living room. "Why is he here? Didn't we just see him at the wedding?"

Ruth gave her father a hug, though he didn't respond. "He's our friend, remember? And besides, we needed him to drive and manage the chair." She gulped a breath. "Where is she?"

Reverend Maclean nodded, swallowing before he spoke. He pointed toward their bedroom. "The doctor just left her there, after she … fell. He didn't see any reason to take her to the hospital. She was already on her way to heaven."

The nearest hospital was an hour or more away. Ruth agreed, but she was desperate to talk to the doctor, to find out more. Could she have saved her somehow? "Can we speak to the doctor?"

"He's on rounds, but he said he'd try to be back around noon." Her father growled, "Make these children stop their infernal howling! I can't even think."

Ruth looked at Meg. "Do you think they could go over to the neighbours? Or the farm? Just until we get organized?"

"Why are you looking at me? I've been with them all night."

Jerry raised his hand. "Who'd like to go for a ride in the car?" The older children all ran outside, leaving only the baby and the two-year-old inside.

"Well, he's of some use then," grumbled Reverend Maclean.

"I'll try and get these two down for a nap," said Ruth. It took a while, as the children were so agitated, but she eventually got them tucked in and resting, anyway. When she returned to the kitchen, the older siblings and their father were sitting around the table, drinking tea. Meg poured her a cup.

Her father was trying to explain things to Billy. "The doctor said she just up and died. She was just expecting, too. We lost the baby. The doctor thinks it was her heart, or maybe some other thing, like a blood clot." He faced Ruth. "What would that be,

Ruth? You should know by now, with all your fancy nursing education."

Oh, oh, thought Ruth. There's a nasty tone to her father's comment. "An embolism, maybe? Those can happen anywhere and cause the body to shut down. One of my patients …"

He flung his hand toward the bedroom. "Your patients, yes. Those precious patients. Well, maybe your dear mother wouldn't be lying there if you'd come home and helped her out. Have you thought about that?" Ruth paled. She wanted to shout about the multiple pregnancies but knew that would just lead to more rage.

Billy coughed. "Shouldn't we be working on the service, Father? I know there'll be a good turnout. What readings do you think would be best?"

Reverend Maclean frowned at Ruth, then turned to Billy. "Yes, we'd better get planning. We'll need some cooking. Meg, you do that. Ruth can tidy and do the laundry."

Right, Ruth thought. The old "Ruth can't do anything right except clean" line. She stood and began tidying away toys and piling clothes for the wringer washer they shared with their neighbour. When she took the clothes out to the lean-to in the back yard, that whole family came outside to offer their condolences. "Do you need me to help with the children?" Mrs. Tindall asked.

"Oh, that would be a blessing. My friend is driving them around, but they'll be back soon."

"When does the wake start?"

"I think noon. The funeral is tomorrow."

"Send them over when they get back. I'll keep them busy while it's all going on."

"Thank you so much, Mrs. Tindall. I'll be sure to save some food for your lot."

Mrs. Tindall leaned in. "You know, she really shouldn't have had that last baby. She bled so much. I was afraid we'd lost her then."

"Thank you," Ruth said, throwing the clothes into the washer and fleeing. She didn't want to hear any more about the things she'd missed in looking at her mother. She couldn't stand any more guilt.

Turning, she saw Meg coming across the yard with another basket and clothes pins.

"Ruth, I'm sorry if I snapped. I'm just so tired. And Father has been … Father. And the children have been wild."

"I'm so sorry I wasn't here. I didn't even know she was sick. Some nurse I am!"

"None of us knew. But don't feel bad. Come here." She took Ruth's hand and walked her away from the laundry baskets and back into the house, into their parents' bedroom. Ruth couldn't look away from the silent heap on the bed. It was so slight … She pulled back the blanket after steeling herself. Her mother looked as if she was asleep, eyes closed, maybe a slight smile on her face. Tears ran, unnoticed, down Ruth's face and fell on the covering blanket. She touched her mother's hand. It was cold.

"You've put her in her best dress. She looks so pretty, and doesn't it look like she's smiling?"

"She can rest now, I suppose," said Meg. "It's strange to see her without mending in her hands."

"Maybe we should put a sock in her hands, and her knitting needles? She might want them where she's going."

"Is there knitting in heaven?" Meg smiled thinly.

"In Mother's heaven, there must be. She wouldn't want to just sit around, 'wasting good time', as she always said." Ruth leaned forward and kissed her mother gently on the cheek. Her face felt cold, like rubber. It reminded Ruth of her patients in the San. Pale and cold and dead. She fought back her sobs. "It's so hard to believe that she's gone. You'd think Father would have been the first, with all his shouting." She stroked her mother's hair, tidying up a wayward strand. "I don't know how we'll get along without her."

"I know. I'm just glad she could see my wedding. If only she'd lived to see you get your cap and senior uniform! She was following every step you made, look!"

Meg threw open the closet door, where their mother kept all the reports of things her children had done that made her proud. In amongst the spelling and math tests and notices of Meg's wedding were all the letters that had been sent to praise Ruth during her hard year the year before. "She kept them all. She was so proud of you!"

Ruth broke down, sobbing, fell to her knees. "I so wanted to do well for her!"

Meg hugged her. "You're doing better this year, right?"

Ruth said nothing. Meg looked at her, tilting Ruth's face up. "You are going to pass, aren't you?"

"I hope."

"No hoping about it. You pass or I swear on Mother's grave I'll never speak to you again. It's not been easy looking after everyone here, you know, but I did it because I wanted you to be free to learn to be a nurse. You don't pass … well, it's all wasted exhaustion. You get your cap and pin, and you show them to Father and you work as a nurse, and you send us money. Got it?" She paused for breath. "What you did for Billy, that counts for something. But you need to get finished. You need to show Mother that she didn't waste her time and strength on you."

"But …"

"She'll know. And I'll know. Look, you know I love you, but it's been really lonely since you left. I had to wash Mother all by myself! And Wayne is wonderful, but he's not my sister."

Ruth hugged her tight. "I've missed you, too, and I've been working so hard."

"So pass and show this whole town you were right to go. They are going to give you grief over Mother, you know."

"I know. I'm sure they will."

And they did. Once the wake started, the public started streaming past Mrs. Maclean, offering prayers and looking askance at Ruth. It was good that it was cold out, so everyone couldn't fit into the small house or stand around outside. They got crowded out of the house before the murmuring about Ruth reached thunderous proportions. Ruth tried to stay either in the kitchen running food out or with the younger children, keeping them busy, but she couldn't avoid hearing some of the comments. It didn't help that she couldn't stop crying and could barely see out of her eyes. People seemed to find that the most annoying.

"Yes, she's been away. In Kingston. Supposedly learning to be a nurse. Well, she could have done some nursing here. Look at her crying now. Feeling guilty, I reckon."

"Imagine! Poor Reverend Maclean! Thankless daughter as well as losing his wife! She's probably out gallivanting with the soldiers."

"Who is going to watch the children now? She should come home."

"A sensible girl would."

"Well, she's never been sensible. She turned down my Chuck. Thought she was too good for him! Imagine that!"

It was awful. Ruth was crushed by the guilt she poured on herself, and every comment added more weight. It didn't help that her father walked by her, not saying anything. He wanted Billy to do one reading. Meg would help seat people at the funeral and had helped pick the music. Ruth was assigned no tasks and she and Jerry floated around, feeling unwanted. Ruth did load after load of laundry. Jerry tidied away dishes and helped Billy navigate around the house. The doctor came by when Ruth was hanging out laundry and she missed him. No one thought to get her. She wanted to yell.

The funeral was worse. Ruth felt like a guest at her own mother's funeral, with no input, no involvement of any kind. Her heart was breaking. As they lined up after the service, the congregation passed her by. She wanted to shout, "It wasn't my fault!"

But it was obvious everyone thought it was.

She was relieved to get into the car to head home, finally able to cry her heart out. Billy listened for a while and then said, "Ruth … Ruth, honey … Mother's death was not your fault. It was that greedy bugger Father, making her push all those children out and then work her fingers to the bone trying to keep them fed. I sent them over half my pension, you know? He's never mentioned it. I've already threatened him that if he makes you move home, I won't be back again, but I'm not too sure that will stick."

"Oh Billy, thank you! I wondered why he didn't tell me to stay! We don't have a lot of time off. I couldn't even take more days away now, let alone stay here for months and months, or at least until they got settled at the farm. He probably expected me to offer. I couldn't. He'd probably say yes, stay here. Then they'd fail me for sure."

"Well, we can't have that, not after all your hard work and that terrible time you had last year. If anyone's earned this, it's you."

Ruth sniffed loudly, looking out the window at the passing trees until she could settle her mind. They hadn't had a big snow yet, and the woods looked damp and as depressed as Ruth felt. "I sent Mother my pay, you know. I didn't want Father to take it to spend it on his things, the church, you know."

"Good idea. Maybe I'll send my money to Meg."

"Poor Meg. I feel like such an awful sister and daughter. I should help more."

"Yeah, well, get your licence first, then reconsider. And besides, once Meg gets everyone moved over to Wayne's place, she'll have it a bit easier. There's a lot more space for everyone to run around, and things for the children to do. And Wayne's parents are more understanding than Father. Speaking of whom, at least there will be no more babies from that front, anyway."

"Oooh, I don't know, my friend. A bunch of the widows from church were making eyes at your father. Did you not notice?" asked Jerry.

"Already?" Ruth frowned.

"Oh, they all aiment beaucoup his sermons. Meg told me. She didn't seem trop concerned. Perhaps she is looking for l'assistance?"

"Wow," Ruth threw herself back against the car seat. "I didn't notice that. But Meg did tell me she'd kill me if I didn't pass nursing. I'm not sure she will ever forgive me for abandoning her here."

Billy patted Ruth's hand. "She's just tired. She loves you."

Ruth wasn't sure. She knew she'd have to work even harder from here on out. She didn't want to disappoint her mother, Billy, or Meg.

TWENTY-NINE

Father visits

Another few days passed, Ruth trying to be efficient but so overwhelmed with sadness she almost felt she should check herself into the hospital for a treatment. She could understand how Mrs. Matthews felt, that covering grey fog that she was struggling to get out from under. Outside, the sun stayed away, and fog and drizzle and a begrudging snow fell. Wet air blew in around her window at Leahurst, despite her stuffing around it with towels borrowed from the hospital. She ended up with a head cold and felt even more miserable. Her housemates brought her hot toddies and lemon tea, but she could barely smile her thanks at them. She didn't dare meet up with Richard in case she passed on her cold, and he was busy with exams, so she didn't even have him to give her support. She was blue, blue, blue.

Then a week later, as she headed home from another dispiriting day trying to get any of the schizophrenics on her ward to speak to her, have a "therapeutic conversation" instead of just yell, there was a telegram awaiting her at Leahurst.

"What now," she groaned. She opened it, fingers crossed that it wasn't bad news. It didn't help her mood. Her father was coming to Kingston for a meeting, and he wanted to see her. It wasn't a request, she knew. It was a demand. Thus the telegram instead of a call.

"What is it?" asked Doris, having seen Ruth's face. The girls were having an afternoon cup of tea in the kitchen and reading the latest serial story in the Whig newspaper. It was another torrid romance about nurses and doctors, and they all ate up every word.

"My father is coming for a visit. Every time I see him, I am so afraid he will want me to move back home and look after the family." Ruth threw herself into a chair and reached for the teapot with a sigh.

"It must be hard for him with your mother gone," said one nurse.

"I'm sure it is. But I don't want to give up nursing."

"Nor should you," said Doris, staunchly. "You are doing so well. We're all plotting how to keep you here!" She passed Ruth the cookie tin.

"That's right," said another student, giving Ruth a hug. "We want you to stay. You remember to share cookies."

Ruth blushed and handed the tin along. "You are so nice, all of you. I may call on you to convince him."

"Why not meet him here? You can show him where you're living and working, and we'll hover in the background in case you need us to parade by singing your praises."

Ruth laughed. "He is coming here. Tomorrow morning. Luckily, I'm off until the afternoon. He never asks if I'm free, of course."

"Parents, eh? My mum is the same way."

"Well, he is heartbroken, probably. I'm not even home, and I miss Mother every minute. Don't let me weaken, will you? It just makes sense for me to finish, but I know the family really needs me as well."

"We need a code word. Like spies. Maybe shout out 'bed pan' and we'll know to come in." The crowd all fell about laughing, even Ruth.

"I think he may notice that ..." she said. "But thanks for that image. I can just see his face!"

The next day Ruth prepared carefully, combed out her hair until it shone, pressed her dress so it looked brand new, polished her shoes, and tucked her aunt's prayer book into her pocket. She waited in the common room, feeling her pulse race as she did, trying to practice deep breathing until she was dizzy. Finally. the doorbell rang, and there was her father.

"Father," she cried out, enveloping him in a hug.

"Daughter," he returned, as he always did. Ruth was surprised to feel him actually hug her back.

"Come in, let me take your coat. Can I get you some tea or coffee? We have some in our kitchen."

"Thank you, but no. I have to get to this meeting very soon." He stood and walked around, finally opened his coat and sat. "I wanted to talk to you first."

Ruth felt her muscles tighten. Was this the request coming?

He cleared his throat. "I owe you an apology," he said, turning his hat over in his hands. He didn't look at her. "I was unacceptably rude to you at your mother's funeral."

Ruth released the breath she was holding. "Oh, Father, don't worry about that. It was such a hard time. We were all so busy and sad and ..."

"No excuse for it." He pulled out a handkerchief and wiped his eyes. "You look so much like your mother, you know. I couldn't look at you. When you are away for a while and come back, it's almost shocking." He coughed, tucked the handkerchief away. Ruth waited, knees jiggling, tears hovering. Was he going to ask her to come back home? "And I was trying so hard not to beg you to come back and stay, to help me with the little ones. I didn't want to do that."

"You didn't?" Ruth's knees stopped jiggling and locked in astonishment.

"Well, of course I want you home, as do the children, but I thought of your blessed mother, may she rest in peace. She was bound and determined that you would be a nurse. She went on and on about it. I can't let her down, no matter what I want." He stood up to walk around the room, looking at the paintings. Ruth had never seen him so nervous. He turned and came back to sit, slapped his hat on his thighs as if he'd decided something. "Of course, if you wanted to come home, you'd be most welcome." There was a long pause. Ruth looked at the floor. He cleared his throat. "And besides, after you finish your training, you can always come back as a parish nurse. We could really use you." Ruth didn't move. He cleared his throat again. "Well, there's lots of time until that decision needs to be made. Right now, you need to finish your training."

She dared to look up. "Oh, thank you, Father! I was so worried."

"I know you were," he said with a little smile. "I know I put a lot of pressure on everyone in the family. But look how you are turning out: Billy a soldier, helping other vets, Meg married and happy, and you here, learning so much. You are all such good examples to the Parish. And the young ones are doing well, too. Wee Thomas told me he wanted to be a preacher like his father! I caught him the other day setting up pinecones in the snow like a congregation, then preaching to them all. Of course, he was preaching about your mother in heaven. Just about broke my heart."

After a pause to gather herself, Ruth asked, "But how are you managing all your work and the children?" She mentally kicked herself. She didn't want to give him an opening to change his mind.

Her father hesitated, coughed a little. "Well … I've been very fortunate. Two of the parish ladies have offered to come and help a few days a week. They are a wonderful support for Meg."

"Oh?" Ruth hid a smile. Jerry had been right about them hovering around.

"Yes, you probably know them. They are both widows, and their children are grown. It is nice having them cook and clean and help with the Parish visits." He preened a bit. "One of them seems quite fond of me, actually. She keeps bringing over treats and offering to iron my shirts."

"Father! What would Mother think?"

Again, the embarrassed cough. "We sometimes talked about what we would do if one of us ascended before the other. With our big family, we agreed that neither of us would mind if the other remarried quickly. It's just too much to manage on one's own."

And whose fault is that? Ruth squelched her anger. In the corner of her mind, she could see an escape door opening. She wouldn't have to go back to Cloyne if her father recruited a replacement for her mother.

They spent the rest of the brief visit telling more stories about the younger children and life on the farm where they were all living. The children were happily learning the farm tasks, feeding chickens, even mucking out the barn. Because they had moved out to the farm, the Parish offered the manse (a rather grand name for a small house with a leaking roof) to a family down on their luck. "With all of us in the farmhouse, it made sense to share our old house. They were living in a terrible place in Napanee. Besides, then I can save some money for everyone."

Ruth felt a pang. That was her growing-up house, where

she'd dreamed and cried and sighed and cheered. Would she ever see it again?

"I must go," said Rev Maclean, standing up and reaching for his coat. "This diocese meeting is important. Billy is joining me for dinner. I suppose you are busy?"

"Yes, I'm on duty at three. It's been good to see you, Father." She ushered him out of the door after another hug, closed it behind him, and was swarmed by a gaggle of girls. They had all been listening behind the door.

"He's a pussycat," said one.

"He was so sweet and sad," said another. "I don't know what you were worried about."

"And he's dating! He must be a catch! Wish we could have seen him."

"Ugh," said Ruth. "He could wait a bit longer before having women stuck all over him."

Dolores chimed in, "Maybe he'll remarry and you'll be off the hook! Just think! You could come and work here after you're done!"

Ruth smiled back at her new friends. They really did pull together. "What makes me maddest is that if he had died instead of my mother, no one would lift a finger to help her."

"Likely true," said Doris. "But let's focus on the good things. He has help, he wants you to stay ..."

"For now ..."

"And we have a full box of cookies in the kitchen. Time for refreshments." She took Ruth's arm and pulled her into the kitchen, where they shared the cookies and tea and laughed together until it was almost time for shift change. Then there was a thundering of feet as everyone raced to get ready.

THIRTY

Christmas shift

Betty glared at Ruth. "First you say you can't come, and then you say you can, and then you cancel out on me. Is that fair? Now I'll have to go with Nancy, and you know she's all flirty with everyone. I'll have to fight to be noticed."

"Betty, I can't go to a party. My mother just died. I'm far too sad to go dancing, and besides, what would people think?" Ruth hugged her friend. "Besides, you are always the belle of every ball. Nancy will have to look out for you!"

Betty preened, consoled somewhat. "I really am sorry about your mother. I don't know how I would manage without my dear mama. How are you doing? You're so good at acting fine."

"Day by day … It's still hard. I keep finding myself crying when I think of some small thing."

Betty sat down, sighed. "I can imagine. I wish there was something I could do to help."

"Oh, Betty, just being a friend is enough."

"Are you're sure? I can stay in if you want."

"No, Betty, I'm fine. You have to go! All those boys are waiting for you!"

"Well, then, can I beg you to help me get ready? It's the last party before Christmas and you know those lovely soldiers will have money and want to spend it on me."

"Sure," said Ruth. "You're going to be careful, aren't you? No more scares like last year?"

"Oh, of course," Betty said, airily waving a hand. "Now, what do you think of these earrings?"

Ruth ran into Alison at shift change the day after the parties. Alison was dancing.

"Thanks for offering to take the Christmas shifts, Ruth. You're an absolute doll!" said Alison. "I usually never get to go home. But don't you want to be home with your family? It's going to be a tough time, isn't it?"

"No, neither Billy nor I are going home. It's just too crowded, and with all the church activities entirely too busy. We decided working would be the best way to honour our mother. Billy and Jerry and my friend Mary and I are all going for a Christmas brunch after the holidays. We'll just pretend it's the real day."

"Well, I sure am grateful. My mother is over the moon! She's baking all my favourite things. I'll bring some back for you!"

"Ooh, yes, please!" Ruth paused. "Do you do Christmas parties on the wards for the patients here? We did them over at the San."

"On our ward, no. It gets them too excited. Sometimes we've done stockings, but then everyone gets to fighting over them. Some of the other floors do, though. The open wards take the observant Catholic patients over to the Church of the Good Thief, for the early service. Here, a minister or priest comes onto the ward like they do on Sundays. Some patients know it's a special day, but many don't."

The Church of the Good Thief was just up the road from the hospital. Built by prisoners from the nearby penitentiary out of local limestone, it was a pretty place, with one tall tower. Ruth always wondered why they had just the one, on a corner of the roof.

"Best thing is that there are no treatments that day."

"That should make things a bit easier," said Ruth.

"Yes, and there are two orderlies on, too — your favourites. Bob and Jim. You'll have a good time."

Ruth smiled. "I hope so. I hate being on all alone."

Alison patted her on her back. "You've done so well when you have been, though. Have you ever thought of being a psych nurse? You could so do it."

"I've still got a lot of training to do," said Ruth. If she couldn't get past the pity she felt for these poor patients, she couldn't be an effective nurse, she knew it. But how to shift the pity to nursing empathy? All she could think of was how terrifying it would be to lose her mind. The other day she'd wept for an hour over one patient. Or was it grief over her mother? She didn't know.

"Well, have a good sleep! Thanks again and have a wonderful Christmas!"

Ruth nodded and headed home to her tiny room above the snow. There was a crisp wind blowing in around her window and the hot water radiator didn't quite heat up this high. She'd brought back an extra quilt of her mother's the last time she was in Cloyne, and she wrapped it around herself and headed down to the kitchen for a cup of tea. The room was packed with laughing women, all trying to wrap presents and trading treats.

"Come in, come in! You must be freezing way up there, Ruth! Let me pour you something hot."

"Give her some hot chocolate. Hey, I hear you're covering

your ward over Christmas! Cheers for the first KGH student to ever do that in college memory!"

Ruth blushed. "Well, to be honest, I needed the hours after my sister's wedding."

"And your mother's funeral. We're so sorry for your loss, aren't we girls?"

Everyone made supportive noises and came to give Ruth hugs.

"Thanks. It would be so depressing at home anyway. And now Meg can be the new wife, running the Christmas dinner, without her big sister looking over her shoulder."

"Well, it's still nice of you to cover. Alison usually does that. She hasn't been home for years. Bet she was happy."

Ruth laughed. "She sure seemed it. Her mother is going wild preparing. Here, let me hold that ribbon while you tie it." She placed her finger on the parcel.

"Thanks! That's me done."

"Me, too. That took forever!"

"I hate wrapping!"

"Almost bedtime, everyone. We all want to look good tomorrow! We just have a few cookies to finish. Here, Ruth, here's the one that looks like you!"

It was a gingerbread cookie, cut out in Ruth's shape and the icing was blueish like her uniform. On her head — her curly hair, and a cap! "Oh, thank you," she said, "But I don't have my cap yet."

"Just a matter of time, my girl. You're certain to get it this time."

Ruth nibbled her cookie as everyone packed up their wrapping supplies and tidied up the kitchen. Just in case, she didn't eat the cap. She tucked it in her pocket. If I get my cap, I'll have it then, she thought. Till then, it's my good luck charm.

"Is anyone going to be staying here over the holidays?" she asked the other women.

"Yes, the super will be here, and a few other students. Most of the grad nurses live elsewhere, though. They may come by for tea and to check on you."

Hmm, thought Ruth. Creepy being here mostly on my own. It was usually a melee of nurses flowing in and out.

"Why don't you move down to my room while I'm gone, Ruth? It's warmer and closer to the w/c. I don't mind."

"Oh thanks, June. I'm quite cozy up in my nest, but I appreciate the offer."

"Well, you won't be alone for long. Most of us just have a day and a half off."

"Why not ask your friend Betty for a sleepover on Christmas night?"

That sounded like fun. Ruth went immediately to the phone and waited until Betty was cleared to speak to her.

"You're here for Christmas, right Betty?"

"Yep — I'm on afternoons."

"Me too! Most of the girls are leaving here for Christmas. They suggested I ask you over for a sleepover. What do you think?"

"Such a sweet idea! I'll bring the wine! I'll take a cab right from the hospital."

"I'll clear everything with the super. Let's find some treats."

"Excellent! See you tomorrow!"

She headed up to bed, warm with the friendship of her fellow nurses. She carefully wrapped the little piece of cookie that had her cap on it and tucked it away in her souvenir box. "Soon, soon," she whispered, as she gave it a kiss.

Ruth woke on Christmas Day with the same feeling of excitement she'd had when she was little. Don't be silly, she told herself. It's not like there will be any presents. She wrapped her quilt around herself and walked down the silent stairs for a hot cup of coffee. She wasn't on duty until the afternoon, so she had some time to putter around. It was glorious to dawdle, knowing she wouldn't have to fight for access to the washroom later.

First, though, she called home. It took her three tries for the phone line to connect. Ruth ruefully recalled the ads in the paper about how the telephone lines would be busy over the holidays and to try to call some other day. When Meg finally answered, it was too noisy on her end to hear anything, so she just shouted, "Merry Christmas!" and hung up. Here, though, it was eerily quiet. The other students left in residence were on days, so they'd left long before. The rest had headed home at first light to reach families. And who knew where the super was?

Ruth went to open the fridge to get some milk for her coffee and what did she see? A little stocking with her name on it! She squealed with excitement and pulled it out. Those girls, she thought, they are really something else. The stocking, a lovely hand knit sock, done properly (unlike Ruth's efforts), had the other sock inside it, and even a new a pair of stockings, bless them! An orange and a chocolate bar filled it up.

There was a note tucked inside, too, wishing her a Merry Christmas and telling her where the popcorn makings were in case she wanted some. Ruth sat, peeling her orange, her heart very full. Even at the San, she hadn't felt so special. The group here really seemed to look after each other. Maybe psychiatric nursing really was in her future.

She shook her head. She hadn't explored the other areas of nursing yet. Mustn't make any decisions yet.

THIRTY-ONE

Escape

That afternoon, as she arrived at the floor and was let in and locked up, she sensed things were not all as they should be on her ward. The charge nurse, Miss White, a second-year from the psych school, was glowering, and the supervisor was holding court in the nursing station. She entered the station quietly after one of the junior nurses opened the door.

"This situation is intolerable. Why didn't you call me sooner?" The supervisor was flushed red with rage. She sat in one of the chairs, legs apart to give room for her sizeable stomach. Her elastic stockings were bunched at her swollen ankles, probably cutting off her circulation. She gasped between angry phrases.

"We did. We left a message for you at the switchboard an hour ago," said Miss White.

"Don't tell me that! I was told nothing!"

The nurses all looked at each other. This supervisor, a retiree frequently called in for relief, never answered her calls.

"What's up?" Ruth whispered to the nurse beside her.

"One of the patients escaped."

"What? How?"

"What's that whispering over there?"

"I'm sorry, Supervisor," said Ruth. "I just wondered what was happening."

"Well, these nurses here somehow let a patient get out through the locked door. He's gone who knows where in this cold. It's on your heads if we find him in a pile of snow somewhere, frozen solid!"

"Should we go look for him?"

"I've sent the orderlies out to look. You'll be starting your shift with no backup. You know who to thank for that."

"I'll stay until they get back," said the junior nurse.

"There'll be no overtime," snarled the supervisor.

"I'm a student," the nurse said. "I'm not paid that way anyway."

"Good. Limited budget. Well, I'm off to let admin know you've lost someone."

"Could you wait for a little while? Maybe he just went out to church or something. It is Christmas," Miss White pleaded.

"I'll give you one-half hour. I need to get home." She stormed out of the door, slamming into Ruth as she went. Her cap bobbed erratically as she trudged down the hall. Everyone breathed a massive sigh of relief as she left.

Miss White called Ruth over. "I let him go, with an orderly. They were supposed to be back by now. He said he wanted to go to church. They were just supposed to go to the Church of the Good Thief. Where can they be?"

It did seem strange. The church was so close that even with the storm brewing outside, it shouldn't have taken much time to get back from the service.

"Who's missing?" she asked.

"Sgt. Turner."

"Oh no. Was he … stable today? He wasn't back to being suicidal, was he?"

"I didn't think so," she put her head onto the desk and moaned. "Please God, let him be okay."

There was a commotion at the locked door to the ward, and the junior nurse ran down to open it. In came three snow-covered orderlies and one smiling patient. Ruth stepped back around the corner. She didn't want Turner to see her right away.

"Thanks, guys," he said. "I owe you one."

Bob the orderly took him by the arm. "Come on, Sgt. Turner. We need to get you back to barracks and warm."

"What took you so long?" Miss White demanded.

The soggiest orderly looked down, holding his damp coat away from his uniform. "You mean, other than the snowfall? It's deep out there. We stayed for Mass, and then he wanted to talk to the priest. The Father obviously wanted to leave, too, but Turner just talked on and on, the two of them sitting in the pews. Seems to have cheered him up, though."

"The supervisor was here." Miss White's tones were icier than the orderlies' coats. "Now I have to call her and explain. I was hoping you'd be back before anyone knew. Now there's going to be hell to pay!"

She picked up the telephone and called the supervisor. "The patient is here, safe and sound. He wanted to go to Mass, that's all." There was a pause. "Yes, just needed to see the priest, apparently." Another pause. "Well, if you feel that way, that's fine with me. The orderlies are just warming him up. Merry Christmas." She hung up. "Well, who'd have guessed? She said that of course he wanted to go to church like a good Catholic man."

The orderlies snorted. "Just didn't want the paperwork, I'll be figuring."

"Exactly. She's 'wiping the day clean'. Thanks all. I'm getting out of here. Want report, Miss Maclean?" And she ran through the patients double-quick.

"Miss White?"

"Yes, Miss Maclean."

"Shouldn't we be a bit concerned about Sgt. Turner and his visit with the priest? Could he have been getting absolution in preparation for taking that big step?"

"Good thinking. Let's put him on suicide watch. Bob, you seem to get along with him. Can you 'special' him for this shift? We can see how he is and perhaps let's increase his sleeping meds overnight."

"Sure thing," said Bob, heading off. 'Specialing' meant one-to-one nursing, usually a requirement for agitated or suicidal patients. It would mean more work for Ruth and Jim. But at least she wouldn't have to worry about Sgt. Turner all night.

Sighing, she started her rounds as the other nurses fled, whispering "Merry Christmas" as they went.

THIRTY-TWO

Advocacy

The evening was long and unusually quiet. Perhaps everyone had spent an exhausting day, not having treatments or other torments to confuse or stimulate them. Or maybe the quiet of the heavy snowfall was making it easier for everyone to rest. The troublesome Sgt. Turner was sleeping soundly, and Ruth hadn't yet had to go in and see him or bring him medications. She wasn't sure if he'd still be furious with her for not killing him.

On one round, Ruth found Mrs. Matthews awake.

"Hi, Mrs. Matthews," she said softly, to not wake her roommate. "How are you? I haven't had a chance to visit with you in so long. Are you feeling better?"

Mrs. Matthews shook her head. "Can't sleep. The insulin is making me all mixed up."

"Can I get you something to help you rest?"

"No! I'll end up all dozy for tomorrow and my husband will be angry. I'd rather be tired."

Ruth couldn't believe she was having a conversation with the previously silent woman, but then Mrs. Matthews started to cry.

"I don't know what to do," she said. "Nothing I do seems to please my husband, Grant."

"But you are doing so well! You've made such progress. I can see it so clearly!"

She shook her head violently. "Not when he is here. He keeps poking at me and poking at me and telling me I look bad and should go lie down, and then he goes and talks to the doctor and they think up new things to do to me."

Mrs. Matthews' ability to speak was a tremendous advance over when Ruth had first met her. She sounded clear and focused and almost back to normal. Except for all her crying. "Can I bring you a cup of tea? Or hot milk? Would that help, do you think?"

Mrs. Matthews frowned at her. "Would you be able to sleep if your husband said he was going to get the doctor to do one of those lobotomy things on you soon?"

Ruth tried to hide her involuntary intake of breath. "Did he tell you that?"

"Yes, yesterday. Everyone was talking about it, and he overheard. He came in and was yelling at me to talk to him. I didn't, there's no point, so he came over and grabbed my head …" She stopped to catch her breath. "He said the new way they wouldn't even have to cut my hair!" She tossed on the bed, tangling herself in the sheets. "As if that matters! He wants to cut into my brain! After all this torture … half the time, I don't remember who I am!"

Ruth stood beside the bed and cradled Mrs. Matthew's hands to keep them from flailing about. "Maybe you misheard. Maybe he just was talking about the surgery like everyone else. You sound so healthy right now."

"I don't think that will help. I think he's tired of me. Doesn't want to pay for more treatments. Or a nanny for the babies." She started crying again. "I just want to see them, Miss Maclean. He won't let me. He won't bring them in to visit, even for Christmas." She paused and wiped her nose. "He wants me dead," she finished, her voice dull.

Ruth started to object but stopped herself in time. Important not to challenge delusional thoughts, she reminded herself. "It must be terrifying to think that. Have you spoken to the head nurse about it?"

"Her? She's always smiling at him. I think he told her he was making a donation or something. He has lots of money." Her voice dripped acid.

"I'll have a look at your chart and let you know what I can find out," said Ruth in her most soothing voice. "I'm here all evening. They won't do anything to you tonight. Please try to sleep. Let me straighten out your bed." She pulled the sheets into shape and covered Mrs. Mathews snugly. "There, that feels better, doesn't it?"

"You're here the whole night?"

"Until almost midnight, and I'll talk to the people on tomorrow to let them know you are worried."

"No, don't. They'll just start more treatments. Just please keep watch over me while I sleep. Don't let them take me anywhere."

"I'll keep a sharp eye out. You can feel safe. I'm sure everything will look better after you've had a good rest."

As Ruth left, she felt queasy at saying those platitudes to a woman who was seriously trapped. What could she do? The husbands had complete power over their wives' treatment, it seemed. Thinking hard, she headed back to the nursing station. She pulled Mrs. Matthews' chart and read the doctor's notes.

"Insulin treatment seems to be working. Patient is more willing to speak and participate in activities on the ward. Patient's husband feels a lobotomy might be a more appropriate treatment. Consult with a surgeon after the Christmas holidays."

Ruth blanched, put her hand over her mouth. She was in a cold sweat when she heard a tap on the nursing station door. It was Richard.

"Oh, thank heavens you're on, too! I'm so glad to see you!"

Richard looked a bit shocked at the fulsome greeting. "Good to see you, too. How is your night going?"

"Look … at … this!" Ruth said, stabbing a damning finger at the doctor's notes with each word.

Richard read the notes. "Seems pretty straightforward. What's up?"

"I was just in with Mrs. Matthews. She's speaking well, focused and active. The doctor even says so. But her husband comes in and yells at her and she won't talk, so he's asking for her to have a lobotomy! It's inhumane! How can this happen to a woman whose brain is healthy, though abused?"

Richard reached out a hand. "Hold on there. Wasn't this the woman who was almost catatonic a few weeks ago?"

"Yes, but she's so much better! She's been getting better bit by bit. He won't even bring her babies in to visit. I think he's horrid!"

"Hey! What became of that nursing objectivity you told me you were striving for?" Richard asked.

Ruth collapsed on the chair. "This is why I find working here so very hard. I feel so sorry for everyone. Mrs. Mathews can't seem to keep them from doing all manner of things to her — but brain surgery? I've got to stop it." She paused. "Can you help?"

Richard looked at his feet. "Well, I am only a junior. They aren't likely to listen to me."

"You could evaluate her, though? Bring in another doctor to have a look at her? Her doctor is off over the holidays, so he wouldn't feel we were overstepping." Ruth kept on at him, her voice rising.

He was silent for a few minutes, while Ruth watched,

impatient. Finally, he scuffed his shoe on the floor, abusing a scrap of paper. He cleared his throat. "It happens I do know the covering surgeon. He's an old friend of my uncle's. He was at the demonstration the other day, so knows what we'd be talking about. I could ask him to come and assess her. But he might just agree with her doctor."

"Oh, Richard, I know, but it's a hope. Thank you! Thank you!" Ruth almost hugged Richard, and he smiled at her so warmly it was hard work holding back.

"There's no guarantee he will come, though. The docs don't enjoy stepping on each other's toes, and her doc is a senior fellow. I'll try," he added, seeing Ruth get ready to speak again. "Now I've got to go. I mainly stopped by to see how you were doing this first Christmas without your mother."

Ruth's eyes teared. "It was so nice of you to send that card. Thank you."

"How are you feeling? How is your family?"

"Oh, that's too long a story to tell. You need to go, and so do I. I have some meds due. It's so good to see you, though. I feel terrible I never called you after I received your card."

"I imagine you've been at least as busy as I have. I'm sorry I haven't been more in touch. I would like to hear about your family sometime, though." He reached out and held her shoulder briefly and Ruth felt tingles all along her arm. "Well, please let me know when you might be free for another date. I really enjoy spending time with you."

"And I with you," Ruth said, blushing "Right now, though, I can't think of anything but Mrs. Matthews."

Richard laughed. "Why do I get the feeling that you'll only go out with me again if I get someone to look at her?"

Ruth smiled and ushered him out of the nursing station. She knew she'd be glad to see him even if her plan failed, but there was no point in telling him that.

Historical Note

WOMEN IN PSYCHIATRIC INSTITUTIONS

If a man tires of his wife, and just be fooled after some other woman, it is not a very difficult matter to get her in an institution of this kind. Belladonna and chloroform will give her the appearance of being crazy enough, and after the asylum doors have closed upon her, adieu to the beautiful world and all home associations.

I ask you, my dear friends, you are wife and mother, what would your feelings were you torn from your children, your home, and all that you hold dear on earth, and thrust into an institution of this kind, and what would your appearance be? Did you ever stop to think? You might plead and beg; it would all be taken for insanity. Yes, all you could say and all you could do would only be some symptom of the fatal disease. If you were quiet and passive, even submissive, you would be reported as a hopeless case; but if you would rave and storm, as almost anyone would, you would be put in the close room. Perhaps you do not know what that is; well, it is called the cell at the asylum, and if you should once get in there it would be very doubtful if you ever came out alive.

When a person is put in the cell, they at the asylum know what it means.

Lydia A. Smith 1865 -1871.*

---

* Jeffrey L. Geller and Maxine Harris, *Women of the asylum: Voices from behind the walls, 1840-1945*. Anchor books, New York, 1994.

THIRTY-THREE

Sleepover

Promptly at eleven-thirty, Betty knocked at the door to Leahurst. Ruth swung open the door with a flourish. "Come in! Merry Christmas!"

Betty struggled in with an enormous basket of food. "I stole this from our cafeteria. There was lots going to waste! And TWO, look, TWO bottles of wine! Let's get started — I'm famished."

"Let's get your coat off first! We can lay this all out and then go into the social room. There's a fire there."

"Fantastic." Within moments, it was done, and the two girls were curled up in chairs in front of the fire, eating their dinner with unladylike speed.

"Cheers!" said Betty. "Here's to almost finishing your rotation! Only a month to go!"

"Plus a couple of weeks! I'll be back for class, and then the capping ceremony. If they give it to me, that is." Ruth scooped out a second helping of potatoes to put on her plate.

"Just be glad you aren't on orthopaedics. I'm so tired from lifting legs in traction and turning people in body casts. There

was some of that at the San, but these patients are much bigger."
Betty took another slice of turkey.

"The blessing of TB, I guess. Skinny bodies." They laughed
immoderately.

"Awful, you. I miss your black humour."

"Oh, Betty," said Ruth as she picked up her glass of wine and
took a long, thirsty sip. "I wish you were there with me at the
OH. I could really use seeing your cheerful face sometimes.
There's still that one patient who wanted me to kill him! He
hasn't seen me again yet. I've been all over and then he was being
specialled by the orderlies. Wonder how he'll react when he does
see me? I pretty well hid from him last night. He's probably still
furious."

"You and your murderous patients! With any luck, they've
shocked him into memory loss. Though who could forget your
sweet face?" Betty leaned over and patted Ruth's cheek. "Where's
that wine? Mine seems to have evaporated."

Giggling, Ruth filled her glass. "So, Betty, what's new on the
boy front? Still going to the base? It seems like forever since we've
had a chance to catch up."

"Well," said Betty, holding Ruth's hand. "You've had a lot
going on. I wish I could have joined you for your mother's
funeral. It must've been grim. How are you? How is the rest of
your family? And your father? Is he pulling out all the stops to get
you to Cloyne to wash and clean?"

"No! He came to visit the other day, and I was so frightened,
but he said mother had insisted I become a nurse. He said he
wouldn't feel right about ruining that. I couldn't believe it!"

"What a relief!"

"Well, he said he wants me to come back as the 'parish
nurse', so I'm not off the hook yet. So, Betty, boy update! I'm not
going to let you get away with not telling me!"

Betty laughed and told Ruth about the Christmas parties, the

RMC cadets fighting over her at the Christmas ball, and even an intern at the hospital who had taken to following her around, doe eyed. "What about you? Any more awful patients falling in love with you? I keep waiting to hear George has been admitted."

Ruth shrieked, throwing her hands in the air. "God forbid! No, no patients falling in love with me. I feel too sorry for them. It must be awful not to be able to trust what you think you see. Can you imagine thinking voices are always telling you what to do?"

Betty snorted and refilled her glass. Through a mouthful of stuffing, she said, "Yes, I can. My mother's voice comes through loud and clear whenever I'm kissing a boy."

"I believe it. My father's voice is often present, too. But he isn't telling me to kill people or follow God … wait a minute…," she burst out laughing. "I suppose he is."

Betty poked the fire, throwing some sparks onto the carpet, and there was some scurrying to scoop them up before anything burned. "Sorry." She burped. "A bit wobbly."

"We are on the second bottle, after all. And I've only had a glass and a half. Maybe I should cut you off."

"No thanks. We're safe and warm here and I need to celebrate, even if I have had exactly zero proposals this entire term. Honestly. I wonder if I've lost my charm." She fluffed her hair. "And you, Ruth, any proposals for you?"

"Well … there is this doctor — a resident…who seems to like me a bit."

"What?" Betty squealed.

"Shh. You'll wake up anyone who is here. Yes, he seems nice. We've been out for tea and chats."

"What?" stage-whispered Betty. "Why haven't you told me this before? What's his name? What's he look like? Is he cuddly?"

Ruth shook her head. "I purposely didn't tell you because I don't know where it's going. He's much senior to me and every once in a while, he tries to lord it over me, which I don't like. But he's really helping me with one patient."

"Who? How?"

"I can't really tell you details. Confidentiality, remember. But I've got to ask you. When you were on your placement, did you notice how the husbands arranged for all the treatments for their wives? Without asking them if they wanted them?"

Betty grimaced. "Husbands sometimes, but the docs were worse. I got really fed up with having to genuflect while they used the patients for experiments. Couldn't say anything, of course."

"This doctor is helping me with a patient whose husband keeps wanting her to have more and more treatments even though she is already getting better."

"Well, they do go back and forth, you know. I'm sure you've seen relapses while you are there."

"I know, Miss Betty Bossy. But this is different. Have you heard about this new brain surgery?"

"Lobotomy? Oh yes, several of the patients have had one there. Seems to help if they are violent."

"Well, there's a new procedure that can be done really quickly. They shock them to sleep and stick a pick in through the back of their eyes to scoop out the brain."

"Oh my God. A pick? Like an ice pick? How horrible! How do the doctors know where they are in the brain? Or what they are cutting out?"

"I don't know, but the surgeon who is doing them seems very sure of himself. And they want to do it on this patient. Who is not violent, just had postpartum depression, and who is coming out of it now."

"Awful! And what's this about shocking them to sleep?"

"The shocking is supposed to be safer than anesthesia, if you can imagine. I'm trying to get the doctor to change his mind. And Richard, I mean Dr. Hartman, he's helping me."

"That's dangerous, you know. You could be fired for insubordination."

"I know." Ruth started banking the fire. "But I can't let it just happen. She's fine. It's her husband who is sick."

"Be careful, you. You don't want another black mark on your record after last year's mess. You know they thought you were insubordinate all the time then. Best not to give them more fodder for that fire. They hate nursing students who offer opinions, you know."

"I know. That's why it's so good he's helping me." Ruth sighed. "Well, I'm full, tipsy, and exhausted. Bedtime?"

Betty stood, weaving a bit. She lifted the wine bottle, shook it back and forth. There was only half a cup of wine left. "That's for you. Better finish it off so I can hide the evidence."

"Okay, fine. Let's clean these dishes and get to bed." Ruth poured the last bit of wine into her glass and tossed it back. "I'm going to regret this tomorrow."

"I'll help with the dishes, but only if you tell me more about this Richard. Is his last name really Hartman? Heartman? It's a sign …" Giggling behind their hands, trying to be quiet, they carried everything into the kitchen.

THIRTY-FOUR

Fighting for Mrs. Matthews

The next morning Ruth and Betty shared a breakfast in Leahurst — just toast and coffee, but they were all still full from the night before and significantly queasy. "That's the last time I drink Chateau-Gai wine. Especially the cheap stuff," said Betty, rubbing her forehead with cold water.

Ruth moaned, inhaling steam from her tea. Coffee wouldn't stay down this morning. After Betty left, many hugs and (quiet) laughs later, she threw herself into a long hot shower, relishing the fact she could dawdle for once.

Ruth wanted to go on early for her next shift, even though she was sure she oozed alcohol smell. Betty shouldn't have brought both bottles of wine. She'd had way more to drink than she was used to. Even at Meg's wedding, she'd nursed one punch most of the night.

But she couldn't stay away, thinking about Mrs. Matthews. Ruth tried to explain in report the previous night how much better Mrs. Matthews was, how she was talking in complete sentences and moving about freely, but also how she was very afraid of being taken for a lobotomy she didn't feel she needed.

The night relief nurse was an old one of the traditional sort who just muttered, "We can't have patients, loony ones at that, telling their doctors what to do. The doctors know best. As do husbands. They are responsible for their wives, after all."

Ruth was going to ask if that held if the husbands were abusing their wives, but she looked at the old battle-axe and realized she'd probably assume that was the wives' fault for not being submissive enough to their husbands. Her mother would probably be alive today if she hadn't submitted so much to her father, Ruth grumbled as she stomped off.

But Ruth was learning to pick her battles, and after all, there would be no procedures that day, so Mrs. Matthews should be safe. Just in case, Ruth decided to come in early to stand guard, alcohol smell or no.

Coming onto the ward, she was glad to see her mentor Allison was the charge nurse for the day shift. "How was Christmas?" she asked her.

"Oh, Ruth — I loved it! My mother cried half the time, she was so glad to have me there. And it's been ages since I went to Mass in the church in Westport. Have you been there? It's this massive ancient church, built on a hill, with a tall, tall spire. I remember when I was growing up there, I thought God lived in the spire and could see everything we did. It's beautiful, and they had it done up so pretty. It was perfect to go to midnight Mass with all my family. Thanks so much for covering for me!" She gave Ruth a squeeze. "I thought of you the whole time I was with my mother. I even lit a candle for yours."

"Thanks, Alison. That was so kind. I'm so glad you had a good time! Was Santa Claus good to you?"

"He was as good as he could be. I've got a gorgeous new quilt for my bed. I'll have to show it to you. And, of course, we had our traditional dinner — tourtiere and sugar pie for dessert. I love having French Canadian relatives! I brought back some butter tarts. I hid them in the medication room for you today. My mother is a pro at making them."

"Yummy! I adore butter tarts." Ruth was quite ready to stop talking about mothers. Tears were hanging just back of her eyes, ready to spill.

"How was your Christmas here?"

"Oh, don't ask. Betty is a bad influence." Ruth rubbed her eyes. "But I wanted to ask you something." She dragged Alison into the med room and shut the door. "What did you think of Mrs. M. today?" she asked.

"She seems a lot better," said Alison. "I have no idea why they'd want to do a lobotomy on her. She's not violent or delusional."

"I know," Ruth almost yelled, she was so frustrated. "I think her husband just wants to terrify her. It's abuse. Can we get someone in to stop him?"

"I see your Dr. Hartman has asked for a referral from the head doc on call today. Did you ask for that?"

"Who, me? And he's certainly not my Dr. Hartman."

"Sure, sure," Alison replied, laughing. "We could also ask the social workers to have a look in. Should I do that before I leave? Just to spread the blame around. After all, I've already graduated. You don't want to get in trouble."

Ruth breathed out. "No, I don't. I just have to do well this time around."

"I know. And you are. Mrs. Matthews loves you, as do a few of the other patients. Even Sgt. Turner might come around."

"How is he doing? Does he still hate me?"

"He seems calmer by all reports. They've been working with him, but he's still being specialled."

"I'd best be off. Got my meds to give out." Ruth gathered up the tray and started going through the medication Kardex, doling out pills.

"You're even getting faster at that. See, all good things." Alison patted her on the back. "Okay, I'll call in that consult. You'll let Mrs. M. know?"

"Sure will." Ruth picked up the tray, took the keys from Alison, and headed out on her rounds.

The ward seemed livelier this afternoon. It turned out some families had visited during the day and patients were wearing new slippers and holding new books. One was eating a chocolate bar with so much pleasure Ruth hated to disturb him for his daily pill. King Leonard had a new sceptre made of padded stockings and he was ecstatic. He knighted Ruth with it.

"Female knights are unusual," he said, "But you deserve it."

Ruth bowed and thanked him.

When Ruth got to Mrs. Matthews' room, she found the woman sitting on her bed, crying. "What's wrong, Mrs. Matthews? Has something upset you?"

"I thought he'd bring the babies in today. It's Boxing Day, after all, and we'd planned for a visit in the cafeteria. An orderly was going to take me down. But Grant called the ward this morning and said the little one had a cold so he couldn't bring them out. It's so mean of him. I haven't seen my children for months now."

Ruth put her hand on Mrs. Matthews' shoulder and gave it a squeeze. She didn't want to get her hopes up, so didn't tell her of her plans, but she hoped she could get some help for her from somewhere. Mrs. Matthews turned away and lay down on her bed, pulling the sheet up halfway as if she couldn't be bothered to do more. Ruth covered her.

She'd just finished testing the urine sugar of one of the

insulin shock treatment patients when she heard a tap on the door to the utility room. It was Richard.

"Any luck?" she whispered.

"I'm afraid you owe me two lunches and maybe a movie as well for this. I got a proper dressing down. But Dr. Oak is coming to see her today. I didn't mention you, thought it might be better if it seemed to come from me."

Ruth beamed. "Thank you, Richard! I do owe you! And Alison has put in a referral to social work. Maybe we'll be able to stop this. He refused to bring her babies in today, did you know? I'm going to have to keep myself from slapping him when I see him again."

"That might be today, too, depending on what Dr. Oak sees. He may call him in to chat."

"Wouldn't it be great if the social worker was here then, too?" Ruth washed her hands after discarding the test tube of urine. She tucked the equipment away, then dried the counter.

"I don't know how quickly all of this will happen over the holidays," warned Richard.

"Well, if we can postpone any decisions, that would help, too."

"Fingers crossed," said Richard, doing so. "Must run. Talk later?"

"Yes. Are you coming up with Dr. Oak?"

"I'll try, but I'm the only resident on call today. Lots of things to get done."

Ruth nodded. "Me, too. I imagine Dr. Oak will call for me when he arrives."

She waved goodbye to Richard, a song in her heart. Now, if only they can protect Mrs. Matthews! She dashed out to be sure to be caught up for when the doctor arrived. She didn't want to miss being there for his assessment.

THIRTY-FIVE

Patient assessment

Dr. Oak swept onto the floor, his lab coat flying out behind him like a cape. He was a tall, thin man, with glasses on a chain dangling around his neck that swung as he walked. His shoes squeaked.

He saw Ruth looking at them.

"I know, nurse. They are noisy. But I find it's less scary for patients if I make some sort of noise as I approach. Of course, I'm not tip toeing around at night like you nurses do." He smiled and Ruth could feel her worries decrease. A friendly senior physician? Why hadn't she met him before?

"Now, where is this patient I hear we are concerned about? Can you bring me up to date on her history, please? Bring her chart, we'll talk there."

Drat, thought Ruth, and here I thought he was sensitive. And now he's going to talk over Mrs. Matthews' head, just like all the other docs.

They entered Mrs. Matthews' room, and the doctor went right up to the bed and offered his hand. Mrs. Matthews reached for it and shook it. Ruth was astonished. This, too, was huge progress for her.

"Mrs. Matthews. I'm Dr. Oak. I understand you've been with us for …," he took the chart from Ruth and flipped through the pages, "… some time now. It looks like they have tried a few things to help you feel better. How are you feeling today?"

Mrs. Matthews sat up straight and looked directly into his eyes. "I am fine, doctor. I feel much better and would like to go home if possible."

"Ok, let's slow down. Usually, people don't go directly from the locked ward home. I know you must be eager to get out of here, but we like to place you on an open ward to see how you fare first." He turned some more pages. "Why is she on the locked ward, nurse? I see no reason for it in the chart."

"I believe it was a request from her husband, doctor."

"Hmm, yes, I see several requests from her husband in the notes. Can you tell me why you are here, Mrs. Matthews?"

"I came in after my second baby was born. I had a terrible pregnancy and then the birth was so painful. They told me I shouldn't have any more children, because of the damage. Well, after that," she added, touching a tear on her cheek to blot it, "I felt so sad. I didn't want to look at my baby, didn't want to move. So I didn't." She sniffed. "But now all I can think of is seeing them. And my husband won't let me! And he keeps ordering more treatments."

"Please don't get agitated, Mrs. Matthews. We're just having a friendly chat here."

"But now he wants them to give me a lobotomy! Wouldn't you be agitated?" Mrs. Matthews spoke loudly but gained control quickly. "I don't want anything more done to my brain."

"Well. Let me just run through the usual set of questions that we always ask to see if you are doing well. Do you know where you are?"

He read through the questions and Mrs. Matthews aced them until he asked for her address. She did not know. "Could that be because of the treatments she's had, doctor?" Ruth asked, timid. She didn't want to make him mad.

"Of course, nurse, but thank you so much for pointing that out." He frowned at Ruth, who moved closer to the bed and held Mrs. Matthews' hand. He wasn't going to frighten her off.

"Are you still feeling sad?" he asked.

"Only about not being able to see my babies."

"And are you worried about anything?" The doctor peered into her eyes, which she turned away from him.

In a tiny voice, she said, "I am a bit afraid of my husband. He gets so angry with me."

"Hmm. Can you walk for me?" the doctor asked.

She did so, did the neurological tests of finger to nose, backwards walking, and more.

"I have to say you seem in remarkably good shape. How are her sugars, nurse?"

"Despite the insulin shock treatments, they seem to be normal."

"Hmm," the doctor said again. "Can you come with me, nurse?" He turned to Mrs. Matthews. "Thank you for being so helpful. I'll be discussing a treatment plan with your nurse. She can explain it to you afterwards."

"No lobotomy?" Mrs. Matthews said in a trembling voice.

"I'll talk with your physician after the holidays and discuss our options." He turned and literally stormed out of the room. His shoes didn't even dare squeak. Ruth squeezed Mrs. Matthews' hand and followed him.

Back in the nursing station, he turned to Ruth. "What are your impressions?"

Ruth, stunned, couldn't answer for a moment.

"Come on, come on, I don't have all day."

"Well, when I first came here, she wasn't moving or responding to anyone."

"How long ago was that?" He flipped through the chart again. "Not long. And now?"

"Now she seems perfectly fine. She was a lot better after the ECT treatments, so I'm not sure why they shifted her to insulin shock. It's almost like her husband wants to try everything on her."

"Perhaps he's concerned?"

"Perhaps he's mean!" Ruth burst out, unable to hold her worry in any longer. "She wants to see her children, and we had it all arranged, and he cancelled at the last minute. I think he is trying to make her sad again."

The doctor frowned at her over his glasses, now perched at the end of his nose. Then he nodded. He nodded! Ruth was spiralling with hope.

"There are a few things that I can do. First, I think we should get a social worker consult. Have them assess the family environment."

"Already requested by the day nurse," said Ruth. He peered at her again. A brief nod.

"And I see no reason she should be in a locked ward. Let's transfer her as soon as possible to an open ward. That will make it easier for her to visit with family. Regarding the treatment plan … I can't override another doctor's orders, I'm afraid."

Ruth started to object, but he put his hand up.

"Now, just you wait. I will write a note here, detailing my exam. I'll say my resident assessed her as being anxious and so I visited, though I suspect you may also have had something to do with it."

Ruth cringed, but the doctor just smiled and took out his fountain pen to write. He wrote for a long time. Ruth was nervous waiting, so she went out and did a few checks on the rest of the patients. Dr. Oak came to find her. "You should have waited," he reproved her. "Nurses usually do."

"I'm sorry," Ruth said. "It's just I'm the only nurse on today, and we've been busy for a while. I just wanted to check …"

"Yes, yes, fine, fine. I have to run. Must keep a sharp eye on that resident of mine. He gets ideas, you know." He winked at her. "The orders are in the chart. I'll try to catch her doctor when he gets back after the holidays. I've left him a note." And he sped off down the hall, coat flapping behind him.

Ruth ran back to the nursing station and flipped open Mrs. Matthews' chart. True to his word, he'd written a lengthy note, detailing how well Mrs. Matthews was doing, the complete mental exam. Even her reflexes were back to normal, he'd said. He ordered her to be transferred to an open floor immediately, and have a social work consult, and he left a note asking for an urgent consult with Mrs. Matthews' doctor before any other treatments were completed. Ruth let out a whoop that made the orderlies race to the nursing station.

"Are you okay?" Bob asked. "I thought you were being attacked!"

"No, but look! Mrs. Matthews gets to go to an open ward. And no more treatments! Isn't that good?"

Bob grinned. "Well done, you!"

Dan frowned. "Her husband isn't gonna like that, not at all."

"Well, let's get her transferred before he visits, then, shall we?" Ruth picked up the phone and called 2A, which, fortunately, had a bed. "Let's go!"

The orderlies and Ruth had Mrs. Matthews packed and rolling in less than fifteen minutes. Ruth went with along with the chart to give a report. It was all done with unbelievable speed, and the three of them celebrated in the nursing station when they got back. "One thing done, anyway," said Ruth. "Now to keep her safe."

It was good they got things settled quickly because they'd just finished celebrating when they heard a knocking on the locked door to the ward.

THIRTY-SIX

Mr. Matthews enraged

Bob went down to open the door, and there was Mr. Matthews. Because, sighed Ruth, we can never catch a break. He went to his wife's room, and of course she wasn't there. He stormed up to the nursing station where Ruth was charting and banged on that door with five sharp thumps.

Ruth was glad to see that Bob and Dan were both hovering in the sunroom, talking with patients but with one eye her way. She was going to miss their protection when she went to the general hospital.

"Nurse! Nurse!" Mr. Mathews hit the door again.

Ruth gathered herself and stood up, opened the door and stepped out, pulling it shut behind her.

"Can I help you, Mr. Matthews, is it? I don't believe we've met before. I'm Miss Maclean." Ruth reached out her hand.

Mr. Matthews looked at it with a sneer. "Who's in charge here today?"

"That would be me."

"You? You aren't even a real nurse!"

Ruth folded her hands and waited. She could see Dan grinning behind the angry man.

"Where … is … my … wife?"

He paused between each word to gather spittle, Ruth thought. She wanted to mop off after he was through. She counted to three, then spoke in her most soothing tones. The ones that frightened her siblings because she sounded like a mean kindergarten teacher they'd once had.

"Oh, I'm so sorry. That must have been terribly alarming to go to her room and find her gone. We haven't had time to notify you yet. Your wife was reassessed, and the doctor said she should be transferred to an open floor as soon as possible. She's on 2A. The doctor felt she would recover quicker, and it would be easier for the whole family to visit if she were there. Were you able to bring your children with you? She mentioned how much she longed to see them." She suppressed a devilish smile. So there! she thought.

Mr. Matthews glowered. "I did not approve this transfer. She is much safer on the locked ward."

"Dr. Oak felt she was ready. It really is up to the physicians."

"Where is her usual doctor? I'm sure he would agree with me. And where's the head nurse? She agrees with me, too. My wife is still a danger to herself and others."

"I'm afraid many of the regular staff are off for the holidays. Would you like me to call the supervisor?"

He grunted. "If I find out this is some kind of trick you are playing to cut my ability to control my wife's treatment, you'll be sorry. I am her husband, and I can say what she needs done."

"With respect, sir, the doctors are in charge of everyone's treatment. They are the most knowledgeable." Behind Mr. Matthews, Dan was making cutting movements across his neck. Taking his cue, she said, "I'm sorry, but I really must get back to work. Would you like me to call the supervisor for you before I do? Perhaps she has a solution for you. In the meantime, why not see your wife? The open wards are so much nicer than the locked ones."

Mr. Matthews stared at her, jaw dropping. "Well, I see no one has taught you how to treat your betters. Snip of a girl, telling me what to do! Yes, call the supervisor. I'll see who is behind this." He turned on his heel and walked swiftly to the door. "Let me out. Now!"

Bob walked casually down to the door, the delay making Mr. Matthews even angrier. "What is wrong with this place? I'll be back with my doctor!"

As soon as he headed towards the door, Ruth was on the phone to floor 2A. "I'm so sorry, Mr. Matthews is on his way, and he's loaded for bear. Do you want me to send one of the orderlies down in case things get out of control? … Yes, I am calling the supervisor, but you know … yes, she's probably asleep. Can you page Dr. Oak? Let me know if you need anyone else."

She hung up, called the supervisor, listened to the ringing, left a message with the switchboard. Mrs. Peters was on and she at least understood the urgency of the message. "I'll keep trying, Miss Maclean," she said, ringing off.

"Bob," Ruth called out of the nursing station. "Could you go around and knock on the supervisor's door? I think we'll need her."

"I'm on my way." He almost ran to the ward door. As he opened it, Richard stepped in.

"What's happening?" he asked, looking at the orderly as he dashed out.

"Mr. Matthews just came in and he's furious we moved his wife to 2A. Dr. Oak was here and assessed her and wrote the order."

"Oh, I'm glad he did that. I should maybe …" He gestured at the door with his thumb.

"The more the merrier, if you can get to her."

"I'll let you know what happens." He vanished out the door.

Ruth paced around the ward, absent-mindedly speaking to each patient and responding, but her mind was a ward away. Fortunately, Dan had set up a big card game for most of the patients, and it kept them busy until it was time to get everyone ready for dinner. Ruth checked the vitals on those patients who needed it, though when she did, she had trouble telling her own bounding heartbeat from theirs.

An hour passed. Bob hadn't come back yet, but Ruth figured he'd gone to 2A and was hovering to protect the patient and staff, as he did so well. Ruth started getting the patients ready for their evening meal. They all played along, still cheery after the family visits, she guessed. She didn't know they also got a special dinner. When it came up from the kitchen, it even smelled edible. It must have been Christmas leftovers from the cafeteria.

"It's good they get some decent grub today. Least we can do," said Dan.

"It's funny, I was told they shouldn't know what day Christmas was. Too exciting. But they all knew it anyway."

"I think some of the other nurses just don't like all the out-of-tune carol singing." He laughed. "Can't say as I blame them."

Just as Ruth thought she'd explode with nerves, Bob came back. They ran to meet him in the nursing station.

"Well?" Ruth demanded.

Bob sat in one of the chairs, heaved an enormous sigh. "I don't know, Miss Maclean. I like you, I do, but you certainly know how to start a mess."

"Oh no! Is Mrs. Matthews still safe?"

Bob sighed again. "It was quite the scene. Hizzoner arrived, threatened the nurse, got surrounded by everyone. Their orderly Adam is a man mountain. It's good he was there. He stuck to the nurse like glue." He ran his hand over his biceps, finding them wanting. "Reminded me I need to go lift something heavy more often. Anyway, then Matthews went into his wife's room. It was a fugging outrage ... sorry miss ... to see how scared she was of him. So, Adam wandered over by her."

"This sounds terrible! Please tell me it worked out?"

He stretched. "Well, the mister raised his voice at her, telling her off, so I joined the party. Then the supervisor finally arrived, and that young fella Dr. Hartman came too. We had quite a crowd in the room. The nurse kept trying to move us along the hallway, but Matthews wouldn't leave his wife. He was holding her hand, but it didn't look friendly."

He spun around on the chair, slowly. Ruth almost bit her own hand with frustration. "Come on, Bob! Is she all right?"

"Sorry. Just need to relax myself after all that. Sometimes it's very hard not to punch people, you know? Anyway, then who should come along but Dr. Oak, who dragged Matthews out into the hallway and started talking hard at him and poking him in the chest with his finger. The nursing supervisor pushed them both off the floor. Meantime, the nurses swarmed Mrs. Matthews, bringing her tea and blankets and keeping her company. She calmed down pretty quick. Dr. Hartman was talking to her when I left."

Ruth relaxed. "Oh, that's good. Where is Mr. Matthews now?"

"They threw him out. Sent him home to calm down. He's not allowed back until the social worker sees the missus."

"Really? How can they do that?"

"We'll manage," said Bob, with a grim expression on his face that Ruth had never seen before. "I hate men who are mean to their women. I know that here, we have lots of people who are mean, but they are out of their heads, they can't help it. That guy, though ..." He made a fist and punched it into his other hand. "I might have to take to walking around the hospital after dark just to see if he's there."

Ruth put up a hand. "No! Don't you get into trouble, Bob! We need you!"

"I can see that!" Bob laughed as he looked into the sunroom. "What happened over dinner? It's a mess out there."

Dan laughed. "I'll get it, Bob. It was a special meal day, remember? Ended up being the usual free for all."

THIRTY-SEVEN

Orienting newbies

Richard caught up with Ruth as she was leaving the hospital for the night. "Hey! How'd the rest of your shift go?"

"Other than the heart attacks, you mean? Thanks so much for looking after Mrs. Matthews. Isn't her husband horrid? I thought he was going to punch me."

Richard scowled. "If he ever tried …"

Ruth pulled on her cape, opened the big door outside. A brutally icy wind blew through, almost knocking her over. She fell back into Richard's arms. The shivers weren't all from the cold, especially when he hugged her before releasing her. "Careful, Miss Maclean. You're precious cargo."

"Cargo? Thanks a lot." She laughed. "Seriously, I owe you a massive thank you. If you hadn't asked Dr. Oak to assess her, if we hadn't transferred her, she'd still be on my ward waiting for her lobotomy."

"I only hope it stays that way, Ruth," he said, using her first name as they were far out of the door now and no one was lingering in the chill. "His pet doctor may change everything back."

"Oh, I hope not." Ruth wrung her hands in her mitts, jumped up and down twice. "Gosh it's cold. I'm freezing. The wind really blows along here. I've got to get inside." She shivered even though the walk was so short, hoping Richard would put his arm around her. No luck.

"When are you off next?" he asked.

"I worked the holidays, so I'm off the next two. How about you?"

"Me, too. What would you say to a movie? You owe me, remember?" he added with a smile that took any sting out of the remark.

Ruth grinned at him. "Well, given that you have proven your worth by rescuing a damsel in distress, I say yes! When?"

"How about tomorrow night? That way, if we have fun, we can maybe go out for dinner the following night."

"Hold on, mister," said Ruth, her hand knit mitten up against his chest. When had he gotten so close? Was he going to kiss her? She wasn't sure about it all and pulled back. "I may not be free."

He took a step backwards. "Of course, Miss Maclean. I'm just excited to spend time with you."

Ruth couldn't speak. Was this for real? Or would he attack her like George had done? She was holding back judgement. Just in case, she was going to call Betty and see if she could come along to the movie as well, sit behind them. She wanted to be alone with him, but didn't want to risk anything bad happening.

"What shall we see?" she asked.

"I'm not sure what's on. Can I call you tomorrow with the choices?"

"Perfect. Talk then. And now I really must get inside!"

"Me, too," said Richard, his lips almost blue. "I still have a bus ride to get through."

Ruth squeezed his hand through her mitts. "Time for a seat by a big fire."

He nodded, pulled his hat down over his ears and ran off, his breath making a cloud behind him. Ruth ran up the stairs, flung herself inside, pulled off her cape and boots in seconds, and ran toward the fire. "It's bitter out! Must be well below zero."

"It is," said another new student, leaning into the fire. "I tried to go shopping but gave up. You don't have any Rinso, do you? I dropped something on my uniform, and it's stained."

"You're in luck, I do for once. I'll get it for you in a sec." Ruth rubbed her hands in front of the fire, grabbed the poker, and pushed things around, increasing the heat a tiny bit. The fire struggled on, despite the lack of coal. It had been banked for the night.

"On the good side, it's supposed to snow tomorrow. That should warm things up."

Oh no, thought Ruth. There had better not be cancellations. She had to go out with Richard to the movie, she just had to!

"I'm Julie, by the way. Just filling in for another student who went home with chicken pox. You've had it, right?"

"Oh goodness, if I haven't, it's not through lack of trying. My parents had seven children and all of us had it at one time or another. Glad to meet you, Julie. Where are you studying?"

"I'm with Queen's. We haven't even covered psychiatry yet. It's my first clinical, too. I'm terrified."

Ruth stretched, turned to warm her back. "I was scared, too, but there are lots of orderlies about and everyone takes care of us. Why don't we grab a tea tomorrow morning and I'll bring you up to speed? Are you off?"

"Oh, thanks, Ruth! I'm not on until the afternoon. I'm on a locked ward! Are they violent there?"

"Not usually," said Ruth, thinking of Sgt. Turner. Would he

be nicer to a different student? She shivered. "Let's talk tomorrow. I'm ready for bed. Just let me get you that Rinso."

Julie nodded. "Thanks so much. See you in the morning! I'm staying here overnight just to get my bearings."

Ruth woke early, slow to get up because of rather warm and romantic thoughts about a certain someone. What would he be like in the movie? Would he be all grabby, like many of Betty's beaus, or would he be more polite and maybe just hold her hand? "Betty!" she said, as she jumped up. "I've got to let her know to come. But which movie?" She tumbled about, her head in a whirl, trying to sort out her feelings and fears. It was still early enough she couldn't hear the bath running, so she grabbed her robe and ran downstairs.

In half an hour she was shined, buffed and in her day clothes. When she went downstairs to get a drink of tea and some toast, there was Julie, waiting for her, her eyes red-rimmed.

"I couldn't sleep," she said, clinging to her teacup and sniffing. "I wish they hadn't sent me over! There won't be any other from my class there, and I hear they hate us."

Ruth patted her shoulder. "Well, hate is a strong word. I think they think you should have longer placements and do some night shifts."

"That's not our fault. Our profs arrange all of that."

"I know. Just offer to help whenever you can and you'll win everyone over. They are terribly short-staffed. And make friends with the orderlies. They are always around and a great help." She pulled out her toast and buttered it, sipped her tea. "What floor are you on?" she asked through the crunches.

"I'm on 2B."

"Oh, that's my floor! We're in luck! I can tell you all about the patients so you'll know them, and the nurses, too. And most of the orderlies on that floor are wonderful. I've had to work alone with them quite a few times and I always felt safe."

"You worked alone? But you're still a probie, aren't you?"

Ruth made a face. "Yes. Remember, they have a lot of missing nurses. So many left after the war was over, and there's no funding right now to hire any more."

"Oh noooo," wailed Julie. "Will I have to be on all alone?" She put her head on her arms. She sniffled.

Ruth rolled her eyes. "Can you give meds yet?"

"No," she raised her head, hope written all over her face.

"Well, then, fasten your boots. They made me do them anyway, even left narcotics drawn up for me to give. The supervisor was supposed to come and check, but they hardly ever did."

Julie moaned.

"Oh, come on. Buck up. They aren't so bad. Let me tell you about the patients, and what the ward routine is. You'll look like a pro." They spent the rest of the morning running through the list of staff and patients, Julie even taking notes. "Let's go over to the cafeteria for lunch," suggested Ruth. "Then I can show you where everything is."

Julie paled but nodded. "Okay."

They suited up and walked over, chattering on the way, Ruth trying to distract Julie from the barred windows and the shouts and smells. After showing her the locker room, the entry door for the floor, and the cafeteria, Julie finally breathed a deep breath and seemed to relax. "Thanks so much, Ruth! I don't normally feel so nervous about a placement, but you hear things, you know? Now that I see it all, it doesn't seem so bad. I used to look after my grandmother before I started school, so I know a bit about bedpans and things."

Ruth held back from rolling her eyes. It was so unfair to send this student here, where things could get scary fast. "Just remember, you are the most junior right now, so be sure to keep your mouth shut and your eyes open. The rumour about you Queen's gals is that you think you are too good for the rest of us, so don't act that way and you'll be fine." A couple of nurses walked by and said a cheery hello to Ruth. "See, they are friendly!" She grinned. "Actually, they are so nice here I'm even thinking of applying here after graduation. Haven't decided yet."

"Really? Oh, I couldn't. I can't imagine not being able to believe my brain like these poor patients."

"I felt the same way," said Ruth, standing up. "But they are people, just like everyone else. They need us." She looked at her watch. "Oh, my goodness, is that the time? I have to get back!" She'd forgotten about Richard's phone call in all the orientation. What if she'd missed it? And it was probably too late to catch Betty, too.

Movie with Richard

When Ruth arrived back at Leahurst, there was a message waiting for her. Richard had suggested *Singapore*, at 6:30 pm, and said he'd meet her there. "Cheeky," said the nurse on duty at the phone. "Not even coming to get you!"

"Well, I wasn't here to arrange it. He probably thought I was out for the day."

"Excuses, excuses. You watch yourself. You need to set the rules out early, you know."

Ruth stuck out her tongue as she headed up the stairs. As if she didn't know that. Though she was a bit disappointed he hadn't bothered to pick her up. Remembering, she dashed back downstairs, signed the book and called Betty. Or tried to. She'd already gone to work and wouldn't be home until midnight. So much for using Betty for protection.

She spent the rest of the afternoon in her room studying and putting together the nursing care plan for Mrs. Matthews, part of her final assessment. It had to be perfect so that maybe the other nurses would follow it and keep her safe. Her book had only a small section on postpartum depression and recovery from it, how best to get the patient to revive herself. There was no recommendation for lobotomy, but maybe her books were out of date. She'd better have a look in the library at the hospital before her next shift.

She so wanted to call the ward and see how Mrs. Matthews was doing, but she knew it wouldn't be welcomed. And there was nothing more she could do for her, really. It was in the hands of the doctors and social worker now, and they were probably still on vacation. So, she toiled on the care plan as a proxy for being able to do something. She couldn't help the occasional tear as she envisioned Mrs. Matthews being dragged for a lobotomy without her consent. In the care plan, she outlined the incredible importance of the patient having control over her life to recovering from depression. She hoped her wishes would become the rules.

Time flew by and when Ruth looked at the clock, it was already 4:30. "Oh no!" she said, patting her hand on her hair. She hadn't dried it properly that morning in her hurry to meet with Julie and it was curling madly all over her head. She sprung up, grabbed her makeup, hairbrush and hairspray, and headed to the washroom to freshen up. She was wrestling with it when Doris came in.

"Look at you, getting all decked out!" Doris leaned into the mirror, frowning. "Oh, I am so jealous of your hair," she sighed, plucking at her straight locks. "Mine just lies flat like a dead thing."

"I'm trying to get it to cooperate. I'm meeting Richard for a movie."

Doris grabbed her hands and shook them. "A real date! How exciting!" She looked at Ruth critically. "Let it curl. It looks so cute, and all the hairspray we use for the wards just makes it feel like a helmet. Not touchable." She fluffed Ruth's hair.

Ruth blushed. "I am not planning on being 'touched'," she said, rather stiffly. "It's too soon."

"Is it? Maybe just a little kiss? A hug? You can't tell me you aren't thinking of those things."

"Well, I am, but that doesn't mean I'm going to let them happen. Remember my last year!!"

"Yeah, but Richard isn't a TB patient or a soldier with serious anger issues, remember."

"So far as I know … meaning the anger … I know he doesn't have TB, thank heavens." Ruth pulled at her hair, trying to give it a perfect curl. Despairing, she flung her hands in the air.

Doris shrugged. "A little kiss is in order, I think. You've been out with him what, three or four times? He's going to want to." She gave Ruth a squeeze and headed out. "Live a little," she added as she left the room.

Ruth shivered. Maybe this movie wasn't a good idea. Could she call and cancel? But where would she call? She wasn't even sure how to reach him. No, she told herself. Stop being silly. Every man isn't out to attack you.

She met Richard at 6:15 in front of the Odeon. She'd taken the bus down early and waited in a cafe until it was time, nervously nibbling a biscuit and sipping tea as the minutes went by. When she made it to the theatre, Richard was standing outside, stamping his feet and slapping his hands together in the cold. He immediately put out his cigarette and greeted her with a light kiss on either cheek, as the French do. Very proper, thought Ruth.

"I'm so sorry I couldn't pick you up. For two reasons. I know it's not polite to ask you to meet me here, and, also, it's bloody freezing out here! Sorry. Let's go in."

"I'm sorry I wasn't in to get your call. My fault entirely. There's a new student who needed my help." They'd gone into the lobby and were shaking their coats free of snow.

"And I was called to do an admission. Busy people, us. Want popcorn?"

Ruth thought. She could just imagine their hands meeting in the bag … but then she also saw herself smiling with a kernel stuck in her teeth. "No thanks, Richard. I've just eaten." Dry biscuits, she thought, but that would have to be enough.

"Right. Let's get our seats. I like to see the news items at the beginning, and the cartoons."

"Me too." Ruth smiled and didn't even withdraw as Richard took her hand. They went into the theatre together, carrying their coats over their arms, "In case it's cold in the theatre," said Richard.

Ruth's lips twisted. She hoped he wasn't going to try and grope her under the coverings. She didn't want to make a scene, and she did like him so. Please don't disappoint me, she begged to the wall as Richard ushered her into a seat before him. She knew Betty had fought off several cadets who were using this technique.

He arranged her cape over her lap and sat down, draping his coat over himself. "I was here the other day, and the wind just seemed to blow through. I froze by the end of the film."

Ruth nodded. He was here recently? With whom? She squashed the tiny jealous monster that threatened to creep out. "What did you see then?" she asked in her most innocent voice.

"Oh, a couple of the guys wanted to see this horror flick. I came along for the laughs. I didn't think you'd like it. It was truly awful, so you didn't miss anything."

The green monster sulked away. The theatre was only half-filled, it being the middle of the week and freezing cold outside. They cheered through the news about Canada's hockey team and Barbara Ann Scott and their wins at the St. Moritz Winter Games and laughed through the cartoon. The main feature started, and Richard reached over and took her hand, softly and warmly. On top of their coats. As they watched, Ruth could hardly focus on the movie. Her mind was totally on her hand. His hand. She wondered if he could feel her pulse as it danced along. Was hers getting sweaty? Should she squeeze his?

When the lights came up, Ruth felt a bit of a loss. He had tried nothing, just held her hand. What did that mean? Wasn't he attracted to her? What did she want, after all? She didn't want him to leap all over her, but she did want a little leaping. Did she? Oh, she was ridiculous.

"What did you think of the movie?" Richard asked as he helped her on with her cloak.

Ruth babbled something about Fred MacMurray, Ava Gardner, her amnesia. She wasn't thinking straight. She'd been distracted through the romantic scenes, wondering if Richard was thinking of her.

"Seemed like a weak plot device to me," said Richard. "The amnesia, I mean."

"Have you ever seen an authentic case of amnesia, Richard?"

"Not yet, except after a set of ECT, and even then, most of the memories seem to come back, without having to be hit on the head again! Would you like to stop for a hot cocoa or a drink before I take you home?"

"Oh, yes, please!" They walked in awkward silence to the cafe Ruth had spent the earlier part of the evening in. Thank heavens the staff had changed.

"I'm going to have a hot cocoa. What about you?"

"Sounds perfectly yummy." Ruth settled into the booth she'd only vacated three hours before.

The cocoas arrived and the awkwardness that had passed between them slipped away as they laughed about the cartoon and discussed the film, giggled about some of the staff at the hospital and all their rules and regulations. It all seemed so cozy.

After an hour, Ruth raised her hand. "I'm having fun, but I really should get back. Speaking of rules, they still check us in and out, and we're almost at curfew."

"Really? That seems so … matronish. Do you ever get late nights?"

"Only one or two a month. I used up a lot of mine with Meg's wedding and my mother's," she paused, "funeral."

"Oh, of course. What an oaf I am. I never even asked about that. How are you dealing with it now? I'd be totally shattered if my mother wasn't here anymore. She's my biggest and probably only fan."

"Not quite the only fan," said Ruth, daring a look into Richard's eyes. They both smiled. The air seemed to sizzle.

"Closing time," called the weary waitress, leaning on the counter.

"Is it? Oh, I am so late!"

"Let's run for the bus," said Richard. "There's one any minute now and it'll be faster than a cab."

They threw on their coats, Richard paid the waitress, and out they ran, catching the bus just as it pulled up to the curb. They jumped on, laughing, and sat at the very back. As soon as they were seated, Richard captured Ruth's hand again. "I've really enjoyed tonight," he said. "Any chance we could visit again tomorrow?"

"I've had a good time, too. I'd love to see you again, but tomorrow I must work on an assignment. It has to be perfect."

Richard frowned. "To be honest, I need to study, too. Thank you, Saint Ruth, for keeping me honest." He squeezed her hand. "Though I'd much rather spend the day with you."

The bus slid to a stop outside the hospital, and they leapt out into the cold. Richard walked Ruth almost to Leahurst, but paused and pulled her into a patch of shadow. "Would you mind if I …? I've wanted to all night."

Ruth tilted her head up to his, and they shared a soft kiss, warm inside, cold outside. It felt magical. Ruth didn't want to pull back. Richard wrapped his arms around her and said, "Wow." They cuddled for a bit, Ruth's head resting on his shoulder. She loved the feeling of his arms around her.

"I had better go," said Ruth, reluctantly unwrapping his arms. "Thank you so much for a wonderful evening. I won't forget it," she tapped her head. "No amnesia here."

"I'll hit you on the head if you develop any. I understand that helps." He watched her as she ran up the stairs to Leahurst, waving through the falling snow. Once she was pulling on the door, he pulled out a pack of cigarettes and lit one, the match flare a light in the darkness. Ruth walked into the hall and almost swooned.

"So?" asked Doris, from her perch by the fire.

"Were you waiting up for me?"

"Well, I knew you were worried. How did it go? No untoward public displays of affection?"

"None whatsoever. He was a perfect gentleman."

"How boring. Did he try anything?"

"Just one wonderful, delicious, perfect, goodnight kiss," said Ruth, spinning around in a circle.

THIRTY-NINE

Fighting again

The next day was spent working and studying. She wasn't sure what her final evaluation might be at the hospital, but she was certain they'd be asking lots of questions, as no one had been there half the time she'd demonstrated a task. The checklist she needed completed to pass the placement was woefully empty. She ran over to the hospital library and spent a couple of hours there, looking through the books and perfecting her nursing care plan. After all that, she couldn't resist going up to see Mrs. Matthews. Was she still on the open floor? Was she okay?

Ruth found her on the open ward, in the sunroom, teaching another patient how to knit. They were giggling together. Ruth wasn't going to interrupt, but Mrs. Matthews spotted her and called her over.

"Can you knit, Miss Maclean?"

"I've been seen knitting, but no, I can't," said Ruth with a laugh. "My mother tried to teach me, but I seem to be all thumbs, and I keep losing count. My socks always end up as dishrags."

"Maybe you can join our lessons," said Mrs. Matthews. "Helen here is getting the knack of it, aren't you, Helen?"

The other patient looked up. Her hair was a wild mess, all short in the front, and her eyes didn't quite focus, but she nodded her head vigorously and tucked it down to look at her knitted scarf. As she did so, Ruth spotted the telltale scar of a lobotomy.

"Yes, she's had the procedure," said Mrs. Matthews. "Thank you so much for preventing me from having it."

Ruth nodded but still felt uncertain if that was going to stick. "Did the social worker come in yet?" she asked.

"Not yet. Tomorrow morning." She pulled Ruth over to whisper in her ear. "I'm just as glad if she delays. It means more days without Grant." She started back into her knitting. "It's so peaceful here," she added in a normal voice. "The patients aren't screaming as much, and I am feeling so well. I hope everything works out and I can see my babies soon."

Ruth squeezed her shoulder. "I hope so, too. I'd better let you get back to your teaching." She smiled at them both and headed off the ward. The charge nurse stopped her as she walked down the hall.

"She's looking good, isn't she?" she asked Ruth.

"Yes. I wonder what will happen when her husband comes in, though."

"You and me both. He's such a pill. The lout called all night demanding to see her, even though we told him the doctor said not until the social worker has seen her. He yells and hangs up and then calls back in half an hour. It's exhausting."

"I'm so sorry you have to go through all that." Ruth felt a wash of guilt about putting this problem onto the other nurses. She knew they were busy, too.

The other nurse grinned. "Oh, we can handle it. We're not fond of him, though. If he tries to come in, I think the entire staff would take him on. And Adam is quite capable of throwing him down the stairs, if needs be."

Ruth considered dropping by her floor to see how Julie had fared, but thought it over. Would she want to be assessed by another student? More than she already was? No, she thought. We students have to stick together. Even if we are from other schools. And Julie hadn't seemed snobby at all. She wrapped her cloak around herself and left the building, heading for Leahurst and a cup of tea. As she came around the front of the building, she could see a man in a heavy overcoat yelling at someone in the front door. Was that? Oh no, it was Mr. Matthews. Dreading another outside the building attack, like the time George had grabbed her outside the San, she turned her head away and was hustling by when the angry man turned around.

"You!" he yelled. "Wait for me, nurse. I have a bone to pick with you."

Ruth tried walking faster, but he ran to catch up.

"What does this mean? Why aren't they letting me see my wife?"

"I don't know, Mr. Matthews. She's not on my floor anymore, so I don't know what they've ordered." She tried her sweetest student nurse voice and even tried to bat her quickly freezing eyelids. He didn't notice. She added a tiny lie. "They don't let students travel between floors unless we are told to. I'm sorry, I can't help you. Have you spoken to her doctor?" She kept walking, him skipping along beside her. She just needed to reach the door to Leahurst …

"He's still away. Honestly, this hospital is a mess. I've half a mind to transfer her to Toronto."

Ruth paled under her hat. "I have to go," she told him.

"Oh go. You're just as useless as the rest of them." He stormed off through the gusting wind and Ruth was happy to see one of his gloves fall and blow across the snow. He ran after it, slipping and sliding, just as Ruth reached the door, and she fell into the hall, laughing. She sobered up quickly, remembering his threat to move his wife to Toronto. How could she protect her then? She had to do something, and quickly. But what?

She was thinking hard and stirring her tea aggressively when one of the senior nurses came into the kitchen.

"Watch it! Those cups are fragile, you know." She poured her own cup of tea and sat down beside Ruth. "Hey, Cloyne, what's bugging you? Missing the trees up north?"

Ruth snorted. "Hardly. No, I'm worrying about a patient."

"When do we ever stop doing that? It's one of the worst things about nursing. You've got to learn to detach from the patients, but it feels like cutting off your arm. Who are you worrying about?"

"Mrs. M. on 2A. Have you worked with her?"

"No, I don't know her."

"Her husband just chased me across the lawn, yelling at me about how they won't let him see her. She's not even on my ward anymore."

"Well, then she's not your problem, nor is he."

"But he says he's going to move her to Toronto."

"Not your problem. Look, there will be another patient you break your heart over tomorrow. You've got to learn to let go, even if it hurts. Because otherwise, this job will kill you. And just you wait until you do your paediatrics rotation. I cried every night."

"I lost a lot of patients when I was at the San. It was sad, but there was nothing we could do. But this patient is being abused by her husband."

"Whoa Nelly! Be careful what you say. Them's dismissal

words, unless you have proof. And even then, husbands have been known to get nursing students fired. Better just forget this patient, focus on your own work. Sometimes there really is nothing you can do for them." She stood, adjusted her uniform. "Well, I'm on. See you later."

Ruth topped up her tea, sighed. There had to be something she could do. Did Mrs. Matthews have any other family? Could she get them involved in any way?

The next day, before her shift, she went over to the open ward and talked to the nurses.

"Do you know, does she have anyone else who could speak up for her?"

"Well, let's see," said the nurse, flipping to the history section of the chart. "Yes, it says she has a sister, in Ottawa. I wonder if they get along. Have you seen her visit?"

"I haven't, no, but I wonder if she knows what is happening to her sister."

"I think when she was on the locked ward, her husband said only he could visit." The nurse smiled, a mischievous grin. "But there are no restrictions now. Maybe I'll give her a call. Thanks for the nudge, Miss Maclean. Mrs. Matthews always speaks highly of you, and now I know why."

Ruth went to her ward with a song in her heart. Maybe Mrs. Matthews' sister could intervene somehow. After all, Ruth was almost done with her placement, and she felt as if she was abandoning her patients already. Thinking of Mrs. Matthews being transferred to Toronto and being experimented upon more filled her with horror.

FORTY

New Year's

It seemed like no time at all until the end of the year approached and everyone was hurrying to get ready for 1948 to start. The entire Leahurst house was buzzing. One or two of the senior nurses were dreaming of an engagement ring on the special day. Ruth didn't have any wish for such a thing, but she was dizzy with excitement after Richard asked her out for the celebrations. They were going to go dancing at the Paradise, a place Ruth hadn't been. Betty told her it was very glamorous, so now Ruth was worried about what to wear. She didn't want to wear the dress she'd had for Meg's wedding, and besides, she'd left it up in Cloyne.

Fortunately, the other women in Leahurst were ready and eager to share, and some of the senior nurses brought in dresses and shoes they weren't going to wear, too. There was a mini fashion show one afternoon after work as everyone tried on different dresses. Of course, a few students were going to be working New Year's, but Ruth was off and felt no inclination to cancel her date with Richard to take on an additional shift, no matter how sadly Julie looked at her.

"You'll be fine," Ruth reassured her. "You've been there for a while now, and you are only on until eleven. They'll eat dinner and go to bed."

"Unless those orderlies get them going! They are so mean!"

"They are great. If they tease you, they must like you. It's like grade eight all over again. Just play along."

Julie sniffed. "I'm just trying to do my job. They should understand that."

Ruth thought she should lighten up a bit but didn't say anything. Julie's feelings were too familiar. Instead, she started thinking of a New Year's bundle she could put out for Julie, like the girls had done for her over Christmas. Julie didn't live in, but she could hide something at Leahurst as she routinely came over after shifts to get organized to go home. She didn't like changing in the locker room. It was creepy, agreed Ruth. Especially late at night. So, she gathered some little treats for Julie and got the other girls to help her set it up.

Meantime, she'd picked a dress in deep blue from the fashion show to wear for the dancing. It had a lovely neckline that almost showed her shoulders, a snug waist that fit her perfectly, and a skirt the exact right shape for swinging out as she danced. The shoes she had for Meg's wedding would do with it, and she had a silk scarf of her mother's that Meg had given her. When she was all dressed up, she and the others who were going out all stood in the social room and admired each other. Young, fit, excited, they were glorious. One of the nurses was grumping, looking at herself in the mirror, turning her head back and forth. "I spent so much on that dimple maker, and it didn't work at all — see? Not a dimple to be found!"

"Just smile, Nancy. You are beautiful, even without dimples."

"I wish we had some mistletoe to hang over the door. When will they let us get it again? What a silly ban. I wonder when they will allow US imports again?"

"Oh, wait, I made a fake one out of paper. Let's stick it up!" The girls quickly dragged over a chair and pinned the paper mistletoe to the arch going into the social room. Unfortunately, it quickly fell apart, leaving little paper balls and crumpled leaves on the floor. The nurse laughed. "Well, I never said I was crafty …"

The doorbell started to ring as one by one they were claimed by their dates. Ruth was a puddle of anxiety by the time Richard arrived, but at least he wasn't the last one. When he walked into the social room, he gasped. "Look at you all! You look fantastic."

Ruth frowned. "But you," he added, turning to Ruth, "you are astonishing. Do I really get to go out with you?"

"Awwwww," said the other girls, as Richard pinned a tiny corsage to her dress.

"I'm so sorry it's so small. It's all I could afford."

Ruth looked down at it. "It is precious. Absolutely perfect." She was already planning where she would keep it, pressed.

He draped her cape over her and ushered her out of the house. There was a cab waiting! "Is that for us?"

"I couldn't expect my princess to walk to the ball!"

Ruth giggled. No one had ever called her princess before.

"Besides, it's freezing, and this tux isn't that warm."

She sighed. If nothing else, Richard was good at managing her expectations. Still, dancing till midnight! She'd received permission to be out late for the night and couldn't wait to mingle with everyone and see what everyone was wearing, and most of all, to dance close to Richard. Hold him tight, even in public. They'd stolen kisses in the shadows, but to be out and seen would make it all seem real.

The hall was crowded, but they managed to get a table with some of Richard's medical resident friends. Some of them were dating nurses, but many had Queen's students on their arms and Ruth started to feel awkward.

"What are you studying?" one of them asked her. "I'm in sociology."

"I'm in fine arts," said another.

"I'm a nursing student," said Ruth.

"Oh, at Queen's?"

"No, at KGH."

"Oh. The certificate school."

Ruth closed her lips over what she was going to say. After they'd figured out where she was studying, the women lost all interest in her. When Richard went to get them both drinks, one whispered to the others, "Richard could do so much better than that! Why doesn't he date a Queen's student, at least?"

"I'd date him," said one.

"Hush, she can hear you," said the other.

Ruth sat back, the butterfly excitement of the ball over. She didn't belong here. Maybe she should leave. Who was she to think that Richard would even care about her? She wasn't a university student. As she tapped her foot and chewed her lip, a bunch of the nurses from her class came running over and pulled her into a hug.

"Ruth! It's been so long since we saw you!"

"Yeah, thanks for abandoning us at the San!"

Ruth hugged the group of them back. She was so glad to see them, but she hoped they didn't say anything about their placement. Now that she was away from the San, she saw how icky it was looking after all those coughing and spitting patients.

"I'm so looking forward to coming back!" said Ruth, trying to distract them.

"I'll bet," said Susan. "You're in the loony bin now, right?"

The Queen's students' heads spun on their necks.

Ruth pulled her friends away from the table. "Shhh. Those girls are from Queen's, and they think I'm lower than a worm."

"Well, phooey to them. We know who runs the wards, don't we, girls. Oh, that's my song. I've gotta find my fellah. See you, Ruth!"

Ruth cringed. The song was "Smoke, Smoke, Smoke That Cigarette!" by Tex Williams, in a rather inexpert cover. Richard finally came back with the drinks, only to be mobbed by his friends. He responded as they talked over Ruth, but saw the look in her eyes and pushed his way over to her, offering her an old-fashioned.

"An old-fashioned for we old-fashioned types," he said. "Shall we cut a rug?"

The song had changed to a foxtrot, "Ain't Nobody Here but Us Chickens" by Louis Jordan, and the entire room was moving. Richard took Ruth's hand and swung her into the melee.

From then on, the night was grand. They danced and danced, sat and talked, walked outside to cool off and have a few kisses, then back in to dance some more. Finally, the band played "I Love You for Sentimental Reasons" by Ella Fitzgerald and they could officially dance cheek to cheek. Ruth could feel her heart swooping up with every touch, every look. The glitter ball spinning on the ceiling couldn't match the sparkle in her eyes as she looked at Richard.

"You are so incredibly lovely," he breathed into her ear, sending shivers up her spine and … elsewhere.

She almost replied, "So are you," but realized that was a country girl thing to do. Instead, she kept her mouth shut and just twinkled her eyes at him, hoping he'd understand. He must have, because he put his hand on the back of her neck and brought her head onto his shoulder. He grasped her other hand

and held it to his chest, where she could feel his heart beating as fast as her own.

"It's almost midnight," he said as the song ended. "What do you say we go see the New Year in looking at the lake?"

Ruth looked around. She wanted to give him his New Year's kiss in front of everyone, especially his snobby Queen's friends.

"There'll likely be fireworks … and I can have you all to myself," he added.

Ruth agreed, though she was disappointed. At least they'd get away from the annoying girls.

Unfortunately, as they gathered their coats to go, the Queen's gang heard where they were going and decided to come with them. They all piled into one taxi, crushing Ruth's corsage. One guy actually sat on Ruth! She wriggled until he shifted over.

Still, when they got to the waterfront, everyone spread out, waiting for the fireworks to start. There was a crowd waiting with them, but an anonymous one, so Ruth and Richard were able to hold each other tight and sneak kisses. Finally, the shout went out to count down to the New Year, and Ruth and Richard joined right in. At the Happy New Year gunshot, Richard took Ruth's hands in his hands, warming them, and pulled her into one of his delightful cold weather kisses. They didn't even notice the fireworks.

Ruth almost swooned. Richard just kept on kissing her, stroking her hair, pulling her in to be close. His friends were all shouting, but he kissed her until she finally had to step back, dizzy and her legs wobbly.

"Sweet," he whispered in her ear. "That was quite the kiss!"

Ruth couldn't help herself. She burrowed into his coat and said, "Best one I've ever had."

"Mmmmm. Me too. Wish we could get somewhere more private …"

Ruth felt a thrill, but also a warning. A lot of her friends were "getting private" that night, she thought, and she really didn't want Richard to think she'd be up for that, good church girl that she was. She knew if they were alone, she might not be able to control what her body was telling her. Meg had written to her about what happened on her wedding night and Ruth had a good idea where her body might lead them.

"Oh, dear Richard," she said. "I can't do that. My curfew runs out soon."

Richard turned away. "Damn curfews!" He turned back, kissed her again, very lightly on her forehead, her lips, her neck. She couldn't stand without holding onto him, she was so shimmery.

"You're shaking," he said.

"I must be cold," Ruth lied.

"Well, perhaps I can see you home, then, let you get warmed up."

"We won't ever be able to get a cab in this mob," Ruth said, looking around. "And I don't know if the buses are still going."

"Good thing you brought your boots," laughed Richard. "I think these shoes won't pass muster when I return them to the rental place."

They started off, walking arm in arm, touching as much as they could through coats and hats and mittens. It was a long, love-filled walk, and Ruth was floating as they reached Leahurst. "Want to come in and get warm?" she asked. "Oh no, dang it. They won't let men in tonight. Too much 'getting private', I think."

"Virginal nurses. Who would have thought it? You have quite the opposite reputation, you know, especially after the war."

Ruth tapped him lightly on the cheek. "Bad boy. You are talking to a good Presbyterian woman. We never misbehave."

He leaned back and looked at her, smiling a slow smile that sent shivers right down to Ruth's toes. "I think whoever gets you to misbehave might be a very, very lucky man." He leaned forward for another thrilling kiss and enclosed her in his arms again. "But I fear an angry God right now, so I'd better let you go."

Ruth felt a sting of regret, but turned and went up the stairs. By the time she turned around, he was gone, leaving a faint scent of cigarettes behind him.

FORTY-ONE

Catching up

Real life had to return, of course. Ruth spent the first day of the new year lying about daydreaming, but she was on duty the second. And it seemed she wasn't going to have a slow day. "Good morning, Miss Maclean." Head nurse Myrna Thomas called Ruth over the minute she arrived on the ward. "I realize I've been a bit lax about completing your assessment form. It's just been so busy."

Ruth nodded. "I have done a lot of the things on that list."

"I'm sure you have. But no one has witnessed you. Did you not get someone to watch you perform the tasks?"

"Who would I ask? It's been so short-staffed here lately that I was on my own a lot of the time."

"Miss Maclean! I've heard you had a tendency to talk back, but I haven't witnessed it until now. Please desist." She sighed. "Be that as it may, you need to be signed off on all these things. I'll partner you with a nurse for the next few shifts and the two of you will work through them all."

Ruth looked over the list again. It had things like recording blood pressures, or testing urine, or speaking with patients. She'd done them all almost every day.

"I won't assign you any patients for today so you can get caught up on the easy things. There are some dressing changes you can do, too. Sgt. Turner has injured his arm. The dressing needs changing."

"Sgt. Turner? Is he feeling any better?"

"Well, he injured his arm breaking a window, so I wouldn't say so. He's in restraints. It will give you a chance to demonstrate your skill with agitated patients, restraints, and dressings."

Oh no, thought Ruth. She resisted thinking the swear words she wanted to say. The last thing she wanted to do was look after an angry Turner in restraints. One thing about spending last year with soldiers and this term with psychiatric patients, she knew a rich vocabulary of cuss words. Now all she had to do was remember to never, ever, let them out. She forced a thought of her father into her head and crushed them.

"Alison. As Ruth's mentor, I'm assigning her to you today."

"But I already have eight patients, and an insulin treatment."

"That seems fine, four each. Off you go."

Alison grumbled as they went to the clean utility room. "I don't mind watching you, Ruth. It just seems a bit late! You've already done all of these things." She gestured at the list.

"I know. But I'm so glad you are helping with Sgt. Turner! I hope he doesn't remember me!"

"Let's get him done first and over with. I'm a bit nervous, too. I haven't seen much of him lately. Just remember to keep your bandage scissors well back and mind the tape."

The two nurses hesitated at the door with their bundles, but when they went in, they were relieved to see an orderly standing by. Bob nodded at them both. Sgt. Turner was lying on his back on the bed. Both arms and hands were wrapped with bandages and attached to the bedside. He had bloody scratches on his face around his eyes.

"Good morning, Sgt. Turner," said Ruth. May as well jump right in.

"You! I remember you!" he said.

Ruth shivered.

"You were so kind to me on my first night here. Thank you for that," Sgt. Turner mumbled.

"You're most welcome," said Ruth. "May we change your dressings?"

"Oh, I don't think so," he said, his voice getting lower, his eyes glittering. "Didn't we have an agreement the last time I saw you?" He glared at Ruth. "But somehow, I'm still here, Miss Nursey-wursey." He spat out the last word.

"You know I couldn't do what you wanted. I could only give you a good sleep," said Ruth. She looked directly at him, staring him down. "Are you feeling any better?"

"No, I'm not!" Sgt. Turner shouted suddenly. "Who could after seeing those people? Seeing just how cruel we are to one another? The images are burned into my eyes. I tried to claw them out, but then you tied me up so I can't even do that!"

Ruth took a deep breath. "Sgt. Turner. I went and looked up what you'd seen after we spoke last time. It was absolutely horrific."

"You damn well better believe it!"

Bob stepped forward so that the man could see he was watching.

Ruth continued, still standing out of arm's reach from the bed. "You don't know me, Sgt. Turner."

"I know you're a bleeding liar!"

"Please don't yell. You'll upset everyone else. Some of them are afraid of loud noises. You don't want to be cruel, do you?"

That shut him up for a moment. Ruth said, "Sgt. Turner, I'm

the daughter of a minister. After seeing what you'd seen, or rather, pictures of it, I had to sit and pray for understanding. I was ashamed of us, we humans. But as I prayed, it came to me that there were also good people. The ones who are trying to save you. The ones who work so hard with all the patients in this hospital to help them get well. I've seen them get better. I know you can, too." She sighed, took a step closer. "We need people like you, people with a conscience. People to prevent that horror from ever happening again. As you already have, fighting in the war."

Sgt. Turner seemed to listen, so she went on. "You can tell other people what you've experienced, convince them, make them listen. You've already taught me so much."

He remained quiet. "Can we change your dressing now, please Sgt. Turner? We just want to make you more comfortable." Alison brought the supplies closer to the bed, slowly.

"I guess," he said, ungraciously. But as they bent to remove the bandage, he darted his hand out and twisted Ruth's hand back hard. It hurt. Bob was there in an instant, freeing it, but it still burned.

"Now why'd you go and do that for, Turner?" said Bob.

"It's Sgt. Turner," he said, angry.

"You don't deserve to be called by rank if you are going to hurt our nurses. Now lay still and let them do their job or I'll be putting you in the padded room, naked. The heating isn't too good in there. You might get a nasty cold. So quiet down. Got it?"

Sgt. Turner calmed down, but his face remained angry. Bob held both of his arms flat on the bed while the women cleaned the glass cuts and re-bandaged the area, being sure to tuck in the bandages well. They changed the restraints and attached them firmly, Alison coming over to Ruth's side to check her work. They gathered up the old dressings and fled.

"Well, that's at least four things I can check off. Restraints, bandaging, dealing with hostile patient, working with orderlies — whew! We'll be done with you by lunchtime! Okay, let's get rid of this stuff and do vitals and meds next."

They strode quickly to the utility room, both of them burning off adrenaline. "Well done with Turner, by the way. You handled him perfectly."

"Oh, I don't think so," said Ruth. "I don't know what we would have done without Bob."

"He's a gem," agreed Alison. "But he didn't need to get involved right away, which I was afraid of when Turner first … 'turned' … on you. Ha ha. We should put some cool water on your hand."

Ruth looked at it ruefully. It was swelling and there were some purple marks forming. "Who knew he could move so fast? Or crush a hand so quickly?"

FORTY-TWO

Exhausted

Ruth dragged herself off the ward at the end of her shift. After dealing with Sgt. Turner, she'd spent the day running around doing things to check them off her list. Testing urine, giving medications, doing IM shots into people whose backsides were tough as old shoes, taking a patient for a bath treatment. She was able to leave an aide with the patient while they were soaking so that she could do more tasks. Set up the autoclave, clean and sharpen and sterilize needles and syringes, same for dressing trays. She felt like she'd done the entire placement's work in one shift, but she had almost everything checked off. Her nursing care plan was left. She'd be bringing that her next shift. Tomorrow, she had to prep and follow up an insulin shock treatment, and the same for an ECT one. All things she had done before, but no one had thought to sign them off, and to be honest, Ruth hadn't thought about it either. She'd been too busy just trying to hang on.

As she came out of the locker room, dragging her feet, she ran into Richard. "I hoped I'd catch you," he said, smiling widely.

Ruth couldn't help an answering twinkle, despite her fatigue. "How'd your day go?"

He made a face. "Got in trouble for Mrs. M."

"Did you?" Ruth woke in a hurry. "What happened?"

"Nothing to worry about. Her regular doctor seemed to think there was some nefarious planning going on to change his care plan. Big dust-up in the nursing station."

"Oh, I'm so sorry! Why didn't you call me? I could have taken the blame."

Richard smiled at her, his eyes warm. "I know you would have, my moxie girl, but you see, I couldn't let that happen. I'm almost done. You are just beginning. They wouldn't dare drop me after all they've already spent on my training."

"Thank you! But what is happening to Mrs. M.?"

Richard looked around. "Can I walk you home?"

Ruth nodded. "I'd like that, short though it is."

They wrapped themselves up and headed out the door.

"I cannot wait for spring. The winds here are like the ones off the lake back home."

They jointly shivered. "So, Mrs. M.," said Richard, after looking around carefully. "Her doctor, that old chrome dome, was furious that she'd been moved and had a social worker referral without his say so. But then the nurses and social worker all ganged up on him and asked for a reassessment. He dragged me along to help him and she was even better than the other day, so he didn't really have much to say."

"Thank heavens!"

"Yes. It helped that the eyeball lobotomy guy already left for the US. The patient didn't recover well, apparently, and no one wants to follow his technique. I'm with them."

"What happened to that patient?"

"She got a brain infection. She's at KGH on the neurology

ward while they try to control the infection. So much for not needing to make everything sterile."

"Oh, that poor woman! She is so young. I hope she recovers! You don't want to try one of those lobotomies, do you?"

"No, in surgery practice, I know I like to actually see what I'm cutting into."

"Well, I'm glad things have worked out for Mrs. M., anyway!" They'd almost finished the short walk to Leahurst.

"What about taking a little longer walk with me?" asked Richard. "I can't stop for long. A bunch of the guys got tickets for the big game tonight."

"The hockey game? Oh yes, all the orderlies were talking about it. At Jock Harty? Boston Bruins against the Toronto Marlboros, am I right? I should know. It's all they've spoken about for days."

"It should be something to see. Do you like hockey?"

"My dad loves the Bruins. He used to make us sit absolutely silent so he could hear their games on the radio. I became a fan, one step removed."

"Have to admit I'm a fan of the Bruins, too. Don't tell anyone here, though. After all, Kingston is the home of hockey, right?" Richard pulled his hat down over his ears. "It'll make a nice ending to this rotation, and my term."

"You're almost finished everything now, right?" Ruth felt a wave of panic. Would she lose him forever?

"Almost. I have to decide where to do my final placement. I'm thinking about going to that hospital up in Frobisher Bay."

"What? Yes, let's walk some more. I want to hear about this. Where is Frobisher Bay, anyway?"

"Don't you remember your high school geography?" teased Richard, tapping her on the nose. "It's way north, above the arctic circle. I've always wanted to see what it's like. And now they have a hospital set up there, on the military base. They are looking for junior doctors they don't have to pay too much to help the Forces ones. A lot of those docs didn't make it through the war."

"Will you be treating the Eskimos?"

"That's the exciting bit. They get treatment at the base too, if it's urgent, but maybe I can do some home visiting, too. It would be so interesting to see how they survive in the bitter cold. I hear some of them are still living in tents!"

"But," said Ruth, a selfish urge pushing her forward, "you'll be so far away!"

"I know," said Richard, putting his arm around her and giving her a squeeze. "But it's only for a year, and you'll be busy being all brilliant, healing everyone like you do, and wouldn't have time for me, anyway."

"Not really," said Ruth. Her throat was getting tight. He was leaving her. He didn't care for her after all.

"Ruth, we have a few weeks left together. Let's focus on those. I promise I'll try to write and get home when I can. My mother has already said I have to, religiously, every week." He pulled up her chin, cupped her face with his chilly mitten. "At least I'm not off to some battle front where you would never hear from me and wonder if I was dead or alive."

"True," sighed Ruth, pulling away. She tried to joke. "But I'll worry that you'll freeze into a snowbank somewhere, your legs sticking up." She poked her fingers up in a V and wiggled them. Walking a little further on, she tried to get control of her tears. They were freezing on her cheek, and she didn't want Richard to see them. It was because she was tired, she told herself. Then she thought of the times they'd had together, the fun times, the long conversations, the understandings they'd shared. She'd miss them. A lot.

She turned on him, surprising him. "Why do you have to go? Why can't you find something different here? There are all sorts of spots! You're needed here, too! And your mother must be heartbroken." Ruth hated a whine that had crept into her voice, but there it was. Please don't sob, she begged herself. "Is that why I haven't heard from you since New Year's? I was hoping for a call. Maybe you didn't enjoy my company?"

Richard recoiled. "Look, Ruth, of course I enjoyed your company on New Year's. I'll miss you, too, but after all, it's my career. I need to get experience that will help me find a decent permanent position. I need to stretch myself. And no, I haven't meant to be distant. Like you, I've been busy. Besides," he added, with a bite to his tone, "I knew our time together was going to be short, and I don't want to hold you to anything if you wanted to move on."

"Ha. Didn't want to hold me, eh? Well, that sounds about right. Why not just say goodbye and go off and be free, if that's what you want?"

Richard walked on, swinging his arms. Finally, he said, "Ruth — I'm so disappointed in you! I thought you'd be happier for me. It's going to be so fascinating!" He shrugged. "And, after all, we've just gone out a few times. It's not like we were official or anything."

"Yes, that's true," said Ruth, her voice as brittle and cold as the snow chilling her feet. His shrug hurt more than anything. "We've barely started to know each other. Why would you need to take my wishes into account? I'm just glad to find out your priorities before I got too involved."

Richard reached for her, but Ruth pushed him away and ran back to Leahurst, stomping up the steps and slamming the door loudly enough the desk nurse shushed her.

Doris found Ruth later, sobbing in her room. "What happened? Everyone says you came in like a tornado."

Ruth wiped her eyes. She could feel righteous anger pour over her. "That … Dr. … Hartman! He's going to go to some way up north place for his next rotation. He'll be there for a year! And he never even asked me about it!"

"Oh," said Doris.

"Obviously, I was just his little plaything for now. And here I stupidly thought we had something more. Oh, I hate men!"

Doris sat down beside Ruth, pulled her into a hug. "You must be so sad."

"Oh, don't try that therapeutic conversation stuff on me. A genuine friend would be as angry as I am."

Doris laughed. "Okay, so he's a real jerk. Let's put his name in our shoes."

"What?"

Doris took a piece of paper and wrote 'Richard' twice on it, then tore it in half. "There, one for you and one for me. Put it in your slipper. Then, whenever you walk anywhere, just stomp a little harder."

Ruth couldn't help but snort with laughter as she tucked the piece of paper under her foot. "And this does exactly what?"

"Makes you feel much better. Here, stand up." They stood, in their house slippers, and stamped the foot with the name in it, twisted it back and forth.

Ruth laughed out loud. "That does feel better!" They twisted a bit more and then fell, giggling, onto Ruth's bed. "Oh, Doris, I'm going to miss you so much when I move back to the residence!"

"I'll miss you, too. Though it was so much quieter before …" Doris grinned at Ruth. "But remember, you can always come back. We could use you, with your 'taught by brother fighting skills' and your persuasive gifts." She sat up and smoothed the covers on Ruth's bed. "Did you have your evaluation yet?"

"Not yet. I think she is waiting until the last moment so she can throw me out with no repercussions."

"I doubt it. She's been talking to all of us, which is a good thing. Usually she doesn't bother."

"I just wish it was over. The evaluation, I mean. Not this placement," Ruth hurriedly added. "You girls have all been so sweet to me! I'll never forget my Christmas stocking-s!"

FORTY-THREE

Mrs. Matthews

The weeks flew past, now that the end of Ruth's rotation was in sight. With any luck, she'd be getting her cap and be seen as a proper nurse very soon. She knew the other nursing students in her class were busily planning for the big day. Ruth didn't have an easy opportunity to help, living as she did far away from the rest of them. So, she plunged along in her placement and worked harder, trying to shine and forget Richard. She tried over and over to get the non-communicative schizophrenic patient to speak to her, walked the obsessives around until they were too tired to tidy, ran stretchers and wheelchairs back and forth between treatment rooms. Everywhere she went, she tidied and wiped so the ward shone. She even tidied the nursing station.

With the additional work she'd taken, and because she hadn't wanted to run into Richard anywhere, she'd been avoiding popping in on Mrs. Matthews. She was trying to keep in mind what the senior nurse had said about having to detach from patients, but was finding it hard. Finally, she couldn't stand it anymore and one quiet night she called over to 2A.

"Hi, it's Nurse Maclean. I'm just calling to see how Mrs. Matthews is doing."

"Hi, Miss Maclean. Mrs. Matthews? We discharged her last week. She's not here any longer."

"What? Did he take her to Toronto? Can we stop him? Did he make her have a lobotomy?"

The other nurse laughed. "Slow down — you really have been out of the loop. Didn't Dr. Hartman tell you?"

"Um … no. We haven't talked much lately." Or at all.

"Well, I've got to run in a moment, but I'll give you the brief report. The social worker came in and recommended she and her husband live apart while she finishes her recovery. Turns out her sister had been wondering what happened to her. He hadn't told her anything. When we called her, she ran right down from Ottawa. They had a wonderful reunion here last week, and her sister is providing her with a place to stay while she gets used to her children again."

"Really? That's all so wonderful! So did she see her children finally?"

"Not when I was on, but I think they came in for a visit. I was just happy to get her away from that man. You owe some thanks to Dr. Hartman for her escape, by the way. He was here advocating for her with the senior most days until he relented. Even I was impressed. Most residents don't care that much about their patients."

Probably needed it for his career, thought Ruth, nastily. We know that's the important thing.

She hung up, saddened that she hadn't had a chance to say goodbye. Mrs. Matthews was the first patient to respond to her, and she vowed to never forget her.

The phone rang. It was the nurse from 2A. "Sorry, forgot to tell you — she left you a note. Didn't want it to go over in the mail in case it caused trouble. She was such a lovely woman, and a success story, too. We all needed one of those. Come over and get it anytime. It's in the nursing station."

"Thanks," said Ruth, her throat closing over with emotion. Mrs. Matthews had thought of her. Ruth hadn't been wasting her time entirely on people who would never remember she'd been there. She was so happy she went out of the nursing station and asked King Leonard for a dance to the songs they were playing on the radio. He, startled, bowed and agreed, and they spun around the sunroom once. "You're quite the dancer," said Ruth when the song was over.

"All part of royal training. We need to dance with emissaries' wives, you know. Remind me, you are the ambassador from where?"

Ruth laughed and said, "The kingdom of KGH."

"Funny name for a kingdom," said Leonard. He walked away, muttering to himself, but Ruth was still smiling. She was going to miss all these characters when her rotation was over.

"Having fun?" The low voice of Sgt. Turner crept across the room. He was sitting in a chair in the corner of the sunroom, restraints in place. Bob looked up from his card game with the other patients when he heard Turner's voice. "Ignorant broad. How do you dare have fun?" the Sergeant demanded.

Ruth sighed. This poor man was so so damaged. She wondered what lay ahead for him. Probably a lobotomy. Sorrow washed over her. That was something she wouldn't wish for anybody.

"Sgt. Turner, I just heard of a patient who is better and able to go home. It made me happy to hear she was doing well, that's all."

He grunted, but subsided.

"I really hope all of you are well one day, and can go home, too," she said to the general room. It was a mistake. Patients immediately mobbed her, calling out, "I want to go home!" "Can

I go home, Nurse?" "Let me out!" "I want to get out!" She ducked their hands and escaped the circle. Over on the side of the room, Sgt. Turner smiled.

Okay, thought Ruth. I'm not going to miss him.

"Look, she's going to open the door for you all," he called, increasing the movement of the patients a hundred-fold. It reminded Ruth of chemistry class, where they talked about Brownian motion. All the patients were shuffling in one direction, bumping into one another, then shuffling in another.

Bob stood in the middle of the melee. "Calm down, everyone. No one is going home today. Go back to what you were doing." Some patients sat down again, picked up their cards like automatons. Others wandered down the hall to their rooms.

"Don't let them leave you here," called Turner. The still moving patients turned around, started wandering towards Ruth.

"Enough," said Bob. "You're coming with me." He grabbed Sgt. Turner's chair and pushed it into his room, closing the door behind him. "Now, the rest of you, settle down."

When everyone finally settled, he came into the nursing station and confronted Ruth. "Rookie mistake, Miss Maclean. Didn't we explain why we don't celebrate Christmas on the ward? I'm surprised at you."

Ruth hung her head in shame. "I guess I was overexcited after hearing Mrs. Matthews had gone home."

"You should know better."

"And I do. I'm sorry." Was she ever going to be able to stop apologizing for silly things she did? She could hear her father's voice reprimanding her for being too loud in church. Suddenly, all that shame slid over her like molasses.

Bob crossed his arms and scowled. "And here I thought you were really learning things here."

Ruth's guilt was tipping over into annoyance. She tipped it back, knowing Bob was right. "I have learned so much, especially from you. I couldn't have made it through this rotation without you and the other orderlies. You've saved my … you've saved me so many times! Though I don't think I can ever forgive you for that pudding man."

There was a moment of silence, and then Bob guffawed. "We got you good that time. You shoulda seen your face. And then you turned it around on poor Ned. He still hides when he sees a needle coming toward him." He wiped his eyes. "Ah, you're okay. Just a rookie yet. You'll do better when you are old and bitter like me."

Ruth looked at him. How old was he? The orderlies looked all sorts of ages, but it was hard to pick which one. She couldn't resist asking.

"How long have you worked here, Bob?"

"Almost twenty years," said Bob, stretching. "Started by running the mail around. Lotta changes, lotta bad things, some good things. Way too many students. But you did ok, gotta admit. Held your own, even with that a … Turner. I'd better go check on him. That new orderly won't have — he prefers to hang out with the quiet ones."

He left the nursing station with a wave.

"Whew," said Ruth. Twenty years! He must've seen so many changes. She bent to do charting.

Suddenly the alarm bell was shouting in her ears. What had happened? She bolted up and out of the station, racing down the hall.

FORTY-FOUR

Sgt. Turner tries again

She raced to the room with the red light. It was Sgt. Turner's. The new orderly followed her. "Call the supervisor," she shouted to him. He dashed off and Ruth pushed her way into the room. The patient was on the floor, his arm restraints off the chair arms and pulled tight against his neck. He was turning red, his lips already changing to blue. Bob was trying to tug the restraint open.

"Damn military sure know how to tie knots. Got scissors on you?"

Ruth felt for her hidden bandage scissors that she didn't let anyone know she carried, pulled them out and handed them to Bob

Bob laughed briefly. "Knew you would." He sawed at the restraint, sliding the blunt side of the scissors up along Turner's neck. Though the blades were sharp, the restraints were designed to be difficult to cut, and it was slow going. The room filled with other personnel, other orderlies and a doctor or two, summoned by the alarm. Ruth was sitting at Sgt. Turner's head, holding his neck in place as Bob sawed. Eventually, the restraint popped open, and they immediately flipped him onto his back. "Get rid of the other restraints," said Bob.

"Already doing it," said Ruth, undoing the ones left holding the patient in place.

"Is he breathing?"

Bob leaned down. "Nope."

One of the doctors pushed in near the patient. "Turn him over. Pull his arms, nurse. We'll try to pump his lungs."

They flipped the poor fellow over and pulled his arms back and forward several times. "Any luck?"

They flipped him back, and the doctor listened to his chest, then sat back on his heels and thumped Sgt. Turner's chest with his fist. Once, twice, then listened again. "One more time with the arms," he directed.

"Probably broke a rib," muttered Bob. "This is going to hurt."

They pulled back and forth and suddenly Sgt. Turner coughed and breathed. "Lift him into the bed! Kneeling on the floor is hell on my back," directed the doctor. Two orderlies lifted Sgt. Turner up and put him gently onto the bed. Sgt. Turner shouted as his broken rib was moved, then woke fully and looked around, his eyes filled with hate. They settled on Ruth.

"You! You stopped me again! I am going to kill you!" he shouted, reaching for her. She leapt back, and the orderlies leapt in.

"Get out of here," yelled Bob to Ruth. "We'll manage it from here," he added in a softer voice. Ruth, tears brimming, fled the room and ran to the nursing station, where she put her head on her hands. After a few tears, she shook herself, pulled out Sgt. Turner's chart, and started writing what had happened while she could remember it. Occasionally she shuddered with fright, but she told herself she would not let him make her cry. As she wrote, she realized she'd managed to separate herself from her pity for the man.

Bob came back to the nursing station. "Call an ambulance," he called through the glass. "He needs to go to KGH."

Ruth did so, putting on her sweetest voice. KGH was swamped with patients as always, and dealing with a suicidal psychotic wouldn't be their favourite task. In fewer minutes than she expected, the ambulance attendants were knocking on the door. She went to meet them.

"You're fast!"

"You got lucky. We were already nearby. What's up?"

"Suicide attempt."

"Oh great, what a way to start the new year. Is he with it?"

"Relatively …," said Ruth.

"Oh, oh. Where?" She pointed to the room and dashed back to finish the charting. The attendants would want to take it with them.

The doctor who did the thumping came into the station. "Here, let me have it," he said, putting out his hand. She noticed it was bruised.

"You must've really hit him hard," said Ruth.

"What? Oh yes, needed to get that ticker going again. Here you go," he added, tossing the chart to Ruth, who caught it before it hit her face. "Sorry, I'm going to have to ride with him to the hospital. Got to get my coat. Can you draw up that medication for him before we go?"

"I still need my narcotics checked. Could you do that with me before I go?"

"Are you the only nurse on here again? This is completely unacceptable. I'll be talking to the Board about this. Okay, let's get going."

They got the drug ready, and Ruth loaded it on her carry tray. How was she going to give it to him? When she got to the door of his room, Sgt. Turner saw her and roared. "I'll fucking kill you! I will! Come over here so I can get my hands on you!"

Ruth quailed, but then four orderlies stepped up to the bed, undid his restraints, grabbed a patient limb each, and flipped him like he was a blanket. In no time, he was lying on his stomach, one orderly on each limb, and they'd pulled down his pants, exposing his buttocks for the shot. Ruth, still trembling, crept close and, taking a deep breath, prepped the needle and stabbed it into him. She barely got the dose in before he bucked, breaking the needle in his skin. Ruth pinched it in her fingers and twisted it out, and said, "Now, that's going to leave a mark," before she ran out of the room. She collapsed in the nursing station, laughing hysterically. The orderlies found her there some minutes later, still giggling while she charted the medication given in shaky handwriting. Soon the ambulance attendants, one orderly, and the doctor grabbed the chart and rolled the gurney with the unconscious Sgt. Turner down the hall and out the door.

Predictably, King Leonard was in the hallway, watching the action. "Good riddance. One of my most troublesome subjects." He told everyone until some of the other patients pulled him into a card game.

"Well," said Bob, collapsing into a chair and threatening to make it crash to the floor. "Let's hope that's the last we hear of him for a while." He pulled the bandage scissors out of his pocket and handed them to Ruth. "These might need a sharpening after all that," he said.

Ruth, giggling, said, "They might."

Bob looked at her strangely. "Anything funny?"

"No," she hiccupped. "I just can't seem to stop laughing. The way you guys flipped him, like a pancake. It was hilarious." And she swirled into laughter again.

"Go get her a cup of sweet tea," Bob commanded. One of

the unknown orderlies went to do so, quickly, which Ruth might have found alarming except she was still laughing.

When the orderly came back, Dr. Hartman was with him. Ruth, giggling, turned away. "I'm fine," she said between hiccups. "It was just funny."

"Drink this," said Bob. "It'll help with the shock."

Ruth obediently sipped the sweet, sweet tea. How much sugar had they put in it, she wondered? Eventually, both her giggles and hiccups stopped. When she looked around, she saw so many concerned eyes she almost started laughing again.

"Whew," she said instead. "That was a good laugh. Thanks for the tea. Did everyone get away all right?"

Deep, relieved breaths all around the room.

"Not surprising that you'd have a reaction to all that," said Richard, using his soothing voice. Ruth seethed. Quietly. She sensed she was under supervision. Not wise to show too much emotion when being assessed or she might end up neighbours with his majesty. She so hated being patronized.

"Well, it was pretty wild. Bob was great," she said, patting his hand. "He knew exactly what to do and saved the patient. Fantastic."

"Well, someone else helped a lot," said Bob, abashed. "All in a bad day's work."

They laughed together, easy with each other. Gosh, Ruth was going to miss this. Richard was watching her, but she ignored him. "And then he had to break the needle off," she added. "At least I was able to get it out."

"That takes real skill, especially while he's bucking like a horse." Bob slapped the counter and stood up. "Well, we'd better get back to the boring work."

"Yes," said Ruth, standing. "Lots to do still."

"Oh no," said Richard. "You're staying here until I'm sure you're okay."

Ruth pushed by him, followed Bob out. "I'm fine and so sugared up I need to move around. Besides, there's only another," she looked at her watch, "three hours in my shift left."

"I'm calling the supervisor," said Richard.

"Good luck with that," said Bob, grinning at Ruth. He came along as she did rounds, and Ruth wasn't sure who was supporting who. They were both feeling wobbly.

"Why does he feel he needs to take care of me?" Ruth asked Bob.

He shrugged. "You seem to be able to handle yourself. But I could use a drink," said Bob.

"Me, too," said Ruth. "Pity we lady nurses can't be seen having one."

"A grand pity." They walked along, checking on everyone, calming them down after the excitement. The only one who couldn't settle was the king. Pills helped.

Thanks

The end of the shift couldn't come soon enough. All the patients were fractious, and Ruth and the rest of the staff were feeling fragile and overtired.

"How do you stand it, Bob?" Ruth sat, flipping through the charts she had to complete and trying to keep the tears from slipping down her cheek.

"What? Being knighted five times a day?" He smiled, but his eyes were sad. "No, I know. It's tough, those people who are so sick they don't want to live. Or even trying to look after our permanent residents. But those folks we can try to do something with. The suicidal ones just scare me. I don't understand them."

"He's Catholic, too. Wouldn't he be worried about going to hell?"

"I dunno. Maybe he feels he's already experienced it. Those pictures from the camps are horrible."

Ruth nodded, tucked the charts into the rack. "I know. They make me sick." She sighed. "I don't understand the cruelty."

The new shift staff entered the nursing station, talking and laughing. They took one look at Ruth and said, "Okay, what happened?"

Ruth wearily started giving report while they settled in. When she got to Sgt. Turner, she couldn't continue, and Bob filled in some of the side bits. The replacement nurse rested her hand on Ruth's shoulder. "You sure have paid your dues here, Miss Maclean. And you are still standing. Good for you."

"I've had such help," Ruth replied, her voice breaking. "It would have been too hard without that. I wouldn't have made it without all of you."

Everyone moved in for a group hug until King Leonard knocked on the door. "I'll go," said the Jim, who had just come on shift. "You get out of here."

They didn't need to be asked twice. Ruth was galloping towards the exit when she remembered the note from Mrs. Matthews. Turning on her heel, she went to 2A and gathered it. She tucked it in her pocket to read at home, not trusting her fragile emotions to handle it in public.

Fortunately, Leahurst was empty when she arrived, and she could head up to her room with no one noticing. She took off her uniform and got into her pyjamas, dug under her mother's quilt. She wished she'd kept a journal for this time in the OH. No one would believe all she had seen. Gathering herself, she opened the note from Mrs. Matthews.

> Dear Nurse Maclean,
> I was finally able to see my babies this morning. They have grown so much! I barely knew them. But they cuddled in to me and I could feel love for them. That hadn't happened before. My sister came and she is going to take all of us to her home to recover. That wouldn't have been allowed except for all the things you and Dr. Hartman did

for me. The social worker told my husband I needed to be away from him. He doesn't know this will be permanent.

I don't know how best to thank you, except to say you are an excellent nurse. I always felt safe when you were around. Please know I will never forget you. Thank you, a million times.

Yours, Elizabeth Matthews

Ruth folded the note over and took a deep breath. If only her mother were alive. She could send her this note to put up in the closet. The day and the past few months all caught up with Ruth, and she cried herself to sleep.

She woke the next morning with crusts in her eyes and her hair spun into a knot of curls. She must have thrashed when asleep. Small wonder. She had today off, but tomorrow was her final evaluation. Ruth couldn't help but think of the evaluation she had after her placement at the San. Lots of positive things, balanced with an equal number of reprimands for speaking out of turn or being too aggressive or demanding too much. And all the problems with George. One of the negative comments was about how she hadn't stood up immediately for a doctor on rounds, but she'd been taking a bedpan away from a patient and she would not leave him lying on it while she posed. He was just skin and bones, and the pressure on his hips must have been sore. She'd tried to rationalize it with Mrs. Graham, but she just raised her eyebrows about her speaking out, so she'd stopped.

Well, there was nothing she could do about things now. She wondered if she'd be docked points for helping Mrs. Matthews. Shaking her head, she knew she wasn't sorry. Points or no.

Today she had plans, though. She was meeting Mary to look for thank you treats for their placement floor nurses. Most of the students didn't do this, but that Mary was so sweet. She'd started doing it with her placements and now Ruth didn't feel she could leave without dropping off a bundle. At least, not without feeling guilty. Ruth wanted to get a present for the inmates, too, something they'd want. She thought a new set of cards, perhaps. They played all the time there and the set they had was getting worn. And those wouldn't be dangerous, like a new ashtray might be.

By the time she got down to the Dieu, Mary was waiting eagerly on the steps of the new nursing residence. "It's so nice," she said, posing against the wall. "Much better than where we used to live."

"I'm glad. I'm going to be glad to get back to the regular nurses' residence. I was freezing half the time at Leahurst."

"I remember. But as senior nurses, we could live out. Are you still thinking about trying to get a job there?"

Ruth hugged herself. She needed the comfort. "I don't know. Last shift, one of our patients tried to kill himself. It was awful."

"Oh, my golly! And scary."

"But everyone was so wonderful, looking after me, making sure I was all right. Even Rich … the orderlies gathered around. They are the most supportive group I've met. I'm really going to miss everyone."

"Everyone? Richard was there?" Mary asked, peering at Ruth.

"Oh yes, he was. All protective, telling me to sit down and rest when I still had half a shift's work to do. Hovering." She tossed her head in annoyance.

"Silly. He cares about you."

"Not enough, apparently. We still haven't spoken about him going up north."

"Whose fault is that?" Mary stomped a lump of snow into a pancake. "Honestly. You haven't spoken to him at all, have you? Except to get offended."

Ruth slumped with shame. She had been hard on him, but if he wasn't interested, there was no point in wasting time on him, was there?

"Look — there's the shop with the cards. Let's go in," she added, glad to stop this line of conversation. Ruth ended up buying two sets of cards, one bigger than the other. "Some of them don't see very well," she explained.

"What else? I always get some chocolates or something." Mary pointed down the street. "Austin's Drugs must have some. Or Abramsky's. They have everything."

"Not since the Christmas sales. Did you see the mob lining up there before Christmas Eve? By the time I got in, the shelves were bare. I wonder if they have had a chance to restock, given all the weather."

Austin's Drugs did have chocolates, but they were expensive enough to take the rest of the money Ruth had. "Whew. That's it for me," she said. "I don't even have enough for the bus."

"Let's get a hot drink. My treat!" said Mary.

When Ruth looked like she'd object, Mary put up her hand. "No fighting. I've got some money, you don't, we're both cold. No arguing," she said, with a merry laugh. "Besides, I want to pump you more about the hospital. Who should I speak to about a job, do you think?"

They spent a cozy hour whispering together over a couple of hot chocolates.

"I can't believe you are nearly all finished, Nurse Mary Lavoie! Soon you'll be a full RN!"

"And you! In a few weeks, you'll have your cap and be ready to take on the world!"

"I hope so," said Ruth. "I'm so sure I'll get into trouble for a bunch of things I did. Maybe they will have forgotten."

"They can't be that bad! What did you do, after all?"

"It's all about the chain of command. I simply can't take that on properly, though I've learned how to be quiet — most of the time!"

"Hope not," laughed Mary. "You're at your best when you are challenging someone. Except boys."

Ruth swatted her with a mitten. "We'd best be going. It's already getting dark."

"Yes," said Mary. "And I have a parting gift for you. Bus fare."

Ruth smiled. "You are the best. My soon to be warm body thanks you. My treat next time."

Mary waved her hand airily and headed off, while Ruth went to the bus stop. While she was waiting, she spotted Richard walking down the other side of the street, but she didn't call out, suddenly ashamed.

FORTY-SIX

Evaluation

The next day, Ruth was up early to iron her uniform, clean her shoes, and wrestle her hair into a bun. It was a windy, freezing walk across the street from Leahurst. By the time she was up to her ward door, she was a nervous wreck and her hair wasn't helping, having chosen to spring out in odd places.

"Come in, come in," Miss Thomas called, as Ruth hesitated at the nursing station door. "We're going to meet in the teaching room downstairs. No one is using it today and it will give us a bit more privacy."

Ruth blanched but took some comfort from the smiles of the other staff in the nursing station. They walked down the endless hallways, Ruth wishing she had some handy small talk, but her mouth was too dry to move. Finally, they arrived, and Miss Thomas unlocked the door. "In here. You just sit over there." They both sat and Miss Thomas opened a file.

"Do you have your checklist?"

"Yes," said Ruth, pulling the mangled paper out of her pocket. She tried to flatten it out.

"Hmm," said Miss Thomas. "Not very tidy."

Ruth was going to explain it was mangled in the Sgt. Turner emergency, but kept her mouth shut.

Miss Thomas looked at her, a twinkle in her eye. "I believe you've been in a few situations where you had other things to think about. Let me look at it."

Ruth pushed it over, shamefacedly.

"Well, it seems like you've completed all of your assigned tasks," said Miss Thomas. "But you've forgotten some things." She bent over the paper, writing furiously. "There, that's better," she said, handing it back to Ruth, who was visibly sweating.

She read: "Acted as lead nurse on several occasions without supervision when the hospital was short-staffed. Demonstrated good judgement and skills. Had no concerns leaving her in this role." And "Assisted with control of a violent patient on several occasions, including helping to prevent a suicide attempt."

Miss Thomas said, "That was particularly impressive. Most students, after one attack, take to hiding in the nursing station. You just kept going out. The staff are singing your praises. But the last one is my gold star." She pointed to the list again.

"Acted as an advocate for a patient in danger, involving other team members and working towards a positive outcome for the patient. Nursing care plan for this patient was excellent."

Ruth read this over and looked up, tears in her eyes. "Oh, thank you, Miss Thomas! I was so lucky to have such a wonderful team with me. I couldn't have kept on without them."

"Noble of you to say so, but if I may beg to differ, I get the feeling you'd have been fine. You seem to have won the entire hospital over."

"Really?"

Miss Thomas laughed. "Well, there's one doctor who wasn't pleased, but he's leaving for Toronto, so I think we can ignore his input. He didn't like your trick of transferring his patient over the holidays. I, however, thought it was brilliant." She blushed, astonishing Ruth. "That doctor kept waving donations in my face, and you know how short on money we are here. I couldn't turn him away, even if it turned my stomach to be friendly to him — to both him and Mrs. M.'s husband, who was also offering money every time it looked like I might stand in his way. We had to get the Board involved. Never tell a soul this," she added.

"I never would!" Ruth sagged, relieved.

"You should also know that this is probably the most positive review I've given to a student for years. Except our own students, of course. Don't let it go to your head. You still have a lot to learn."

"I know," said Ruth, her heart tap-dancing in her chest. She felt like bursting with joy.

"That said, if you continue to do well with the rest of your training, you'd be most welcome to come back and join us. If that interests you, of course. I know a lot of nurses don't want to work in a place like this."

"With this team? And these patients?" Ruth gulped. "I'd be honoured. Of course, I still have to finish my training."

"And something else may call to your heart," said Miss Thomas. "I only mention it because you fit in so well here. Your calmness in the face of various storms was noted. And the orderlies enjoyed working with you."

"For that calmness in the face of disaster, I have to thank my family," Ruth smiled. "But the orderlies were the best," she added. "Even if they tried to scare me on my first night shift."

"What?" Miss Thomas turned to her, serious.

Ruth realized her mistake. "Oh, it was just a little tease. No harm done. We all laughed."

Mrs. Thomas shook her head. "I told them to stop with the chocolate pudding trick. They must have really liked you if they dared do it again."

Ruth laughed to herself. Just big boys, those orderlies. Big, extremely helpful boys.

"Well, do you have anything to say to me?"

"Yes." Ruth caught her breath. "Thank you so much for this experience. I was able to see so much, participate in so many treatments and interventions. I feel like I've learned way more than I expected to. Thank you for trusting me with the patients. It was a great placement. If I had anything to say, it would be about the supervisors …"

"Say no more. The walls have ears. But I know to what you refer. Believe me, between some of we nurses and the physicians, there will be a change in the ranks very soon. Especially if we get some replacement nurses on staff …" She winked at Ruth.

"I think my friend Mary Lavoie is thinking of applying," Ruth said, realizing she shouldn't have as soon as it popped out of her mouth. When would she learn to keep her mouth shut?

"That would be delightful. I think she did very well. Tell her to write to me and I'll see if I can expedite things."

"Oh, could you? That would be wonderful."

"Well, I must get back to work. It has been a great experience having you here." She stood and offered her hand to Ruth. They shook hands, Ruth barely believing her luck.

"I need to get back, too. I'm way behind on my rounds."

"Not you, my girl. You've got the rest of the day off."

"But … am I to come back later?"

"No, unfortunately. Your placement is over. Time to pack up and return to the nest."

"Really?" Ruth felt herself on the edge of tears. "Can I come up and say goodbye?"

"No one would speak to me again if I didn't let you! Shall we?"

The walk back to the ward seemed shorter, but perhaps that was because Ruth was floating gently along on happiness. When they got back, Ruth picked up a bag she'd tucked into the medicine room and dealt out the chocolates and the packs of cards.

"Perfect," said Bob. "The other cards stick together and they all cheat." He smiled, with a little sad twist and a trace of chocolate in the corner of his mouth. "Hope to see you around," he said. "It's been fun."

Ruth hugged everyone to the frowns of Miss Thomas, who eventually joined in. She left the nursing station to make one more turn around the floor, stopping to see all her patients one more time. She couldn't tell them she was leaving, of course, but she mentally told them farewell and said a quiet prayer over them.

Finally, she went to the locked door and Bob let her out. "You take care of yourself, now."

Ruth swallowed. "You, too. And ... thanks for everything." She fought not to cry. She already missed everyone.

She fled down to the locker room and was packing up her uniform bits and pieces when Richard appeared in the hallway.

"I see you're done," he said, shortly.

"Yes."

"Ruth," he began.

"Thank you for all your help, Dr. Hartman. And the best of luck up in Frobisher Bay." She tried to smile, but couldn't, and ended pushing past him to exit the hospital. Her heart still ached about him. Ruth spent the rest of the morning saying goodbye to the housemates and packing up her tiny room. She quite loved it, chill wind, tiny closet and long run to the washroom and everything. She and Doris vowed to keep in touch, Doris saying she'd pump Alison about the situation with her patients. They set up a time to meet the following Saturday.

But she wondered. Would she be able to fit in with her old classmates? It seemed like they'd been separated forever. She'd missed a bunch of dances and the Christmas singing and so much else. Would they hold that against her?

FORTY-SEVEN

Back to the nurses' residence and KGH

She needn't have worried. When she got back to the residence, carrying her bundles, she was sprung on by Betty and a bunch of the other students, all cheering and waving her along. Her room had a big "Welcome back!" sign on it, and someone had pressed up a cap and perched it on her bed.

She burst into tears and hugged everyone so much they begged for breath.

"How was it?"

"How did you survive?"

"Was it scary?"

"Did you meet anyone nice?"

"Did any of the patients try to marry you?"

Ruth's head was spinning trying to answer questions, but she laughed at that one. "No, but I was knighted. I'm official now. Subject to the whims of King Leo." She put her hand up. "Enough about me! What's been happening here? Tell me everything!"

More confused talking from everyone until Betty took pity on her and dragged her to the kitchen for a cup of tea. The noise gradually decreased as the other students wandered off.

"Everyone is so glad to have you back," said Betty. "We really missed you at the San. Even the patients were asking about you!"

"Oh, how nice of them, but also, how sad they are still there."

"Yes, even with the streptomycin, it takes a long time to clear up. And many of the soldiers there are dealing with injuries and shell shock and TB. I'm amazed they even try to get better."

"Will they end up at the OH, do you think?"

"Some will, that's for certain. Of course, they can't go there with active TB."

"I can't imagine. Poor patients."

"Yes. It was tough watching some of them struggle but that's nothing new for you. Now that you've become a TB and mental health expert, when are you going to get caught up with your other placements?"

"I don't know," said Ruth. "I've missed a chunk of time. I'm afraid they'll put me on something tough by myself or something. It would be nice to be with my class for a change." Ruth put her head in her hands. "I feel like I am soloing through my program."

"Well, at least we're in classes for the next while, before the big capping! Are you excited? You'll for sure get it this year."

Ruth put down her tea, afraid of spilling. "I don't want to say anything, but yes, I think I might!"

"I should think so. You've put up with a lot."

"Tis the fate of every nurse," intoned Ruth, rolling her eyes.

Betty snorted. "You are soooooo right. We start classes tomorrow. I hope you kept up your studying! We're all counting on reading your notes."

Ruth laughed. "Let me get settled first. Thanks for decorating my room, by the way."

"I've hidden some chocolate in there. Just don't tell anyone or they will all want some."

"You're a doll, Betty. I'm so happy to be back."

The rest of the evening was spent catching up with all the latest news about beaus and head nurses, doctors and medical students, dances, soldiers, RMC cadets, and the plans for the capping ceremony.

"It's all very hush-hush," said one student. "It's going to be a bit more of a ceremony than before, with the padre and everything. Gosh, if I fail, it is going to be so embarrassing."

Ruth agreed. "Who was the person who expertly pressed my cap? I've got it perched carefully in my closet in case I need it."

Everyone laughed and cheered. One student piped up, "That's Susan — she's a pro. Gets all the folds just right. She did it for free this time, especially for the ceremony, but she usually charges for every press. Then she buys treats for us, so we get our money back, anyway."

Susan bowed her head. "That's only because you'd kill me if I didn't. The amount of peanut butter you gals eat!"

By the time Ruth was ready for bed, she was all talked out. Everyone seemed so excited, probably because they'd just come off placements and were looking forward to sleeping in a bit. Ruth was so overwhelmed she almost forgot to call her family and let them know she'd moved. She tiptoed downstairs to where a student watched over the phone. "May I make a call?"

"Sure, just write the time and date in the book and sign your name."

Ruth did so and tried to phone home. This time she got right through. "Hello, Father! How is everyone? ... I wanted to let you know I'm back at the KGH nurses' residence." She passed on the number again, vowing to write it in a letter to Meg the following night because she was sure he'd lose it. "Say hi to Meg for me?" she asked, but he'd already hung up. Phone calls were expensive, she knew, but he didn't have to hang up so fast. Besides, she was paying for this one.

Saying goodnight to the duty student, she dragged herself upstairs, quietly unpacking the rest of her belongings. She remembered her awful night the previous year, when the matron came stomping down and yelled at her for squeaking her cupboard door. Smiling, she thought of the thorny matron, who eventually became head of the Sanatorium, and sometimes even complimented Ruth. So much had happened since then.

Suddenly, her stomach fell. First thing the next morning, she'd be meeting with her new supervisor, hear if she might get her cap, and perhaps be told how she'd be making up her extra placement. Awash with dread, she pulled out her aunt's little blue prayer book and read some prayers to herself. And a few for Mrs. Matthews and King Leo and even Sgt. Turner. And even more for her friends over at the hospital. She missed them already.

The prayers didn't help her anxiety. She still twisted and turned in bed, but after the busy day, so emotion-filled, she couldn't worry for long. Soon she was wrapped in her mother's quilt and heavy slumber.

FORTY-EIGHT

Meeting the head

The morning dawned and Ruth dressed carefully again, checking for runs in her stockings (they would run, always when she wasn't expecting it). Fortunately, she hadn't worn her Christmas stockings yet, and they were in perfect shape — until she pulled them over her toes. Drat. She had a tiny sharp edge to her toenail she'd meant to trim, and it bit into the stockings. She quickly painted the toe of the stocking with nail polish and waved her hand over it to dry it off before she put on her shoes.

It wasn't completely dry when she had to go, and she said a silent prayer that she'd be able to take her shoes off without the stockings sticking and tearing more. The number of pairs of stockings she'd gone through was seriously impacting her budget.

When she went downstairs to the nursing office, she expected to see Miss Acton, the Superintendent, but instead a supervisor she didn't know greeted her.

"Hello Miss Maclean. I am Miss Westcott. I supervise your class group. I haven't had the chance to meet you before. Mrs. Balch, who you met in the fall, retired."

"Oh. Hello!" Ruth stood awkwardly until Miss Westcott told

her to sit. She pulled her uniform tight as she sat, to hide any wrinkles. She could feel her toes sticking to her shoes. And her stockings pulling at her toes.

"I have here your report from your placement in the Ontario Hospital."

Ruth bit her lip to keep it from quivering.

"It seems you managed to stay out of trouble this time."

Gosh, thought Ruth. Will they never let that go? She looked down in case her eyes showed her impatience.

"In fact, you seem to have outdone yourself. Your head nurse is singing your praise, and even offered you a position in their program, should you want it. How did you feel about the placement?"

Ruth's head was spinning, but she gathered herself. "It was an excellent placement, Miss Westcott. They allowed me to see and participate in lots of procedures, from ward work to lobotomies. Everyone was extremely helpful, and I feel as if the twelve weeks of placement gave me enough time to really understand what they do at the Ontario Hospital."

"Prettily said, Miss Maclean. Were you safe at all times?"

"Well, there was one dangerous patient, but the orderlies made sure I was always safe."

"I heard. Now, there was one complaint about you from a patient's husband. Can you tell me about this?"

Ruth broke out into a sweat, but tried to explain what had happened, the support of the other nurses and doctors at the hospital about the situation.

Miss Westcott remained silent until Ruth had finished. "Yes, this is what your head nurse has written here. I wanted to ask to see if your recollection was the same. We know you've had problems with men before."

"Only ones that push themselves at me," retorted Ruth, before slapping her mouth shut. There was an evaluative pause.

"Fair enough. I think we should expunge the experience you had at the San from our records. After all, you were technically not our student then. I see no reason to include it in your permanent record."

"Oh, thank you!" Ruth held back a tear of relief.

"Unfortunately, a lot of the people around Kingston heard the story, so it may take a while to live it down. If you keep up excellent work like this, I'm certain that eventually no one will remember it."

"Are you saying …"

"Yes, Miss Maclean. Congratulations. You have won the right to attend the capping ceremony, provided you pass your exams in the next weeks."

"I will, I will," Ruth said, her voice high and excited. She could barely sit still.

The supervisor smiled at her. "You may go."

Ruth burst out of the room and flew up the stairs, where she crashed in on Betty, who was just finishing dressing. "I'm in! I'm getting capped!" Betty grabbed her hands and jumped up and down with her.

"Shh," another student going by said. "Remember, some are sleeping."

"Oh, yes," said Ruth, crouching down to be smaller and make less noise. "Are you ready for class? I feel like I'm going to explode if I don't get to run around."

"Yes, let's go. You can scream and yell when we cross the street for breakfast."

They raced out, capes flying, and hopped and danced across the street while the few people outside watched in bemusement. When they got to the cafeteria at KGH, her classmates came up to see what the excitement was and joined in until one grumpy doctor told them to shush. After that, they whispered in giggles, everyone excited about the upcoming capping ceremony.

"Hope we all pass!"

"Me, too," said Ruth. She didn't want anyone to suffer what she and Betty had been through. Betty had to repeat after being reprimanded for too much partying with the boys. She'd assured Ruth that wasn't going to be a problem this time. Ruth hoped she was right. Nursing instructors have long memories. If any of them had seen Betty with a fellow, they would be likely to form the wrong impression. And Betty hadn't told Ruth what her evaluation results were.

"Well," said Betty, "We'd better go. Don't want to miss out by being late for class."

Everyone stood and cleared their places, trying not to speak too much as they passed the shushing doctor. They ran back to the residence, this time through the tunnel that linked the residence to the hospital.

"I sure missed this over at Leahurst," said Ruth. "I hated having to get all dressed up every time I went from one to the other — but it was so cold!"

After Ruth and Betty hung up their coats, they ran downstairs, arriving at nine on the dot.

"What are you? A herd of elephants?" The instructor said, frowning mightily. "And close that door. Where were you raised — in a barn?"

Not a good way to start, thought Ruth, but soon they were talking about surgical care, and it was all so fascinating she had no problem staying focused.

"Is Miss Maclean here?"

Oh, oh, thought Ruth. She raised her hand.

"I understand you observed a transorbital leucotomy when you were at the Ontario Hospital. As it is not likely to be performed very often, I'm wondering if you could share the procedure with us while it's fresh in your mind."

"It was … quite awful to watch," Ruth said. "And the doctor

was not a fan of aseptic technique. He didn't even wash his hands."

Gasps filled the room. The instructor was drawing a head on the board. "Could you come up and show us how it worked? I'm quite fascinated myself."

Ruth talked them through it, discussing how the bone behind the eye was very thin and that made it possible to access the brain easily.

"This is why I wanted you to talk about this. As nurses, we need to be aware of where the weaker parts of our bone structure are, in case of injury. When I was at the front, we saw lots of eye and eye orbit injuries, probably a few leading to inadvertent lobotomies. We need to be aware to assess any damage." The instructor gazed at her drawing, pointing out the various places that could be easily damaged.

"You were at the front?" one of the students asked.

"Oh yes. Probably the best professional years of my life." She paused. "But so so sad. I hope never to have to experience that again."

The rest of the class leapt in, asking questions about where she'd been stationed and how it went and what she saw and who she worked with, and the instructor quickly realized the lesson was over for the day. She turned her chair and sat, calling for questions. After about half an hour, she dismissed them with a, "Remember to study, girls. You aren't through yet."

"What an interesting life she's led," said Betty. "I wish I could have served overseas."

The instructor heard her. "Let's hope you don't get the chance. From what I hear, the Russians are still refusing to settle to the Marshall plan. Looks like we might be back at war sooner than we want." She sighed. "Believe me, we don't want to go through that all again."

"I sure don't want rationing again! We're still getting over it."

"The UK is even worse off. Perhaps we can put together a parcel to send. I know some people who are mailing sugar."

"Really? Oh, let's do that. My aunt lives in Brighton. She could share it around." The student, Cherry, turned to the rest of the class. "It wouldn't cost us much."

"All right girls, off you go to study. We can talk about this later."

They scampered to their rooms and soon all that could be heard was the turning of pages, and some whimpering from one of the younger students.

FORTY-NINE

Exams

The weeks up to the exams flew by. Ruth enjoyed doing the academic work. It reminded her of when she studied in high school and how things would suddenly become clear. The students gathered in groups and reviewed nursing care and treatments and assessment skills needed for care on the surgical wards. When exam day finally came, most of them felt ready. They trooped down to their classroom and sat, pencils sharpened, waiting for the exam. The room had been set up in exam format, with chairs and desk as far apart as possible to prevent any cheating. Each desk had an answer book on it, ready to be filled in. Every student was silent, trying to hold on to what they'd learned. Ruth knew that if she talked to anyone, bits of what she'd learned would fall out.

Miss Westcott brought in the exam papers and handed them out, face down. She set up an alarm clock with an unpleasantly loud tick on the front desk, set the alarm, and then told the students, "You may flip over your exam papers. Good luck everyone." As Ruth worked her way through the exam, trying to ignore the ticking sound that seemed to get louder and louder with each passing minute, she realized there was still so much she didn't know. The others had much more experience on KGH's wards than she did. She had a moment of panic and gazed up at the clock, envisioning tossing it into the lake. Gritting her teeth, she finished the questions she knew and then went back to puzzle out the less familiar ones. If she failed now, at the gate, she decided, she was going to give up, head back to Cloyne, marry some sweaty unsuccessful farmer and just drudge her way through her life. Right?

No! She shook her head and looked more closely. Surely she knew this stuff. After all, she'd helped with the surgeries at the San, and the treatments at the Ontario Hospital. She plucked what she could find out of the back of her mind and finished just in time, laying her pencil down as the alarm on the cursed clock went off.

Everyone paraded quietly out of the room, as Miss Westcott called out, "I'll have your results by two this afternoon."

No one seemed happy. They sat around, quietly sipping tea and gazing at the floor until Betty said, "I'm not waiting around for the axe to fall. Who's up for a walk downtown? We can have a celebratory lunch just for finishing!"

Quite a few of the girls stood up and went to get their coats, somewhat unenthusiastically. It was sleeting out, and the temperature was uncomfortably cold, but once they left the building, Ruth could hear them shouting and laughing together. She stayed back.

"Not going with Betty?" asked another student.

"No. I'm too nervous. You're staying in, too?"

"Can't afford another outing. My father has been sick, so I've had to send whatever money I get home."

"Oh, I'm so sorry to hear that! Can I help in any way?" Ruth walked over and sat beside the student on the couch.

"You could come to lunch with me at the hospital? I hate going alone."

"Sold. Let's go. Maybe if I eat something, these butterflies in my stomach will settle down."

They ran through the tunnel to the cafeteria together and gathered some stew and bread. Over lunch, they talked about everything except the exam and their families, ending up laughing together. Ruth was astonished she didn't really know her, but then she'd been away for so long.

"I know you, but I'll bet you don't know me. I joined up after you went to the OH."

"Oh, that explains it. I was feeling terrible."

"I'm Sandra Page. Glad to meet you."

They shook hands, laughing. "Look at the time!" said Ruth, checking her watch. "The exams should be back."

"That was fast. Thanks for waiting with me."

"Let's go get it over with, then." They both stood and slowly, filled with apprehension, headed back to the nurses' residence. As they arrived, they saw their classmates running towards them, late and panicking. Everyone crowded through the door, oddly silent as they hung up their cloaks, removed their boots, and put on their shoes.

Miss Westcott was standing in the hallway, and the girls screeched to a stop in front of her. Ruth wrung her fingers while she waited for everyone to settle down. "First, I should tell you that everyone passed." A whoop went up from the class until Miss Westcott put her hand up. "It was a close thing for some of you. I hope you will go back and revise before we head back to the wards." She paused until she had complete silence. "Since you all passed, you will all be invited to our new capping ceremony this weekend. You are welcome to invite two friends or family members. It will be at 7:30 PM on Saturday in the great hall at KGH."

Everyone looked at each other and whispers broke out. "You mean we won't be seeing Miss Acton individually?"

"No, we are trying something new this year. You all deserve something special. We've noticed how many times you have had to work beyond expectations because of staff shortages. Now, I've hung the list of marks downstairs in the classroom. No running!" she added as the class as one turned to go downstairs.

It took several nervous minutes for Ruth to push through to the list. She scanned it from the bottom up, terrified she'd ended up there, but no, she was right in the middle of the class. "Thank heavens," she said to herself as she pushed herself through the crowd. She'd seen Betty's mark, too, in the top third. She went to her room to congratulate her.

"Not surprising," said Betty, smiling widely. "It's my second time through, remember? Some of it must have stuck. It's amazing how much easier studying is with no boys around."

"Are you inviting anyone to the ceremony?"

Betty picked at her blanket. "I suppose I'll invite my parents, just to show them I didn't mess up this time. What about you?"

"It's so close to losing mother. My father probably won't want to come."

"And Billy? He can come, can't he?"

"It's too difficult to get his wheelchair through the snow and ice piles. He's been trapped in the Legion for weeks. It's hardly fair. I'll go show him my cap after the ceremony. Jerry was going to come, but he's been down with the flu for the past week. Poor guy — he's got hardly any lung left. I hope he doesn't end up in the hospital again. Billy doesn't want to leave him alone."

"Well, how about your sister? You could give her an excuse to get away from the family for a day."

"Brilliant idea," said Ruth. "I'll call her right now." She had heard little from Meg in the last few weeks, and it would be wonderful to have her visit and share her success. She scampered off to find a phone and waited while her classmates called their families. Finally, it was her turn, and she called the farm. After a brief talk, she hung up and turned away from everyone, heading up to her room.

"Oh, oh," said Betty, running after her. "What did she say?"

"I think she was tired out. She said she 'didn't have time to go gallivanting anywhere.'" Ruth pushed her knuckles into her eyes to block her tears. "She sounded just like Father."

Betty frowned. "Well, at least we'll all be here cheering you on!"

"I know," said Ruth, her eyes bright with unshed tears. "I just wish my mother …"

"Oh honey, I know. I know it's not anything, but I bought a chocolate bar when I was downtown — want some?"

Ruth laughed. "You and your chocolate! Yes, please!" Arm in arm, they went to Betty's room and shared the bar, discussing the upcoming ceremony and wondering what it would be like until Ruth almost forgot about not having any family there.

FIFTY

Capping

By the time Saturday arrived, the excitement in the residence was almost too much to bear. Susan was pressing up everyone's caps and there was a panic when one went missing, only to be found behind her bed. Everyone fought for the bathroom to wash and set their hair; some went downtown to the hairdressers. Near the end of the day, a delivery truck from the Chinese laundry arrived, full of starched and glaringly white uniform cuffs and bibs. The nurses fluttered into the mix like a flock of starlings, calling out and handing things around. The noise was unbearable, and the poor student on the phone reception could barely hear when people called. Ruth was hoping against hope that there might have been a call from Meg, changing her mind, but no call came.

They all ran to get a light dinner. "I'm not eating much," said Sandra. "I'm so afraid something will disagree with me in all the excitement." Everyone else seemed to feel the same way.

At long last, it was time to get dressed and ready. There were a few swears around the residence as they did so, followed by running feet as everyone shared stockings. Ruth had trimmed her nails extremely carefully the day before, and filed them, so she wasn't too worried, but she still took forever to get her stockings on. She had to hide the hole from the other day, and it kept twisting up.

"Come on!" yelled Betty. "We're going to miss the ceremony!"

"It's only seven," said Ruth. "Calm down." She stood and looked at herself in the mirror. For fun, she perched the cap on her head. There I am, all in my best bib & tucker, she thought.

"Beautiful," Betty knocked on Ruth's doorjamb. "Now, can we go?"

The sleet was still blowing horizontally, so they opted to take the tunnel. At night, it was cold, damp, and creepy, the bare concrete walls seeping moisture, but at least they could keep their hair and caps dry. When they got to the hall, they could hear the murmuring of the guests.

"Now girls," said Miss Westcott. "Line up alphabetically by your last name, please, and no fooling around. We'll wait out here in the hallway until everything gets started and then you will walk in one by one, slowly. Think wedding march slow. Miss Acton will return your cap and once you have it in place, go to the seats that are open for you. Sit in the order of your name there. The senior nurses will guide you. Now give me all your caps."

Betty and Ruth were close to each other in line, making it easy to share the excitement. The professors were all lined up in front of the students and they marched into the hall, looking very serious in their uniforms and caps.

Then the students started their procession. As they entered, they noticed the senior nurses were already lined up in front of the chairs. The juniors paraded slowly in, and when they had all arrived, the Superintendent started calling out their names, one by one, after instructing everyone to hold their applause until the end. Each nurse shook Miss Acton's hand, and had their cap put in place with the aid of a senior sister. After they were all capped, applause broke out in the room.

Ruth couldn't stop thinking of her mother, all she had done to help her reach this moment. She swallowed a sob.

"Now students, please stand for the prayer. Padre Laverty, will you lead us?" There was much scraping of chairs as everyone stood for the prayer.

He cleared his throat and began, shaking holy water over the class. "I anoint you in the name of the Father who created, loves, and sustains you, the Son who redeems you, and the Holy Spirit who empowers you. May your words and actions always bring comfort and healing to those you touch, to the honour and glory of God. Amen."

Each student and all the professors then received a candle. Miss Acton lit the first one, then the room lights were dimmed, and the candlelight was passed to the professors, then the senior students, and finally to the juniors.

"This represents the light of knowledge we pass through the ages of nurses. The light of sisterhood. The light of nursing, much as Florence Nightingale carried her lamp through the wards." Miss Acton was in her element, speaking in very serious tones.

"Now girls, please join me in reciting Florence Nightingale's pledge."

They all recited the pledge, something they were expected to learn on very their first day. The voices rang out, the candles flickered. "I solemnly pledge myself before God and in the presence of this assembly, to pass my life in purity and to practice my profession faithfully. I will abstain from whatever is deleterious and mischievous, and will not take or knowingly administer any harmful drug. I will do all in my power to maintain and elevate the standard of my profession, and will hold in confidence all personal matters committed to my keeping and all family affairs coming to my knowledge in the practice of my calling. With loyalty will I endeavour to aid the physician in his work and devote myself to the welfare of those committed to my care."

As she repeated the words, Ruth saw a parade of her patients in her head. Had she done her very best? For all of them?

Following the pledge, there was more applause and a few cheers from some boisterous guests.

"Now, class, you are officially student nurses, no longer probationary. Congratulations!" More applause, whistles, yelps. Ruth thought it was just as well her father wasn't there. He didn't like applause at serious events.

They turned up the lights, and the families joined the group to see their nurses. A few boyfriends planted kisses on their girls, to everyone's scandalized looks. Ruth didn't look around. There was no one she expected. The students extinguished their candles but were told to keep them as a reminder of the light of knowledge.

"Good for lighting cigarettes, too," said the student beside Ruth, but Ruth didn't respond. She was too wrapped up in the moment. Betty came up beside her and hugged her.

"Wasn't that beautiful?" she said.

"I don't think I'll ever forget it."

"Well, I must see the parents. I just wanted to say congratulations to you!"

"And to you!" Ruth replied. She turned to get her cloak, when she felt a hand on her shoulder. She spun around, startled.

It was Richard, carrying a bouquet. "I was going to bring you roses, but I understand that's for graduation."

"Richard! What are you doing here? I thought you'd be long gone by now."

He leaned forward and gently touched Ruth's cap. "I couldn't possibly leave before you were capped, now, could I?"

Ruth teared up.

"Oh, please don't cry. You look so beautiful. It would be a pity to ruin it. Is your family here?"

"No, they were too busy to bother, I'm afraid."

"Well, I am doubly glad I came, then. Shall we head out for a hot cocoa or something? I'd love to visit with you."

Ruth could see Betty nodding wildly behind Richard. "That would be lovely," Ruth said. "Thank you so much for these. I'll just run over and put them in some water and get changed?"

"I shall wait with bated breath," said Richard, taking her cloak and gently wrapping out around her. When he touched her neck to fasten it, Ruth still felt the shivers.

Darn it, she told herself as she ran downstairs and through the tunnel again. I was going to be all sensible and distant.

FIFTY-ONE

Walking on

On the way back from their lengthy visit and friendly chat at the cafe, Ruth couldn't hold it in anymore. "I'm so sorry I gave you grief over going north. It was very selfish of me."

Richard turned around and pulled her into his arms. "Well, I'm a bit selfish when it comes to you, too. All those orderlies singing your praises was one thing, but when Dr. Oak started …"

He leaned forward and kissed her, gently, then more firmly. Ruth leaned into him, loving the feeling of his arms about her, the warmth of his breath, scented as it was by hot chocolate.

"Mmm, you taste like a chocolate bar," said Ruth. "I love these winter kisses — cold outside, warm inside."

"Well, we'd better have another one, then."

Some minutes later, even the lovebirds had to admit the cuddles weren't keeping them warm enough.

"We'd better get walking before we freeze," Ruth said, regretfully. She could kiss him forever, she thought. Except that her fingers and toes were aching.

Richard paused and lit a cigarette. He puffed a few times before he spoke again, nervous about something. "Ruth, I need to know. Will it be all right with you if I go north for a year? I really want to learn about the people there. But I don't want to lose you again. Could we still be together while we are far apart? Go steady, or something?"

Ruth breathed out in relief. She thought he was maybe going to propose, and married women couldn't take nursing. Or work, at the moment. Not that she'd object forever.

"Well … will you write?"

"I'll write and call as often as they'll let me. Will you write back?"

Ruth paused, put her hand on Richard's cheek. "You are the best thing to happen to me. Of course I'll write. You first, though."

Richard smiled, took her hand, and placed it in his coat. "Cautious Ruth. You have my heart," he said. "I'll be wearing out my pen."

"All right. I suppose I can let you go then," Ruth said. She kissed him lightly and stroked his hair. She'd miss him like crazy. "When would you have to leave?"

"Beginning of March. It's easier to get us up there when the land is frozen. I get to fly up in one of the Beaver planes! How exciting is that?"

Ruth laughed and bent down to make a snowball. "Now you're just trying to make me jealous." She tossed it at him. He caught it and juggled it for a minute.

"Well, they are looking for nurses, too," he hinted. "Maybe you could come up for a visit."

"Let me feel warmth again before I even contemplate such a thing. I'm frozen."

They'd reached the nursing residence, and Richard bowed over her mittened hand. "See you soon, m'lady," he said in an English accent, then chuckled. "In case you were missing the king." He straightened up. "Might you be free this weekend?"

"I believe so. We won't have started our next placement yet. I should be able to go out. Unless, of course, I have to fly off somewhere. Without talking about it. Maybe south. A warm place. All by myself."

Richard put up his finger in a tsk tsk motion, then wrapped her in a last hug. Ruth didn't want to let go, and it seemed Richard didn't either. "I'm missing you already," he said. "Let's spend as much time as we can together before I have to go." He kissed her, long and heavenly, then took her shoulders and turned her to face the residence door. "Now go get warm! I'm off for a drink by the fire."

Ruth floated up the steps and pulled the door open, only to be grabbed by Betty. "There you are! Are you back together? It sure looked like it!"

"Mmm." Ruth undid her cloak. "I simply can't talk about it tonight, Betty. This whole evening has been absolutely magical."

"Magical enough to see you through your next placement? They've posted them. They've put you in maternity, you poor thing. Demanding mothers, blood and screaming babies. Ugh. And you've already had to help with deliveries before, haven't you? At home? I've got medicine, which means I'll be looking after diabetics and lots of pee. Still, could be interesting …"

Ruth walked away. Time enough to think about that later. For tonight, she was going to focus on her capping and those extraordinary kisses. She hoped Richard wouldn't be practicing them on anyone up north. Well, she told herself, she'd just have to charm him enough he'd never even think of it.

She changed and settled herself under her covers, stretching out her toes in pure joy. In one minute, she'd jumped out again. She ran to her cupboard and pulled out her souvenir box and opened it. She dug under the pressed corsage and the letters from Mary and Meg. Underneath, still carefully wrapped, was the head piece from her Christmas cookie, showing her hair with a cap in place. She kissed it and then popped it into her mouth. The blessing had worked and now she was a full-fledged, non-probie, soon to be advanced nursing student! Only one more year to go and she'd be a real and for true nurse. Smiling to herself, she tucked herself into bed, her heart full.

Historical Note

MENTAL HEALTH TODAY

Canada is the only major western country with no national mental health strategy, muddling along instead with the patchwork of fragmented, underfunded, uncoordinated services, all suffused with the rhetoric of personal responsibility. Everywhere, ongoing care and support are undermined and derogated.[*]

---

[*] Barbara Taylor, *The Last Asylum. A memoir of Madness in our Times*, Hamish Hamilton (Penguin), Toronto, 2014. P. 256

Bibliography

Want to learn more? Here are some references I used in researching this book:

Behnken, Priscilla Booth, and Elizabeth Good Merrill. "Nursing Care Following Prefrontal Lobotomy." *The American Journal of Nursing* 49, no. 7 (1949), 431–34. https://doi.org/10.2307/3458259

El-Hai, Jack. *The Lobotomist*. Wiley, New Jersey, 2007.

Freeman, Walter, and James W Watts. *Psychosurgery In the Treatment of Mental Disorders and Intractable Pain*. 2nd edition. Charles C Thomas, Springfield IL, 1950, p xvii

Geller, Jeffrey L. and Maxine Harris, *Women of the asylum: Voices from behind the walls, 1840-1945*. Anchor books, New York, 1994.

O'Donnell, Dennis. *The Locked Ward. Memoirs of a psychiatric orderly*. Jonathan Cape, London, 2012.

Suleman, Raheem, "A Brief History of Electroconvulsive Therapy." *American Journal of Psychiatry Residents'*, Volume 16, Number 1. https://doi.org/10.1176/appi.ajp-rj.2020.160103

Taylor, Barbara, *The Last Asylum. A memoir of Madness in our Times*, Hamish Hamilton (Penguin), Toronto, 2014.

In addition, *Canadian Nurse* has been completely digitized, and it is fabulous to wander through their site. It's astonishing what they recommend for treatments back then.
 https://www.canadian-nurse.com/archive

And, of course, the Museum of Health Care:
 http://www.museumofhealthcare.ca

Acknowledgments

Writing a book is both a solitary pursuit and one requiring the help of many. I would especially like to thank Tim Covell, publisher and editor at Somewhat Grumpy Press, for his infinite support and cheerful assistance. I'd also like to thank my beta readers, especially Catherine M, and Heather L, who wrote back swiftly with detailed suggestions. Special thanks to Wendy C and Stephanie G-R, who caught some significant errors that everyone had missed. You all added so much to this book, and I love you all.

Thanks too to my children and grandchild and other friends who have been endlessly encouraging, (or at least not discouraging) as I work on these books. I am often absent or distracted or given to talking about revolting things, and I appreciate your patience.

I would also like to thank Rowena McGowan and the staff at the Museum of Health Care in Kingston, Ontario. This fascinating place holds so much interesting stuff that a researcher could spend days there looking at medical equipment and learning the stories. Everyone there is knowledgeable, helpful, and enthusiastic, and will go the extra step to find that little detail of reference that adds truth to a fictional document. If you are writing medical history, there is no substitute for seeing the 'real things.' If you can't go for a visit, check out their on-line gallery! https://www.museumofhealthcare.ca. They also provided the photos for the cover.

My optometrist would also like to join me in thanking the Kingston Whig-Standard, whose issues are recorded on microfiche in the Kingston Library. From these, I was able to find out details about the times, look at the ads to identify popular items, and more.

Finally, I would like to thank my cousin, M-D V., who supplied the means to get even with someone, described in one of the later chapters. I never think about it without giggling.

A portion of the proceeds from this book will be donated to the Museum of Health Care.

About the Author

Dorothyanne Brown is a retired nurse, writer and editor. She lives in Kingston, Ontario, with a large orange cat named Norm. He is very insistent she only writes until 3 pm every day. She is a chronic volunteer, obsessive reader, and occasional ukulele player. Dorothyanne teaches editing at Kingston Seniors, and offers editing through DABEditing. She can be reached through her web site, www.dorothyanneb.ca

Bib & Tucker is her third book. It is second in the White Stockings Series, the first being *Spit & Polish*. Her books, including *Recycled Virgin*, are all available through Somewhat Grumpy Press, https://somewhatgrumpypress.com.

Help independent authors and small presses by leaving a review at your favourite online retailer or review site, or sharing on social media.